"You want me to get on ... that?"

Allison eyed the motorcycle as if it were a fire-breathing dragon.

"Yes, Miss Crawford. I want you to get on *that*. It won't kill you. HomePlace is just a few blocks away." J.T. swung one long leg over the bike.

It should have comforted Allison a little that she'd at least gotten close to her target destination. Instead, all she could think of was sitting on that motorcycle, her body cupped around the back of J. T. James's hard-muscled frame. The image was enough to make her throat close.

"Mr. James ... I ..."

"What's the matter, princess?" he asked with soft mockery. "Scared?"

Her eyes narrowed at the challenge, and she stalked to the motorcycle. She grasped her skirt, pulling it up high enough on her thighs so she could mount the bike.

She felt the heated flicker of J.T.'s gaze on the tops of her stockings, just a glimpse of lace and slip hem reflected in his eyes. Then something in those eyes went dark and dangerous....

Dear Reader,

As always, it's difficult to know where to begin when talking about this month's Intimate Moments lineup. We've got so many wonderful books and authors that I guess the only place to start is at the beginning, with Kathleen Creighton's American Hero title, *A Wanted Man*. And I promise you'll want Mike Lanagan for yourself once you start reading this exciting story about reporter-on-the-run Mike and farmer Lucy Brown, the woman who thinks he's just a drifter but takes him in anyway. Like Lucy, you'll take him right into your heart and never let him go.

In *No Easy Way Out*, Paula Detmer Riggs gives us a hero with a dark secret and a heroine with a long memory. *Days Gone By* is the newest from Sally Tyler Hayes, a second-chance story with an irresistible six-year-old in the middle. Kim Cates makes her first appearance in the line with *Uncertain Angels*, the story of a right-side-of-the-tracks woman who finds herself challenged by a do-gooder in black leather. In *For the Love of a Child*, Catherine Palmer brings together a once-married couple and the voiceless boy whom heroine Lilia Eden hopes to adopt. When little Colin finally speaks, you'll have tears in your eyes. Finally, there's *Rancher's Choice*, by Kylie Brant, whom you met as our 1992 Premiere author. I think you'll agree that this book is a fitting follow-up to her smashing debut.

Enjoy!

Leslie Wainger
Senior Editor and Editorial Coordinator

Please address questions and book requests to:
Reader Service
U.S.: P.O. Box 1325, Buffalo, NY 14269
Canadian: P.O. Box 1050, Niagara Falls, Ont. L2E 7G7

UNCERTAIN

ANGELS

Kim
Cates

Silhouette® ▼™
INTIMATE ▼ MOMENTS®
Published by Silhouette Books New York
America's Publisher of Contemporary Romance

SILHOUETTE BOOKS

ISBN 0-373-07550-2

UNCERTAIN ANGELS

Books by Kim Cates

Silhouette Intimate Moments

Uncertain Angels #550

Silhouette Special Edition

The Wishing Tree #687
A Sky Full of Miracles #777

KIM CATES

is an incurable fanatic, addicted to classic tearjerker movies, Chicago Cubs baseball and reading and writing romances—both contemporary and historical. Married to her high school sweetheart, she divides her time between her writing career and enjoying her daughter, Kate, from whom, Kim insists, she learned everything she knows about the temperament of royalty.

To the *real* Ostrom boys—my cousins, Craig and Terry, Ric, Jeff and Jim—who really do ski on canoe paddles and dared me into doing the same. Thanks for taking the fish off of my hooks, for going frog hunting in the swamp and helping me climb up the fire tower even though I was scared to death of heights. You are the greatest cousins a girl ever had. I'll always remember the times we shared.

Chapter 1

J. T. James leaned a leather-clad shoulder against the wall of the Chicago hotel ballroom, his gray eyes as predatory as a wolf caged in a kennel full of lapdogs.

Rangy and street tough, he had the aura of a man fate had kicked in the teeth with great regularity, but one who had come up fighting every time—and not by the gentlemanly code adopted by the tuxedoed men who were escorting their ladies to this charity affair. No, J.T. had learned early that you had to fight dirty just to survive. And when all the glitz and sequins were stripped away, survival was the only thing that mattered.

He saw that survival instinct every day in the eyes of the kids who prowled garbage cans for something to eat, the winos and the homeless, wandering around with their shopping carts filled with junk. He saw it every time he dragged a runaway child out of the rain, and gave the kid food and a decent bed to sleep in, away from a world that made this whole society-page event seem surreal and disgusting.

Then what the hell are you doing here, James? a gritty voice inside him jeered. *The charity organizers snap their fingers and you race over here to perform.*

It hadn't been for the money. J.T. had learned a long time ago that once people opened their pocketbooks and threw some money at a cause, they wanted a say in how the operation was run. And he wasn't about to give anybody else that kind of power over HomePlace, the unorthodox shelter for runaways that he had carved out of the heart of the inner city.

It had been blackmail, pure and simple, that had dragged J.T. here tonight.

Blackmail of the most unforgivable kind—applied by Lieutenant Mike Flaherty, a baby-faced third-generation Irish cop who had literally set the department on its ear five years ago when he devised his own drug resistance program. A man who had made the badge on his chest stand for more than law and order. Decency, hope, a way out for kids in trouble, a way into a kid's psyche for parents at their wit's end.

Flaherty had always been ruthless when it came to fighting drugs and gangs and child prostitution. He was also the best friend J.T. had ever had. That, combined with a knowledge of exactly how to push J.T.'s personal buttons, had resulted in this upcoming debacle tonight. Inner-city savior served up with lobster pâté. Guru of the street kids to be lavished with praise by people who had probably never seen a three-year-old bleeding to death on the concrete after a drive-by shooting.

"I should have told Mike to go to hell," J.T. muttered, glancing down at his battered diver's watch. But Mike had used the one argument J.T. hadn't been able to dismiss.

You think only poor kids run away, J.T.? You think only poor kids put .45s in their mouths and pull the trigger? Give these parents a chance. If you can save one kid's life by talking to these people...

One kid. Hadn't J.T. spent his life trying to save the world one kid at a time? Nothing ticked him off more than when Flaherty got him in a stranglehold by using J.T.'s own words. And the one thing J.T. had never overcome in the years since he had roamed the streets himself was a temper that could hold its own against the meanest junkyard dog in Chicago.

His only consolation about the whole thing was that when he was finished giving his talk tonight, he doubted many of these toothpaste-ad smiles would still be flashing. And the hotel cook would probably be insulted by the gourmet meals that were left barely touched on the plate. Mixing hard realism and lobster pâté could cause one hell of a case of indigestion.

He started to jam scarred fingers through the thick, dark hair that usually fell in a primitive mane about his jaw. But he stopped, remembering that the shoulder-length masses had been caught back with a leather thong at his nape, his only concession to the formality of tonight's occasion. A black T-shirt stretched across his broad chest, his bomber jacket, the once-stiff leather soft with age, was slung over his shoulders and a tiny gold hoop pierced his left ear.

"Hey, J.T.!" Flaherty's jovial voice broke into his thoughts. "You gotta quit scowling like that, man. The waiters think you're some kinda nut case getting ready to take the hotel hostage or something."

J.T.'s upper lip curled more in a snarl than a grin. "Tell 'em to set down the helicopter in the ballroom. If I could get out of here it would almost be worth doing the time."

Mike was rigged out like the rest, but at least he looked as if his tie was strangling him. "Don't worry, man," Flaherty said, slapping J.T. on the shoulder. "You'll be back to fighting drug pushers and pimps in no time."

"While you sip champagne with the rest of the beautiful people?"

Mike flashed him a grin, saluting him with a crystal stem full of something bubbly. "Ginger ale, pal. It's a tough job,

but someone has to do it. By the way, you really shouldn't
have gone to so much trouble with what you're wearing."

"Go to hell."

"Yeah, well, I think the ladies as a whole are impressed.
You look like one dangerous dude, James. That *is* the look
you were going for, isn't it? Early Hell's Angels?"

"Did they come to look at me or to listen to what I have
to say?"

"Actually, I think they came to get their pictures in the
society pages this weekend. They don't have a clue what we
have in store for them. Now, quit acting like you're going
to take a bite out of the plaster and come meet the lady
who's responsible for this whole thing."

J.T. arched a thick brow. "I already hate her."

"You'd have to be dead not to appreciate this lady. Her
name is Allison. Allison Crawford. Andrew Crawford's
daughter."

A band of iron seemed to tighten around J.T.'s forehead. His temples throbbed. "Crawford? The millionaire's daughter?" He gave an eloquent snort. "You'll
forgive me if I forgo the pleasure."

"But she asked specifically to meet you. She's introducing you to the crowd. Allison's okay, J.T. I've known her
since we were kids. Just because her dad has money doesn't
mean she—"

"Yeah, Mike. I bet she played stickball in the alley with
you and the rest of your friends."

"She wasn't allowed to play with much of anybody, as I
understand it."

"You her personal confidant, Flaherty? What's Danielle think about that?"

Flaherty grinned at the mention of his fiancée's name.
Two days and he would be taking the bright-eyed Danielle
to Vegas, to get married in the most outrageous wedding
chapel they could find. J.T. felt a twinge of regret. They
had wanted him to go with them, to be the best man, but
there were some zoning problems with the new facility he

was starting on the other side of the city. Mike, as always, had understood.

"Dani loves Allison," Mike said, "even though I did use her to make Dani jealous when that business exec was giving her the eye. Allison and I met when we were kids. My dad was one of the guys who found her after she was kidnapped."

"Kidnapped?" J.T. couldn't stop himself from repeating.

"Yeah. She was seven years old. Wandered right out from under her nanny's nose while they were at Willowshade Park. She was missing for three days before they found her. Pretty ugly stuff, I'm afraid."

The thought of any kid terrified, victimized, made J.T.'s gut knot.

"She was in bad shape, understandably. When they got to the station, my dad called up my mom and had her bring me and my sisters down to play with Allison until her father could get there. She had these big, green eyes. And she was scared. So scared. She acted like she'd never seen another kid before."

J.T. fought hard to hold on to his acid cynicism. "Nobody met her father's social standards, I bet. So what happened? Did they ever get the guys who kidnapped her?"

"There was a shoot-out, and the bastards were killed. Unfortunately, Allison saw it all."

The image wasn't pretty. J.T.'s jaw clenched.

Mike shook his head in astonishment. "I can't believe you never heard any of this, J.T. It was a media circus. It got nearly as much play as the Lindbergh kidnapping. You would have had to be buried alive not to have heard anything."

Buried alive... J.T. looked away, unwilling to let even his best friend see the expression in his eyes. He had been buried alive, in lies, in the misery induced by the neglect of his mother. Where had he been when Crawford's daughter was in such danger? Had he been in the care of strangers, paid for the trouble of trying to straighten out a kid who was headed for juvenile hall? Or had he been on the streets, trying desperately to find his mother?

The image of Crawford's privileged daughter being swept into the millionaire's arms, carried off to swimming pools and mansions and private beaches to recover from her trauma, when he had run headlong into more agony as a child, made a knife of unwelcome envy cut into hidden places in his heart. He crushed the pain, ruthless.

"I keep telling you that poor kids don't have a corner on the misery market, J.T." It was one of Mike's favorite litanies. At the moment it only poured gasoline on the fire of J.T.'s temper.

"Yeah. They don't have a corner on the misery market. It's just that, when they *do* get blindsided by life, they land in Malibu penthouses instead of in the gutter."

"You're being a total ass."

J.T. arched his head back, his chest heaving in a sigh. "I'm glad your precious heiress had someone to catch her when her world caved in. Glad she's safe. I just . . ."

Wish there had been someone there for me, when I was alone and scared. Wish that my mother had given a damn about me. Wish that every kid had the kind of emotional security that Andrew Crawford's cherished daughter obviously had. . . .

The thoughts raked across J.T.'s carefully maintained defenses. He grabbed on to the surly attitude that had always protected him, and held on, tight.

"You're breaking my heart, Mike," he snapped. "I can tell you a hundred stories that make Allison Crawford's three days of hell look like a garden party in comparison. But I don't have time to be exchanging street stories, unless I'm on the damn podium over there. I just want to get this thing over with. If making small talk with Miss Crawford will facilitate that, let's do it."

There must have been something in his face that betrayed what he was really feeling. Mike's steady blue eyes filled with empathy. The Irish cop knew better than to put his understanding into words. Instead he gave J.T. an affectionate slug in the arm.

"Trust me. You're going to love Allison," was all he said, then he started wending his way through the throng. If J.T. had been in a better mood it might even have been amusing, watching the sea of people part, as if they were afraid they'd catch something from him. As it was, he couldn't refrain from pinning them with his most surly glare.

They had nearly reached a wall of gilt-framed mirrors when Mike nudged him with an elbow, then nodded to where a woman stood, tucked in the corner, her back to the crowd.

Her slender figure was draped in gauzy white, old-fashioned lace icing the elegant back that scooped low beneath her shoulder blades. Her hair, a thick candle-shine gold, had been caught up in a loose knot at the top of her head, glossy strands escaping from their pins to lie in silky ribbons against the delicate ridges of her spine.

But it was her face, reflected in the mirror, that hit J.T. like a fist in his gut. It was the kind of face J.T. had seen on Christmas-tree angels—elegant, sensitive, soft. Big, serious eyes, a remarkable green-gold, stared earnestly into the silvery surface, her full lips moving slightly as if she were a kid rehearsing a speech for English class.

He felt a stab of naked longing, surprising in its intensity. It had been a long time since he'd been with a woman, any woman. With HomePlace to run he counted himself fortunate when he got to take a five-minute shower uninterrupted, let alone found privacy enough to make love to someone. Not that he'd ever attempt to drag a woman into his life. He'd decided a long time ago it wouldn't be fair.

Yet that resolution obviously had no effect on pure male urges. He gave a wry smile. What was it one of the women he'd been briefly involved with had said? Who would'a figured a guy whose eyes ooze raw sex would be such a monk?

At the moment abstinence was the last thing on his mind. His reaction to the woman in the lace dress was as elemental as it was disturbing. As surprising as it was unsettling.

J.T.'s lips curled in bemusement as he stared at her reflection. He'd seen Andrew Crawford's face a hundred times—the brilliant businessman and ruthless political supporter, totally unfazed by cameras or scandals. This fragile angel of a woman couldn't possibly be the man's daughter. Or was she Allison Crawford? The little girl who had cowered, terrified, in the precinct office with the rowdy Flahertys so many years ago?

Any doubts were laid to rest as Mike reached out and laid a hand on that half-bared shoulder, something about the gesture making J.T.'s fist tighten. The woman wheeled as if Mike had caught her stealing candy.

A hand gripping a computer printout was pressed to her breasts. "Michael! You scared me to death," she said with a breathless smile. "I can't wait until this is over!"

Mike heaved a sigh. "The enthusiasm I'm confronted with here is about more than I can stand. I wanted to introduce you to someone."

It was as if she hadn't even noticed J.T., half-hidden by Flaherty. When he stepped into the clear, those incredible eyes widened, her mouth falling open in what could only be shock as she took in his long hair, his clothes, her gaze finally clinging to the earring. The outrage J.T. had felt on behalf of the child, Allison, dissipated a little. This Allison Crawford was all woman. The price of her ivory satin pumps could probably have fed the kids at HomePlace for a month.

"Allison, I want to introduce you to J. T. James. The guy who has single-handedly kept more kids out of body bags than anyone I know."

She swallowed hard, a tear-shaped diamond the size of J.T.'s thumbnail glinting in the hollow of her throat. "M—Mr. James. I've read so much about you."

"Have you, now, sugar?" His lips ticked up in a smile, his eyes boring into hers with the intensity he had used to make people uncomfortable for years. "Where would a *lady* like you hear about someone like me?"

"For crimminy sakes, J.T.—" Mike cut in in disgust.

"I've read a great deal about HomePlace, Mr. James," Allison Crawford said. "Articles in *Practical Sociology, Progressive Parenting Magazine, TeenSpot.*"

"*TeenSpot?* Don't tell me. You buy that for the posters of the latest heartthrobs to pin up on your bedroom walls."

Her cheeks went scarlet, and J.T. grimaced inwardly. He was being a bastard. He knew it. Affairs like this brought out his mean streak major-league. He forced his smile to warm a little, to take out the sting.

Allison Crawford looked at him uncertainly through lashes as thick and silky as sable, then she smiled a bit herself. "Actually, I'm in charge of all my father's charitable contributions. I work very hard to keep up with people like you."

"I see. And just what kind of person am I?"

"Involved. Aggressive in dealing with problems of kids. Actually, you're a bit controversial, but Michael insists that you're a miracle worker."

"Yeah, that's me. A miracle worker. Well, *Michael* said you wanted to meet me. Here I am, in the flesh. Let's get this thing on the road so I can get back to tend the destitute and downtrodden."

Flaherty was swearing again, under his breath, but J.T. was surprised when Allison Crawford's voice cut in. "Mr. James, if you think I take the problems you face lightly, you're mistaken. I have the greatest respect for anyone who—"

"Allison? Allison, dear?"

The voice was cool and cultured, insistent. J.T. glanced over in disgust to see who was approaching, certain that this new "polite conversation" would postpone his speech even longer. What he saw slammed into his gut like a sledge-hammer.

His whole body went rigid with recognition, and his eyes narrowed. If there had been any way to get the hell out of there without looking as if he was running away, he would have taken it. Instead, he stared into the exquisitely made-up face of the woman approaching.

Fiftyish, her face unlined, her body sheathed in black sequins, she looked sleek and satisfied as a pampered cat. J.T. had heard it said that selfishness and greed left indelible marks in people's faces. But maybe plastic surgeon's knives were able to carve off that kind of hard edge, along with sagging skin beneath the eyes.

"Allison," the woman trilled out in bell-like laughter. "You've outdone yourself again. This is the most wonderful affair! I haven't the slightest idea what cause you are championing this time, my dear, but you know that the senator and I would never miss a chance to support you."

Allison gave the woman a weak smile. "We're dealing with the runaway problem tonight, Mrs. Alexander."

"Lovely. Lovely. You can be certain I brought my checkbook! And you'll never guess who else I brought! My son, Peter, insisted on flying in from Miami the minute he finished his bar exams, just so that he could see you again. You simply must come sit down for a nice cozy chat."

"Maybe later," Allison said. "I'm always a wreck before these things. In the meantime, may I introduce you to our speaker?"

J.T.'s body went rigid as the senator's wife raised gold-shadowed eyes to his for the first time. He leveled his gaze at her with a relentless intensity that made the older woman go pale.

"This is Mr. James," Allison Crawford continued, "the founder of HomePlace."

A heavily ringed hand fluttered to the older woman's throat, and for just an instant her eyes were pleading, almost vulnerable, before those emotions were shuttered away behind a mask of plastic politeness. For a heartbeat J.T. almost felt sorry for her, but the woman was a master of the quick recovery.

"Mr. . . . James? Is that what Allison said your name is? How lovely to meet you. I'm Senator Alexander's wife." The woman extended a beringed hand.

"I know who you are." J.T. pointedly stuffed his fists into his pockets.

The woman's smile faltered, and she let her hand fall to her side. "When one is in public life, I suppose that's not surprising. I regret to say I haven't made your acquaintance before."

"We met a long time ago. But then, I suppose it would be ridiculous to expect you to remember such a trivial encounter."

"You may be certain that I will make amends for the oversight by making a most generous contribution to your organization. What was it called?"

"HomePlace. It's a house for kids with nowhere else to go."

"I see. I—"

"And as for your money Mrs. Senator, keep it," J.T. snarled, furious that he was letting the woman get to him. "I wouldn't want you to break a nail digging for your checkbook."

Allison almost choked on her outrage as Mrs. Alexander gasped. "I'm sorry, Allison. I believe I'll return to my table. The senator and I are—are so eager to catch up on all the wonderful things our son is doing. You understand?"

"Of course." Allison laid a soothing hand on the older woman's arm. "Tell Peter I'm looking forward to seeing him again."

Mrs. Alexander nodded, then fluttered off into the crowd.

For a moment Allison just stared after her, seething inside. She had never enjoyed the glittering parties so many other people did—and gatherings like this one had always made her feel as if there were a hot rock lying in her stomach. But she had forced herself past her innate shyness because she had felt it was important. Because she had wanted to help.

And now this man with his scorn-filled eyes, and his sneer, and his blasted superior aura was making her feel totally incompetent.

"Great job, J.T.," she heard Mike snap.

But before he could let loose a tirade Allison went toe-to-toe with the surly man before her. "Tell me, Mr. James, are there any other important guests you'd like to alienate before the program begins?"

James only shrugged one leather-clad shoulder, those disturbing, icy gray eyes seeming to pierce hers. "None that I can think of offhand," he drawled.

"Good. Because we're not here to feed your ego or let you vent your social-class prejudices. We're here for the kids, Mr. James."

His eyes flashed, molten silver, dangerous under spiky dark lashes. "Thank you so much for enlightening me, Miss Crawford. Since you're not here to feed my ego, and I'm not particularly fond of the company you keep, you can either introduce me now or find yourself another speaker."

Allison tossed her head, feeling more strands of her hair cascade to fall about her neck as she stalked through the crowd. Questioning murmurs welled up around her, but she didn't care about anything except getting this over with so that she could choke down another handful of antacids to calm her stomach.

As she mounted the stairs to the speaker's dais she glimpsed James ambling behind her, his mouth curved into something that looked like diabolical amusement at her anger. She wanted to turn and slug him.

No wonder he had so much success getting runaways to return to their families. An hour in his sunshiny presence and those poor kids probably raced to get back home.

Still fuming, Allison cast her notes onto the podium. Usually she was shaking by now, so light-headed she was afraid she was going to faint. But tonight she didn't even bother sucking in a cleansing breath before she plunged into her speech.

"Ladies and gentlemen, if I could have your attention please?" The guests slipped into their seats, the conversation fading until an expectant hush fell over the room. "Our speaker tonight," Allison continued, "is the founder of HomePlace, a most extraordinary program for runaways that has returned over ninety percent of its children into the mainstream of society—some back to their parents, others on to responsibility and independence."

James cleared his throat, obviously wanting her to stop. She clenched her fingers on the wood of the podium as if she half expected him to bodily pull her away.

"Named *NewsMaker*'s man of the year in 1989, and awarded *TeenSpot*'s coveted Change the World award, Mr.—ouch!" She gasped as a sharp-toed boot collided with her ankle. Glaring up at James, she tightened her grasp on the podium, determined to finish. "I urge you to open your purses wide for Mr., uh—" she paused for a heartbeat, glancing at her notes "—James. Jesse James."

The instant the words were out of her mouth a roar of laughter went up from the crowd. Allison's face flamed. What was it Mike Flaherty had said? Never, *never* call J. T. James by his real name. Oh, God, if only the man hadn't gotten her so blasted furious!

"Uh—Jesse T. James," she stammered out. "Mr. Jesse Tyler James..." Instead of making things better, she was making them worse, the audience growing even more amused at her discomfiture.

She looked helplessly at James, pale beneath the golden layer of his tan. Those lips that could be so sardonic were thinned, his eyes steady, but a wisp of vulnerability clung to the corner of his mouth as he stepped up to take the microphone.

Using his first finger like a six-gun he pointed it at the crowd. "Bang," he said, then held his finger to his lips to blow away imaginary smoke. The crowd erupted in applause.

"Yeah," he said acidly. "It's true. My name is Jesse James. As you can tell, my mother didn't like me very much."

Even through her fury and embarrassment Allison felt a sharp sting behind James's supposed joke.

A ripple of laughter went through the assemblage.

"When I was in school I made a habit of knocking out the front teeth of anyone who called me Jesse, but since Miss Crawford here has such pretty teeth, I'll make an exception for her. Historically speaking, we outlaw types have always had a weakness for a pretty..." He paused, letting his eyes trail suggestively over Allison's body. "Ahem, *face.*"

Allison's fists knotted at her sides in abject embarrassment as appreciative applause drifted from the audience. She lowered herself woodenly into a chair at the edge of the stage.

The crowd's chuckles faded, and J.T.'s smile went brittle as glazed ice. "As for Miss Crawford's plea for money on my behalf, I don't want a dime from any of you. If you want to assuage your liberal guilt complexes, come down into the city and visit HomePlace. Leave your charge cards at home, and spend an hour or two of your valuable time talking to the kids, hearing what they've been through. But be warned. It's ugly on the streets. Ugly in a way I hope your children never have to experience."

Allison wanted to hate him for his arrogance, his hard line attitude that seemed bent on alienating the very people powerful enough to advance his cause. But as the lights dimmed, and images were flashed onto a screen to James's left, she found herself losing her grip on her anger toward him. She listened to J. T. James speak about life on the streets, and outrage burned inside her for the children he worked with—kids who were not only physically hungry but starving in spirit, as well.

He talked about Jenny, a girl who had become pregnant and was so terrified to tell her parents that she had spent two months in dead winter sleeping under an interstate overpass. He told of Jameel, who had wanted to escape the gangs in his housing project. He'd been so terrified about the backlash on his family that he had staged his own "death."

J. T. James had the eyes of a zealot—fierce, intense—and as Allison watched his face, listened to that gravelly voice, she felt as if he had sucked her into his world.

Several women got up and left the room, the stories no doubt too grim for them to endure. Some part of Allison wished she could leave, too, but the stories he told were so compelling she couldn't leave without knowing what had happened to the kids involved. And as he began to draw hope out of the hopelessness, courage and strength and resourcefulness out of kids who had seemed lost forever, a giant fist seemed to close about Allison's heart. Her eyes burned.

J. T. James wasn't bragging about his program, or his accomplishments. No, it was the kids who were the heroes and heroines in his stories—kids that Allison felt somehow she knew personally after hearing J.T.'s words.

When the screen went blank, and James's voice stopped, Allison tried to collect herself, willed herself to stand. The whole room was silent.

"I wish I could give you more happy endings," J.T. said. "The truth is, there are too many runaways in this city every year. At any one time about fifty are living at HomePlace. You do the math. Even if you never think of

my kids again, go home tonight and tell your own kids that
you love them. Even if they did screw up on their science
test, or wreck the car. Listen to them, damn it. As closely
as you listen to your stockbrokers or financial planners.''

Allison was stunned as J. T. James's voice broke. ''Most
people you know want to expand their programs, enlarge
their facilities. There is nothing I want more than to close
HomePlace's doors forever. Because all the runaways that
have been wandering the streets have someplace better to
go. Home.''

. He turned away, and Allison got to her feet. Her cheeks
were wet, confusion and astonishment racing through her.
Jesse James, hard-talking bastard, arrogant jerk, who had
been so disgusted with these proceedings, had somehow
shifted into a man whose heart seemed torn open by the
pain he witnessed every day.

As she looked at him she could almost see him yanking
the shreds of his bristly exterior around those raw places,
trying to hide them away.

She approached him, her voice unsteady. ''Mr. James,
I...thank you. I've never heard anyone speak so elo-
quently about the plight of these kids.''

''Well, Miss Crawford, when you've eaten out of garbage hoppers yourself, you tend to remember what it tastes
like.''

She felt as if he'd slapped her. She steeled herself and
went on.

''I just wanted to tell you how sorry I am for...for my
mistake when I was introducing you. I was just so flus-
tered, and—''

''It's my name. I'm used to it.''

''Are you?'' The question slipped out before she could
stop it. J. T. James looked down at her, and she could see
scars that went far deeper than the lean angles and planes
of his face. She wanted to look away. She stared, mesmer-
ized, into wolf gray eyes.

"Mr. James, I'm certain that after what you said tonight you'll get the donations you asked for. People will come see your work—"

"Sugar, I bet you still believe in Santa Claus, don't you?" J.T. gave a bitter laugh. "None of these society people are going to come down to HomePlace." His eyes bored into hers long minutes in challenge. "Nobody, sweet thing. Not even you."

"You're wrong, Mr. James."

"About you, Miss Crawford? I doubt it." His eyes roved over her again, with a scathing sensuality that made her feel as if he'd raked those work-rough hands over every nerve ending in her body.

"If I were you I'd stay as far away from HomePlace as possible. It's dangerous as hell down there," J.T. said in a low growl. "Just look at me."

"I'll bring a whip and a chair." The words slipped out before Allison could stop them, and she was appalled at herself. A smile that was pure sex spread over J. T. James's face.

"Sounds kinky, Miss Crawford." She was stunned when those long fingers reached out to capture a ribbon of golden hair that lay softly against her neck, the gesture incredibly intimate, sending fire shooting through to her most secret places.

"If I ever had the hots for you, sweet thing, an army couldn't keep me away. You'd better stay tucked up in your ivory tower, princess. No telling what might happen if you ever come down."

With that he turned and strode out of the room.

Allison watched him, her whole body shaking with anger, and something more, her skin sizzling with sensation where he had touched it.

You'd better stay tucked up in your ivory tower, J. T. James had warned in that dusky-smoke voice. *No telling what might happen if you ever come down....*

But as Allison watched him disappear into the crowd she wondered what he was warning her about. The dangers of the world he lived in? Or the dark, seductive danger in his own storm gray eyes?

Chapter 2

Millionaire's Daughter Found Dead In Dumpster.

With a twinge of guilt Allison reached over to check the power door locks of her luxury compact as the imagined headline flashed across her mind. Her fingers tightened on the steering wheel, her palms sweating as she drove deeper and deeper into a world that seemed as foreign and surreal to her as the movie set of some doomsday techno-thriller.

A maze of crumbling buildings obliterated the sky, their walls scrawled with graffiti, their steps laden with vacant-eyed old people and hostile-looking teenagers. Children who looked as if they had never seen the inside of a bathtub were caged behind the chain-link fencing of broken-down playgrounds, their eyes far too old in their faces.

Emptiness, hopelessness.

It thickened the air until Allison could hardly breathe, layering itself over everyone, everything.

Why in the name of God would J. T. James choose such a hideous area to house his runaways? she wondered with a sick lurch of her stomach.

A person could disappear in this place and no one would even know, the residents here were so lost in their own hard-eyed pain.

She looked at a post where a street sign had once been, but the last three signs she'd passed were no doubt decorating some teenager's wall.

Groping for the crumpled map on her seat, she attempted to drive and count roads at the same time, trying to imagine herself rolling down her window to ask directions.

Excuse me, could you tell me where HomePlace is located?

I'll be happy to, ma'am. Go up three streets and turn left. Third building on the right. Have a nice day. . . . She felt a bubble of nervous laughter clog her throat.

Catcalls from a cluster of youths on the street made Allison swallow hard, excruciatingly aware that her expensive car stuck out from the dingy, dented vehicles all around her like a diamond in a pile of coal.

And for the dozenth time since she'd pulled out of the parking garage that morning Allison wondered what had possessed her to come here.

She could imagine her father's reaction if anything should go wrong—blustering, furious. *Why the devil did the girl have to be so stubborn? If she had used the car and driver I put at her disposal this never would have happened. . . .*

But Ernie Bevens, balding ex-secret service agent and father of six, would never have consented to drive her here. He would have found some way to talk her out of it, and Allison had been so emotionally exhausted after her encounter with J. T. James last night that she hadn't had the energy to run head-to-head with anyone else.

But even a rare bout of stubbornness wasn't enough to have precipitated this trip. An unwelcome shiver went through Allison. The car itself had been a revolution. She'd bought the vehicle in direct opposition to her father's mandate, yet had only rarely taken it out of the garage.

But today... today she'd felt an uncharacteristic fit of defiance, brought on by a pair of intense gray eyes, a cynical yet inexpressibly sexy mouth. A gravelly voice that had broken when it spoke of the kids lost in the war zone to be found in the rotted heart of the city. A man who had dared her to come out of her tower, and feel the pulse of the hopeless for herself.

But when he had seen that she intended to take his challenge, the man had done an inexplicable about-face, doing everything in his power to keep her away.

Jesse James—a renegade with a thousand secrets thrumming just under his skin. A dangerous enigma who claimed to have clawed a tiny haven out of the misery around him.

The man had hypnotized her with his primitive, animal attraction, had infuriated her with his biting sarcasm and had frightened her more than a little with the almost savage scorn that had been in his face. Then he had broken her heart with the stories he told, the pain that had been reflected in his eyes. He had set her off balance. Jeered at her safe, protected world, and left her shaken.

Oh, God, what had she done? She'd been an idiot to come charging down here, alone, without the slightest idea where she was going. Hadn't that been what her father had hinted so many times? Hadn't he all but told her she was as inept as a child when it came to such things? But then, there was hardly any reason to learn directions when a limo and driver awaited the crown princess's every command....

She felt an unwelcome chill scuttle down her spine, the shadow of a recurrent nightmare. She fought against the sensations—the suffocating darkness of the trunk of the car where she'd been held captive, the gag, thick in her mouth, and raw terror so deep she couldn't have screamed for help even if she'd been standing in a crowd of a hundred policemen.

In the years since the kidnapping she had made certain that she always played by the rules. She'd been careful to listen to her father's warnings. After all, none of that horrendous terror would have happened if she hadn't disobeyed, and gone charging off on her own.

"Stop it, Allison!" she berated herself aloud. "Things are bad enough right now, without focusing on gags and car trunks."

She swiped furiously at a sudden moisture in her eyes. This whole thing was crazy. She should just try to get out of here as fast as possible. Stop at the safest place she could find, and call Ernie. Ernie would come get her and she could forget about this whole disaster.

The mere thought was enough to make her stiffen her spine. She could picture her father's reaction and, worse still, J. T. James's triumphant sneer at her retreat.

Even being found dead in a dumpster would be preferable to admitting defeat.

A block ahead she saw a convenience store. It looked more like an armed camp than a shop, but its tumbledown appearance was somewhat less forbidding than the rest of the area. Surely a public place would be safe enough. She could get out and ask for directions. And for some tranquilizers, she thought a little hysterically.

She eased the compact into the far end of the parking lot, squeezing it between a truck that was more rust than metal and an ancient luxury sedan covered with stickers of heavy metal rock groups.

Looping the strap of her shoulder bag over her head and tucking it beneath her arm, she drew a deep breath. What was it she had heard on the self-defense talk shows she'd seen? *Whatever you do, don't look like a victim.*

Mustering a false aura of bravado, she pasted on a smile and climbed out of the car.

Three teenagers were loitering beside a battered pop machine that was caged in chicken wire. Allison accidentally caught the eye of the one who seemed like the ringleader, a muscular youth with a black stocking cap pulled low over his forehead. The cap alone was enough to wilt her smile. The headgear reminded her all too vividly of the ski masks her kidnappers had worn.

Awkwardly locking the car, she gripped her purse more tightly and started walking toward the store.

"Hey, babe," the teenager with the ragged sweatshirt called, "that's one fine-lookin' car."

Allison walked faster.

"Yeah, an' she's one fine-lookin' woman. But I guess they don't teach 'em manners uptown."

Allison couldn't help glancing over her shoulder. It was a mistake. It gave the leader just long enough to dodge in front of her. She almost crashed into the teenager's chest, the waves of body odor coming off the kid mingling with the smell of Allison's own fear, making her stomach churn.

Her heart was trying to beat its way out of her chest. "Excuse me," she said, starting purposefully around the youth.

The kid merely moved, blocking her way, the other two closing in like a school of sharks scenting a kill.

Allison's hand trembled, and she feared she was going to pass out.

What's a pretty little rich girl like you doing, running through the park all alone. Don't you know how danger-ous it is? Bad people hang out in parks, little girl, just waiting to hurt kids like you.... We'll help you find your daddy....

The echoes from that long-ago day rippled through her, rocking her to her core.

"Please, let me by."

"I'd like to let you do a helluva lot, pretty lady. Get in the back seat of that car of yours, and find me somethin' sweet under that skirt. Unfortunately, my friends here would rather have somethin' else."

As if on cue, the kid in the sweatshirt grabbed her purse strap, yanking savagely.

Allison screamed, stumbling forward in the youth's wake, but despite his strength the expensive leather held firm. She crashed to her knees, pain exploding through her as he tried to run, dragging her across asphalt littered here and there with shards of broken glass.

Desperately Allison struggled to disentangle herself from the purse, only too happy to let him have it if it meant they would leave her alone.

But just as the strap slid over her head a roaring sounded in her ears, deafening her. A scream clogged her throat as the teenagers skittered back, trapped against the side of a car.

Flat on the ground, Allison tried to push herself up, her eyes catching sight of a black front tire and the gleaming chrome of what looked to be a vintage motorcycle. A black leather boot, worn down at the heel, was planted inches from her face, and she could see jeans weathered a pale blue-gray encasing a long leg, the denim knee ripped out to expose a wedge of tanned skin.

Great, Allison thought hysterically, trying to shove her hair out of her eyes. Some motorcycle gang member was no doubt coming to show these juvenile delinquents the proper procedure for mugging someone.

"What's up, guys?" A gravelly voice came from the back of the bike. "Helping the lady with her purse?"

Allison had been scrambling to her knees. At the sound of that voice she tried to sink back into the concrete.

Oh, God.

"J.T. Yeah. We…we were just, uh, just heading over to shoot some hoops, and this lady fell." The ringleader sounded like a kid caught smoking by the school principal. "Nardo here was just helping her up."

The teen in the sweatshirt took her arm as if she were his aged grandmother, and helped her to her feet. He brushed ineffectually at the torn linen of her skirt.

"You guys are real Boy Scouts, you know that?" James said. "I want you to know that I won't forget this. This lady is a personal friend of mine."

"Oh."

Allison half expected the three to go scrambling over the hood of the car.

"Hell, J.T., we . . . how were we supposed to . . . to know that . . ."

"Get out of here."

He kicked the bike into reverse, backing it up just enough to let the teenagers file through.

"By the way," he said. "You lost your basketball."

"What?"

"You were going to shoot hoops, remember?"

Without a word the boys ran, all but trampling each other in their haste to get around the building.

"They w-were trying to rob me," Allison stammered out.

J.T.'s brows shot upward in feigned shock. "No kidding?"

"Damn it, it's not funny!" Allison could not—*would not*—bawl like a baby in front of this man. "We have to call the police."

"So they can go to jail and learn how to be really good criminals?" James asked smoothly. "You're not much worse for the wear. The way I see it, a pair of ruined nylons is hardly worth having them arrested."

"But they were trying to rob me," Allison repeated, as if he were a particularly dull-witted child.

J.T. shrugged. "I might have been tempted to try it myself. You come down here in your fancy car, dripping money. Why not just walk down the middle of the street with a sign around your neck—Rich Bitch Victim, Mug At Will. Honey, someone would knife you in a heartbeat and not even blink to get hold of that diamond you're wearing around your neck. And that's the friendliest thing that could happen to a pretty lady like you."

"Don't patronize me! I . . ."

He was doing it again, throwing her completely off balance. Her lips quivered. "What are you doing here, anyway? Patrolling the streets like Clint Eastwood, or something?"

J. T. James's mouth ticked up in a smile that was satin-sheet sexy. "Haven't you ever heard of the cavalary, darlin'?"

Allison gave an unladylike snort that would have appalled her boarding-school teachers.

"Actually, I'm picking up some medicine for somebody. Lucky for you, huh?"

"Oh, yes. My luck is just amazing."

"Now, why don't you tell me why you're down here slumming it, princess?"

"You should know. You're the one who invited me. I was trying to find HomePlace, but the street signs were missing, and—" She stopped, not about to tell him what a bumbling idiot she had been.

"I warned you not to come. Mike should have better sense than to let you come barging down here."

"I don't usually call Michael for permission before I go out of the house, *Jesse.*" She used the name on purpose. It was a low weapon, but it was the only one she had at the moment. James's eyes sizzled, and he swore under his breath.

"Fine, then, princess. You want to see how the other half lives? It's all right by me. I'll just get what I need here, first."

He strode away, entering the store. For a moment Allison considered staying where she was, but there was a big difference between stubbornness and stupidity. Her instinct for self-preservation won out. She entered a dozen steps behind him, and stood by the counter.

A few moments passed before he returned, looking more than a little sheepish. He put his purchases on the counter, trying nonchalantly to shield them from her eyes with his shoulder.

Allison looked away hastily. What would a man like J. T. James try to hide? Neon condoms? Strawberry-flavored body oil? *Forget it, Allison,* she warned inwardly. *You wouldn't want to know.*

But at that instant a plaintive squeak split through the murmur of J.T.'s conversation with the clerk. Allison spun around. A wall of solid lead couldn't have kept her from finding out what he was buying now.

She craned onto her tiptoes and peered around him. There, on the counter, was a popular liquid pain reliever for children and, even more astonishing, a squeaky toy of a famous cartoon frog, wrapped in a cellophane bag.

Allison's gaze darted from the frog's silly grin to J. T. James's sulky face. He glared at her as if daring her to say anything.

"Get a lot of three-year-old runaways, do you?" she asked.

"We had a mom and toddler come in last night. We don't have a facility set up for them yet, but..." His hair was loose, tangled in a wild, delectable mane around his face. He jammed his fingers through it. "We do the best we can. The baby's got a fever."

He grabbed the bag with the toy, shoving it into his jacket pocket as if he was embarrassed by it. The frog let out a bleat. Color flooded J.T. James's cheekbones.

Allison's heart melted a little. Who was this man? This hard-edged renegade with a squeaky frog in his pocket? The hot-tempered, arrogant bastard who had all but blamed her for getting herself mugged? This motorcycle-riding savior of the inner-city kids, who had contempt for anyone who wasn't stained by poverty or misery or want?

He was Mike Flaherty's best friend. But he had raged at her when she was hurt and scared, the aftershocks of her terror still exploding through her, her palms and knees burning and stinging, sticky with blood. He hadn't even asked if she was all right. He probably figured that rich people didn't have any nerve endings.

He stalked out of the shop and Allison followed, fishing in her purse for the car keys. When J.T. saw what she was doing he snatched them neatly out of her hand, pocketing them himself. "I'm not about to let you go tearing around here, getting any more kids in trouble," he said acidly.

"Me? Get *them* in trouble?" Allison blustered, outraged. "I was the victim in that little scenario, Mr. James."

"Right. I forgot. Just get on the bike, before you and your diamond incite a riot."

"You want me to get on . . . that?" Allison eyed the motorcycle as if it were a fire-breathing dragon. Her fingers clenched in her pencil-slim linen skirt.

"Yes, Miss Crawford. I want you to get on *that*. It won't kill you. HomePlace is just a few blocks away." J.T. swung one long leg over the bike, and slid into the seat astride it.

It should have comforted Allison a little that she'd at least gotten close to her destination. Instead, all she could think of was sitting on that motorcycle, her body cupped around the back of J.T. James's hard-muscled frame. The image was enough to make her throat close.

She was shaking more than when Nardo and the boys had been "helping her across the street."

"Mr. James . . . I . . ."

"What's the matter, princess?" he asked with soft mockery. "Scared?"

Her eyes narrowed at the challenge, and she stalked to the motorcycle. She grasped her skirt, pulling it up high enough on her thighs so that she could mount the bike.

She felt the heated flick of James's gaze on the tops of her stockings, just a glimpse of lace and slip hem reflected in his eyes. Something in them went dark and dangerous. He let fly a low whistle as she flung her leg over the bike and slid into place behind him.

"If that's what you wear to visit runaway kids, babe, I'd love to see what you put on for an all-night party with one of your society boyfriends."

The barb stung, more than J. T. James could ever know.

Allison welcomed the roar of the motorcycle as it came to life, the wind whipping her face as he whizzed out into the traffic pattern.

J.T.'s long, dark hair teased her cheeks, the restless heat emanating from every sinew in his body penetrating the thin layer of her silk blouse. Her inner thighs, forced apart by her position on the seat, gloved J.T's narrow hips, the soft fabric of his jeans abrading her delicate skin.

And the scent of him—wind and wildness, danger and primitive strength—filled her, taunted her.

And reminded her all too clearly of her own failures.

She swallowed a lump in her throat at his reference to society boyfriends. This ride on the motorcycle with him was more intimate than she had been with a man in years.

The street blurred, and Allison thought she would have given every stock and bond in her father's portfolio just to be soaking in a hot bubble bath in her apartment that moment.

The motorcycle made a smooth turn, and she was forced to grab J.T.'s waist. Her vision cleared, and she was stunned to see the grimness of the neighborhood soften—what seemed to be a small oasis in the middle of the city.

Houses from before the turn of the century lined the street, in various stages of restoration. Several, refurbished to their former beauty and grandeur, sat like disapproving grande dames presiding over wayward children. Gingerbread dripped in charming wooden accents, iced in impossible color combinations that were dazzlingly beautiful. Intrepid trees reached toward the sky—a sky you could see, blue and serene above. Allison could almost believe it was a different sky from the one that suffocated the rest of the area.

Friendly calls from neighbors made J.T. raise a hand in salute as he guided the bike to the front of the largest house of all. A sprawling Victorian that had once been a show-place meandered over a grassy lawn bordered with white-painted fences. Wide porches with swings and rocking chairs, sports equipment and bicycles bordered the front, while a group of boys, really shooting hoops, went one-on-one on a basketball court a dozen yards away.

HomePlace.

The sign over the door was warm, welcoming, and as Allison looked at the place J. T. James had created for his kids she couldn't help but be awed.

She sat on the motorcycle, staring, long minutes after J.T. pulled it to a stop. He slid off the motorcycle and walked to the opposite side, calling to a lanky kid about seventeen years old.

"Hey, Nate, ever drive a Mercedes?"

"Sure. In my dreams."

James fished her keys out of his pocket and tossed them to the boy, flashing Nate the first genuine grin she'd ever seen on James's face. "Consider me your fairy godmother, kid. It's parked up at the Stop Mart. Take a spin in it and impress all your friends, then bring it back here for the lady."

"All right! Jeez, J.T. Thanks!" He turned back to his basketball opponent. "Yo, Ben, come on, man. This is going to be great!"

Allison wanted to protest at J. T. James's high-handed attitude about her car, but she could only be relieved that she wouldn't have to go back to that horrendous place herself.

"Is it . . . safe for those kids to . . ." she started to ask.

James looked at her, askance. "Nate and Ben have been places a hell of a lot worse than the Stop Mart." He extended a hand toward her.

"Better get off the bike now, sweetheart. I've got impressionable teenage boys hanging around here. With your skirt like that, you wouldn't want to tempt—" The words ended in a pithy curse as he looked down at her leg, visible beneath the hiked-up hem of her slim skirt.

He dropped to one knee, his hand cupping her calf. The contact sent lightning jolts of heat to the juncture of her thighs. "Son of a bitch! You're bleeding!"

There was a sense of outrage, accusation in his face. Allison couldn't keep from lifting one brow in an exact mime of his actions in front of the shop. "No kidding."

"Why didn't you tell me you were hurt?" The gray eyes were tempestuous with anger, and with . . . could it be self-blame?

"I was being dragged across the concrete when the cavalary arrived. I guess I just assumed that you wouldn't be interested. After all, according to you, I asked to be robbed."

J.T.'s hand tightened on her calf, and she couldn't help but shiver at the image of that strong, tanned hand against her torn stocking, those scarred fingers, suddenly so gentle.

"Rich people don't feel pain, right?" she asked sweetly. "We pay someone else to suffer in our place."

"I was an ass. I'm—" he hesitated for an instant "—sorry."

"Ouch," Allison said. "That really did hurt, didn't it?"

He leveled that intense gaze on her for long seconds, and she was amazed to see that sexy mouth curve into a bone-melting smile. "Yeah. But not as much as it's going to hurt you when I get to put disinfectant on those scrapes."

He levered himself to his feet and helped her off the motorcycle, his hand still crooked under her elbow as they navigated the stairs.

He called greetings to a bear of a man called Buck at the front desk, then wound his way through the house. The walls were covered with murals, signed, no doubt, by the kids who had stayed here. Graffiti, filled first with hopelessness, then hope, were painted at will. And as Allison skimmed the messages, the one universal message in all was gratitude. Gratitude for J.T. James.

You Pulled Me Back From The Edge, Man.

I Was Scared Before You Showed Me How Strong I Can Be.

Drugs Make You Forget, one line said, above a drawing of a stoned teenager. Forget Your Future, Forget Your Pride.

And the paintings were even more eloquent than the words. A hand reaching out into what Allison recognized as the inner city's skyline, cradling kids in a giant palm. Awkward lettering underneath simply said Thank You.

"We let 'em draw on the walls here. Get their feelings out," J.T. explained as he steered her toward a room with HealthPlace painted above it.

The infirmary was spotless, cheery, a half dozen smaller rooms opening into a central area filled with medical supplies. At the moment only one of the rooms was occupied. A girl of about seventeen sat in a rocking chair, a child Allison guessed to be nearly two years old cradled in her arms.

The girl seemed almost a child herself, clothed in a flannel nightgown, her short blond hair tumbled around cheeks that were still baby smooth. She looked as if she belonged at a slumber party in someone's rec room, experimenting with makeup on her friends, holding fake séances or telling ghost stories.

Allison's chest ached at the sight of the girl, here. Alone and bewildered, the toddler in her arms.

Allison watched as J.T. took the bag of medicine from his pocket and gave it to the girl, then took the baby from her with amazing gentleness, nestling the little one against his own broad chest. The child nuzzled in, its fingers tangling in the long strands of J.T.'s hair, as if he were a lifeline.

Allison felt something wrench in her chest.

There was something heartbreaking in the sight of J.T. patting the toddler's back with those large, tough hands. And she wondered what he was murmuring to the mother, their conversation too hushed for her to hear.

When the girl pulled the squeaky frog from the bag she grabbed J.T.'s hand and began to cry.

Allison felt her own throat thicken with tears as the man laid the baby back in the girl's arms, then gently stroked the runaway's hair. "That kid of yours had better enjoy it." J.T.'s teasing voice was barely audible. "Buying this thing has probably ruined my reputation."

Allison heard the girl give a watery laugh.

"You both better get some rest now. Another volunteer nurse will be here to check the baby in an hour or so."

He slipped out of the room, closing the door quietly behind him. Allison couldn't help staring at the tiny wet place on his gray sweatshirt, left by the child's soft little mouth.

But the J.T. James who had tended the runaway had been left behind the closed door. The one who came out to deal with the "rich bitch victim" wore a forbidding scowl.

He went to the cupboard, taking out supplies, then gestured to a cot. "Climb onto the bed, sweetheart, and let me get my hands on that leg of yours."

There was enough suggestiveness in his tone to stiffen Allison's spine. But she did as she was told, excruciatingly aware of the feel of sheets under her hands, the soft give of the mattress beneath her and of J.T. James's hands that would soon be touching her.

J.T. dragged over a three-legged stool and sank down on it, those steamy gray eyes at knee level. Allison was suddenly aware that she had never felt so vulnerable in her life.

Instinctively she tried to pull down her skirt hem, but the slender sheath of fabric would go only so far. At her action, he chuckled. "What's the matter, sugar? Afraid I'm going to look under your skirt? We just have to strip away your panty hose, unless, of course, you want it fused to your wound."

Panty hose? Allison all but choked on alarm. She had always had a weakness for frilly, feminine underclothes, her one secret indulgence in a world of linen suits and formal occasions. But the idea of exposing to J. T. James the wisp of ice white garter belt frosted with pink ribbon that she wore at the moment made her want to sink into the floor.

"I can take off my own stocking," she snapped briskly.

"Okay. Go for it." He leaned back a little and crossed his arms over his chest. She had hoped he'd give her the courtesy of a little privacy, but she should have known better. His eyes never left her, giving her no quarter.

She tried to fumble the garters loose through the layer of her skirt, hating the way her cheeks flamed, her hands shook. It was as if the dainty fastenings had been stuck together with super glue, or melted down by the heat in J. T. James's hooded gaze.

He let her struggle for what seemed an eternity, then he cursed, low. He firmly grabbed her hands, shoving them away. "At this rate it's going to take you three days to get those things pulled down. You have absolutely nothing to fear from me, I promise. I'm totally immune to leggy blondes with trust funds. Let's just get this over with."

Deftly he curled those fingers into her skirt, easing it high on her thigh. Cool air touched the skin above the edge of her stocking, and Allison shivered at the contrast as callused, strong fingers slipped beneath the lacy garter. J.T.'s eyes burned her from beneath his thick lashes. "Garters?" His voice was thick, low. "I'll be damned. I didn't know anyone wore these anymore, except in men's fantasies."

Fantasies? Allison reeled at the ones that were whirling in her own head at the moment. The thought of J. T. James's fantasies was far too potent for her to consider. She started to reach for the garter, but at that instant J.T. grinned.

"Of course, my fantasies are a helluva lot less bloody." He flicked the fastening open.

Heat flooded through her, unwelcome, embarrassing, as he began to skim the silky fabric down her thigh, slowly, carefully, his fingers leaving a trail of burning sensation wherever he touched. She winced when the stocking clung to the scrape, J.T. pulling it free with astonishing gentleness.

His head was bent, his mane of dark hair obscuring his features. But as he continued to slip the silk down her calf, Allison sensed something different in his touch, the slightest tremor, a hesitation.

When he was finished he cupped her ankle in his palm and settled her bare foot on his thigh. He groped for the antiseptic, knocking the plastic tube off the cot. He cursed, shifting on the seat just enough to grab the bottle. The side of Allison's foot bumped into a firm, jean-covered bulge, any doubts about his indifference to this particular leggy blonde with a trust fund vanishing from her mind.

She tried to yank her foot away, but J.T. grabbed her ankle, a stubborn jut to his jaw. His cheeks were flushed, his mouth set in a determined line. He looked the way Odysseus must have, lashed to the mast of his ship while the Sirens attempted to seduce him onto the rocks.

But Allison was definitely no Siren, and the mere thought of seducing a man as dangerous as J.T. was enough to make her want to throw herself into the sea.

With his hand still locked around her ankle, his thigh muscles still bunched beneath the bare bottom of her foot, Allison groped for something, anything to say to break this silence that was laden with so many undercurrents.

"The girl in there," she blurted out, "the one with the baby. She looks so... so young, and so scared."

"As opposed to what? A slut who screwed half the football team for fun, and got what she deserved?"

"I didn't mean that!" Allison recoiled as if he'd slapped her. "Contrary to what you might think, you don't have a monopoly on simple human compassion, Jesse."

J.T. grabbed the antiseptic and glared up at Allison. He took up a washcloth, starting to clean the bits of glass out of her knee. It stung, but Allison was so furious she could barely feel it.

J.T. worked ferociously for long moments. Then the stiff set of his shoulders eased. When he spoke, there was reluctant apology in his voice. "I didn't mean to jump all over you like that."

Allison swallowed hard, the image that husky voice stirred up in her mind far different from J.T.'s meaning.

"Girls like Annie happen to be one of my more dangerous buttons to push. The girls are always the ones who get blamed for the pregnancy, but I remember when I was that age. A ball of raging hormones. Seems to me that the girls were the ones who were trying to say no, and the boys, well, let's just say they'd stoop to about anything if it meant they'd get a taste of sex."

Allison looked into J.T.'s face, rugged, reckless, unabashedly sensual, and wondered what he had done to get his share. She would have wagered the bank that he'd had droves of girls flocking around his high school locker, and that he'd never had to work very hard at convincing them to give him what he wanted.

Allison felt her blood heat, a tremor coursing through her as he dabbed disinfectant on her scrapes. He bandaged her knee, smoothing the tape with the tip of his long, strong finger. Instead of drawing away when he was finished, he glided his thumb in a slow circle on the inside of her knee.

She knew she should pull away, but the feel of his caress was so warm, and she sensed it was affecting J.T., as well.

He looked up at her, his voice a little shaky. "Any other wounds, princess?"

Allison knew she should shake her head, rearrange her skirt and step back onto solid ground. Instead, she stunned herself by lifting her other foot, and setting it on J.T.'s thigh. Her throat was swollen shut. She pointed to her other knee, like an injured child. J.T. groaned. "Mike is going to beat the hell out of me next time he sees me, and I won't blame him."

"You weren't the one who dragged me across the parking lot."

"I might as well have been, the way I've been acting. In case Mike hasn't told you, I have a hell of a temper, Miss Crawford."

"Really? And you hide it so well!"

The self-deprecating grin he shot her was intoxicating as warmed brandy. "That's me. A master of subtlety."

Allison's smile faded, and she looked into those compelling eyes. Her fingers reached out of their own accord, slipping a tendril of J.T.'s dark hair behind his ear. "From what I've been able to see, you're a master of a lot of things. This place is... incredible."

If anything, J.T. looked even more uncomfortable. As if to distract himself, he slipped her skirt up again, reaching for the second garter. But the contrast of the fragile lace to his tanned skin made something coil more tightly, low in Allison's stomach, a sensation that was mirrored by the sizzling tension in J.T.'s eyes.

His fingers tightened on the garter. His Adam's apple bobbed convulsively in his throat, and despite her inexperience Allison could feel a low throb of desire pulsing in that rock-hard thigh.

"Allison, I think that..." He moistened his lower lip, like a man parched with thirst. A particular brand of thirst that was all too evident in his rigid features. "I think that maybe you should take care of this yourself." His fingers tightened over the garter.

But Allison's hands were numb, lifeless. All sensation was centered in a hot, thick pool under the backs of J.T.'s fingers.

J.T. gave a raspy chuckle. "Guess I'm not as immune to a leggy blonde as I thought."

Crash!

The hall door banged open with a decibel level to rival cannon fire, and both J.T. and Allison jumped. But J.T. couldn't disentangle his fingers from the lace and elastic that held up her stocking.

Allison all but fainted with embarrassment as a gangly boy of about thirteen slammed to a halt, midbounce into the room, his eyes wide under a mop of carrot orange hair.

"Whoa!" he gasped, stumbling a step backward. "Sorry, J.T. Didn't know I'd be interrupting something."

"You're not interrupting anything, Sonny." J.T. worked to get untangled from the garter, but it was as if it had turned into Chinese handcuffs, holding him prisoner. In desperation Allison ripped it free, yanking down her skirt.

Her face was burning up. But so was Mr. Tough-Guy James's.

"Sonny, Miss Crawford, here, hurt her knee. We were just putting on antiseptic and bandages."

"I see." The kid's tone left no doubt that he *did* see. All too well. "If you have to bandage any more, um, interesting places, J.T., don't forget to be a good boy and wear your raincoat."

"Raincoat?" Allison shot J.T. a look of pure confusion.

He looked as if he wanted to cram a wad of medical gauze into the boy's mouth. "Damn it, Sonny, did you need something in here, or did you take a wrong turn at the basketball court?"

Sonny's smile faded, and the boy jammed his hands into his jeans pockets, suddenly looking even younger and more vulnerable than he had before.

"Yeah. J.T., there was something." Sonny's eyes filled with unease. "I thought you ought to know that...well, there might be trouble."

"Trouble?"

"Eli Ramsey is back. And he's high enough to be steppin' over buildings, instead of walking around 'em."

"Perfect. Just perfect." J.T. cursed, jamming himself to his feet. "Allison, stay here." He snapped the order, then bolted out the door.

Chapter 3

Allison stared at the doorway for long moments. The uncomfortable-looking Sonny was shifting from foot to foot as he glanced at her, then down the hall. There was just enough fear in his expression to set Allison's nerves jangling with alarm.

"What's going on?" Allison demanded.

The sound of a distant crash made Sonny jump, and he looked down the corridor as if he half expected something to be charging toward him.

"Um, J.T. kicked Eli out of HomePlace three weeks ago. And, well, Eli wants back in."

Allison's brow creased in confusion. "I thought HomePlace took in all runaways."

"Yeah. Um, until Eli—" He stopped, turning red.

There was something more. Allison could sense it. But Sonny was already so edgy she didn't want to push him any farther.

The sound of shouting outside intensified, and Sonny chewed at his lower lip.

What was happening out there? J.T. had faced down the three muggers at the Stop Mart without so much as blinking. But it had been evident in his face that he was as uneasy about this Eli Ramsey's return as Sonny was.

Unable to endure sitting in the room another second, Allison grabbed up her shoes and slipped them on her stockingless feet. Catching up her purse, she slid off the cot and headed for the door—J. T. James and his autocratic orders be damned.

"Miss Crawford, I don't...don't think you oughta go out there," Sonny warned. "J.T. said—"

"J.T. isn't my guardian. Maybe I can help."

"Help?" The sick laugh Sonny gave made her skin crawl. "No, ma'am. I wouldn't count on that."

Before she lost courage she zigged around the boy and hurried in the direction of the door.

She had expected to see a bloody brawl, or some kind of wicked knife grasped in the paw of a kid over six feet tall.

What she saw was J.T. towering five full inches over a youth who was sobbing piteously, his fingers clenched in J.T.'s sleeve.

There was none of the compassion J.T. had shown Annie in those gray eyes. Rather, they were flinty, his face unyielding.

A dozen other kids were in a ragged circle around them, their features showing a range of emotion from outright loathing to empathy as they looked at Eli Ramsey.

Allison hurried down the stairs and crossed the lawn to where J.T. stood.

"Get out of here, Eli." J.T.'s voice was as hard as it had been when he'd spoken at the charity event the night before. "I don't want to see your face again."

The words lashed at Allison, mingling with the youth's wrenching sobs.

"I'll be good this time, J.T. I swear, man, I—"

"Don't waste your breath. I'm not buying it. You want someplace to stay, go to the rehab center."

"But they kicked me out, too. Where am I s'posed to stay?"

"That's your problem." There was a gritty edge in J.T.'s voice, his face pale. "We all make choices, Eli. You made yours."

"I'm sorry! I'm sorry!" Eli shrieked. "How many times do I have to say it?"

"You don't have to say it at all. You just have to get the hell away from HomePlace. Now." J.T.'s mouth tightened, a muscle working in his jaw. "Before I call the police."

"But I—I'm hungry, J.T.! Goddamn it, I—"

The scene was agonizing, even the kids in the yard looking sick. Allison feared she was going to retch, or cry, or do both. She didn't have any right to interfere. And yet, how could she just stand here and do nothing with that poor, terrified kid sobbing and alone? About to be thrown back out on the streets?

Confusion and anger welled up in her, a sense of betrayal at J.T.'s cruel indifference toward this particular boy.

"Mr. James?" Her voice was far steadier than her nerves.

J.T. whipped around, his eyes flashing warning. "I told you to stay inside. This isn't one of your charity functions, Miss Crawford. Don't stick yourself into a situation you don't understand."

"I understand that this boy is hungry, and obviously frightened. He has nowhere to go. Surely there must be some way to help him."

"There isn't. Just take your checkbook and your bad judgment back into the house and out of my way."

Her checkbook. Allison froze.

Seeing more sympathy in her face, Eli released J.T.'s shirt and wobbled a step toward Allison. "Please, lady. I haven't eaten for three days. I got nowhere to sleep. He won't... won't let me in! Bastard won't help me."

There were real tears coursing down the boy's face. Allison looked from J.T.'s rigid back, turned half away from her, to Eli's desperate eyes. Her fingers clenched on her purse strap for a heartbeat, then she flipped her purse open, fishing out two crisp hundred-dollar bills.

"Here," she said, extending them to Eli. "This will get you a room somewhere. You can call your parents."

"Damn it to hell!" J.T. wheeled, his eyes locking on the money. He made a furious grab for the bills, but Eli was faster, snatching them from Allison and crumpling them in his fist.

J.T. dove for the boy, but Eli raced away, astonishingly steady on his feet. The tears suddenly evaporated into a sneer of triumph so ugly that it stunned Allison.

"Go to hell, J.T." Eli shouted the taunt over his shoulder as he ran. "I don't need a bleeding-heart loser like you anymore."

J.T. stopped, fists clenching and unclenching. "Yeah. This is your lucky day. Your luck runs out the next time I see you anywhere within five blocks of here. Do you understand me?"

The boy made a crude hand gesture and loped down the street.

J.T.'s back was to Allison, and he stood there for long minutes, his shoulders as stiff as if they'd been cast in iron, not even the shoulder-length waves of his hair moving. The rest of the kids had drawn back, silent, waiting.

They didn't have to wait very long. J.T. turned on Allison, and she'd never seen such fury on anyone's face before. "Are you happy now, Miss Fix-It? Feel like you've done your civic duty for the day, providing for the destitute?"

"I was just trying to—to..." Allison took a step back, then bumped her chin up a notch in defiance. "*You* weren't going to help him!"

"That's right. I'm a real bastard." J.T. was inches from her face, so close his breath seared her, his eyes burned her.

"Luckily for you, Eli's pusher is a real prince of a guy. I'm sure he'll appreciate your contribution to his bankroll."

"Eli's...pusher?" Allison echoed the words, feeling the blood drain from her face.

"Even you must know what that means, princess. The scum of the earth who sells drugs to kids, gets them hooked and bleeds them dry."

Allison's anger wilted beneath J.T.'s merciless glare, the whole scene shifting into focus—J.T.'s anger, his refusal to allow the boy entry to HomePlace, and the anguish she could now see, buried deep beneath the rage in his eyes.

Her fingers clenched around her purse strap, and she was aware of a dozen pairs of solemn eyes watching her with quiet condemnation.

"I didn't know. I—"

"Why the hell did you think I told you to stay inside? I knew this was going to be ugly. Way too ugly for your precious little eyes to see."

"But what about a drug program? There must be some way to help."

"Were you listening to anything the kid said? I entered him in the best rehab available, and he trashed that chance, too. You can't help someone who's determined to go to hell on the fast road. It's impossible. That's reality, sweetheart. One I had to learn the hard way."

Allison started to speak, but there were no words to say. She swallowed hard, a lump clogging her throat. The scene in the shelter yard had been the most horrible thing she had witnessed since that long-ago day she'd been kidnapped—raw emotion, stripped of its civilized gloss. She had spent the years since her own trauma cocooned in safety, living in a calm, predictable world, where kids went to prep school instead of into prostitution, and two hundred dollars meant a trip to a trendy boutique instead of a drug buy.

She hadn't understood what was happening here, but it didn't matter.

Even the runaways who had been sympathetic to Eli blamed her for butting in where she had no right. She had intruded and made things even worse than the horror that had been inevitable from the moment Eli Ramsey had turned up at HomePlace's door.

Allison's knees started to quiver, and she struggled not to let J.T. see how badly shaken she really was.

"Mr. James, I . . ." Her voice broke. "I'm sorry. I—"

"So am I. I'm sorry I did the damned charity event. I'm sorry I dared you to come down here. And I'm sorry as hell that when I found you at the Stop Mart I didn't haul your little Saks Fifth Avenue butt back to wonderland where you belong. Climb back in your Mercedes, princess, and get the hell out of my life. I don't have time to play footsie with you anymore."

With that, J.T. stormed away. She watched him in silence as he stalked out of the fenced-in yard onto the street, picking up speed with his long, jean-clad legs. He hit the cracked sidewalk running. Running with the fierce, almost primitive beat of a man lost in rage, trying desperately to outrun some inner demon that was always with him.

Allison glanced at the rest of the runaways, all of them starting to drift away, quiet, subdued, until only the man called Buck was left.

She wanted to turn, run away from all this as fast as J.T. was. Climb in her car and floor the accelerator until she reached her apartment, a place where she didn't make disastrous mistakes, where she wasn't battered by rage and pain and gray eyes so intense it hurt her to look at them.

She turned, fully intending to rush into the driveway to her car, but only J.T.'s motorcycle stood where he had parked it. With a sick wrenching in her stomach, Allison remembered him joking with one of the boys, tossing him her car keys and telling him to take the car for a spin.

She pressed a trembling hand to her mouth, not wanting to complete her humiliation by bursting into tears.

"Missy?" The gruffly gentle voice and the beefy, comforting hand that lay on her shoulder were almost her undoing. She turned to see Buck, his head swathed in a piratelike bandanna, looking at her with sympathetic eyes. "Don't pay any attention to J.T. He just gets all torn up inside when he has to turn any kid away. Even a hard case like Eli. Takes it out on anyone stupid enough to get near him."

"I don't blame him for being furious. It was idiotic for me to—to think I understood what was happening."

Buck's mouth spread into a grin that would have done a doting grandfather proud if it hadn't been for the spider tattooed at the corner of his mouth. "Listen, little girl, you couldn't have known. Got a good heart in you. I can tell. Hell, if I hadn't known the truth, I woulda been tempted to give old Eli the five bucks I have in the bottom of my cookie jar."

Allison blinked back the tears, and allowed herself a wobbly smile at her unlikely comforter. "What did happen? With Eli, I mean? Was it just that he was an addict?"

Buck's bushy brows lowered over a hawklike nose, his face suddenly somber. "Never saw J.T. turn anyone away unless they broke one of the three rules. No stealing. No drugs. No weapons. Even so, he was doin' his best with Eli. Hell, never knew anyone give more of himself than J.T. does. He was fightin' hard for that boy—so hard it took him longer to see what the rest of us already knew."

"That Eli was on drugs?"

"Naw. That Eli was just plain bad. I thought somethin' was rotten the first couple weeks the kid was here, but I couldn't put my finger on it. J.T. said it was just adjustment time. Said to give the kid a chance." Buck grimaced. "Eli took his chance, all right. He was tryin' to push drugs to the younger kids. And when that wasn't workin', he switched to terrorizin' them, stealin' what little bit they had of any value. J.T. caught him one night after lights out.

Sonny had been takin' a late-night trip to the bathroom. Eli had him at knife point, and was tryin' to steal the gold Star o' David Sonny always wears under his shirt.''

Allison thought of Sonny, so small, so young, unable to hide the hero worship when he looked at J.T. She'd felt a gun barrel jabbing into her own side when she'd been helpless and small. She'd never forgotten the sensation, or the terror that had rioted through her veins. "My God."

"Even then, J.T. didn't kick him out on his butt, like I would've. No. Finds a rehab center that'll take him. Drives Eli there himself, and pays a helluva chunk of change to enroll the kid—money that came out of J.T.'s own pocket. But in the real world the good guys don't always win. Eli's back on the street, and J.T., well, it's killin' him to cut the kid loose, even though he knows there's no other choice.''

Allison looked back to the street where J.T. had disappeared moments ago. Had that been what J.T. was trying to escape? His own glaring sense of failure?

"Mr. Buck, J.T. wanted me to leave," she said, "but my car isn't here. One of the boys was bringing it back from the store where I had problems, and—''

"J.T. didn't mean it. He's just mean as hell when he's mad at himself. Why don't you come on in with me, and I'll give you the grand tour. After all, I figure you didn't drive all this way into the urban war zone to take in the scenery.''

"No. I wanted to talk to the kids. But I doubt J.T. would appreciate that now.''

"I can handle J.T. God knows, I've been doing it since he was sixteen himself." Buck laughed. "These kids have some stories to tell. And if you want to hear 'em, well, come along with me, missy, and old Buck'll fix you right up.''

He herded her along like a fussy mother hen, and Allison felt some of the tension inside her ease. Maybe it would be better to wait, stay until J.T. returned—calmer, hopefully. That way, she could apologize to him in person. The thought of facing J.T. at all was daunting enough. It became all but unendurable when she mixed it with the memory of the heat that had shown in his storm-cloud eyes when he'd stripped away her stocking in the infirmary.

Even so, she owed the man an apology before she returned to her calm, predictable life. And she wouldn't be a coward when it came to giving him one.

Steeling herself, she followed Buck into J.T.'s world. A world with halting tales of courage told by children who had faced more misery and pain than Allison could ever have imagined. Kids who were confused about who they were, where they fit in and whether or not their parents loved them. It was a rainbow of personalities, from shy to boisterous, hostile to obsequious, frightened to energized.

Allison would never be sure how many hours passed. She would only remember the untamable cowlick on an eleven-year-old who had fled an abusive father, or the pale dusting of freckles on a girl who had run away from home because her parents had objected to her boyfriend. The girl was one of J.T.'s success stories. She was now anxiously waiting for her parents to fly in from Tennessee to bring her home.

But the story that had broken Allison's heart the most had been told to her when she had wandered back into the infirmary, to check on the girl named Annie and her baby. In a voice that was almost a whisper Annie had confessed to being agonizingly shy throughout grade school, teased mercilessly by her classmates as her father, a career officer in the navy, had moved from base to base. Lonely and unsure, she had never had a boy pay attention to her until they had moved to a base in Yuma, Arizona. There she had met Trace McKenna, a senior with a full ride athletic scholarship to Arizona State hanging in the balance—a baseball player with a bad boy reputation, a grade point average far below where it should have been, and a pair of bedroom eyes that had half the girls in the school trailing after him in a daze.

Honor student Annie had been drafted to be Trace's tu-
tor. The coaches had expected their star to be able to pitch
come spring. Teachers had expected Trace to pass English
and Math. What no one had suspected was that an emotional trauma would hurl the two kids into a physical relationship, that would leave Annie pregnant. Trace had been
fiercely determined to marry her, but Annie had been convinced that marriage would only trap Trace, force him to
sacrifice everything he'd wanted, needed. The shy, gentle
girl had loved him too much to allow that to happen. When
her parents had discovered the truth they had confronted
Trace's, making the whole thing sound ugly and tawdry.
Her father, as unyielding in his moral standards as he was
in troop discipline, had been furious, insisting that she have
an abortion or give the child away. Heartbroken, betrayed, Annie had been on the run now for almost three
years. But during that time one thing hadn't changed.

Allison could still see her, hear her, as the girl had looked
up from the rocking chair, her eyes liquid with tears.
"There'll never be another Trace," she had choked out. "I
love him. I still do."

And now Allison herself sat in the rocking chair by the
window, cradling in her arms the daughter Trace Mc-
Kenna had never seen. She had sent Annie to eat dinner
with the rest of the kids, warning that the girl herself would
get sick if she wasn't careful.

There had been gratitude in Annie's face, and relief to
have her responsibilities eased even for an hour. "I love
April a lot, really. But I worry." She'd hesitated, her next
words more eloquent than she could ever have known.
"Babies need so many things. Clothes, food, medicine. I
don't know how I'm ever going to give her what she needs,
let alone what I want for her. A house, with a big golden
retriever in the yard and a swing set. A place she'll never
have to leave."

The toddler fussed a little, and Allison reached up her
fingertips to stroke the child's dark hair, her throat thick.

And she wondered how much a little house with a swing set would cost, and how much Annie and her baby had already stolen of her heart.

What chance did they have, pitted against the ugly world J.T. had shown her today? Whoever Trace McKenna was, in that moment, Allison hated him.

There had been a time when Allison herself had hungered for a baby. Someone to love her, carry her off to a white picket fence and a garden of her own. But white picket fences didn't have security systems, and the men Allison had met had been far more interested in her stock portfolio than babies who would put fingerprints all over their BMWs. She had put away that dream as quietly as she had so many others, slipping it between the pages of her memory like a delicate rose that had never blossomed.

She lowered her lips to kiss the toddler's forehead, humming a snippet of a lullaby one of her nannies had sung a long time ago.

She barely heard the door opening, or the footsteps drawing near her. She never even felt the tears that trickled down her cheeks.

"Allison?"

She turned her head to see J.T. standing there, his hair tousled, his eyes brooding—but not in anger. There was a lost quality in them, a kind of confusion and regret that reminded her of the emotions she had seen in the eyes of his runaways.

A tear plopped onto the baby's blanket, and Allison was suddenly aware she was crying. She sniffled and tried to mop away the moisture by leaning her cheek against her shoulder.

J.T. crossed to her and knelt, catching the dampness with his thumb. She saw him swallow hard, and he extended his hand to the toddler, gently curling the tiny fingers around his long one.

"Annie told me you were in here." He seemed so different, stripped of his outward armor of anger and fury, of

toughness and scorn. There was something almost vulnerable about the curve of his mouth, the shadows beneath his
eyes. "I . . . God, Ali, I'm sorry."

She tried to smile at this J.T., this outlaw with the soul of
a guardian angel. "Me, too. Buck told me about Eli. I
didn't understand."

"How could you have known? Especially when I didn't
tell you. I wanted you to be a hard, cold ice queen. Or one
of those do-gooders who only care about getting their donations listed in an appropriately conspicuous place on the
social register. But you aren't any of those things, are you?
You're just . . . just what you seem. A beautiful, sensitive,
caring lady with far too much class for a hardcase renegade like me."

Allison hugged the toddler more tightly, and looked into
J.T.'s face, half-hidden by his long, dark hair. Her fingers
trembled, but she reached out and laid the very tips against
that stubborn, square jaw, felt the heat of J.T.'s skin melt
against her.

"You can cut the tough-guy act with me, mister. You
forget that I know you carry squeaky frogs around in your
pockets."

J.T. laughed, the sound a little sad. He turned his face
until his lips were beneath her fingertips, and Allison was
amazed at how warm and soft such an unremittingly sexy
mouth could be.

His eyes drifted shut, thick fans of sooty black against his
tanned cheekbones.

"J.T., what's going to happen? To Annie and
April?"

His eyes fluttered open, and J.T. pushed himself to his
feet. She'd seen him furious, sexy, obnoxious, teasing.
She'd never seen the weight of weariness that stooped his
shoulders now, and shadowed his rugged features. He
scooped the child out of Allison's arms, his hands brushing her breasts. Quietly he turned to where a Portacrib was

set up, and snuggled the toddler into the nest of blankets. He tucked the frog beneath little April's hand.

"What's going to happen to them? I don't know." His back was to Allison as he leaned over the crib, his head bent. "I talked to Annie's parents yesterday, tried to talk some sense into them. She's welcome to come home, as long as she gets rid of the baby. The shame of an illegitimate child would be too much for the colonel."

"Give up the baby? But she worships that child. Surely, if her parents saw April, they'd change their mind."

"I doubt it. No, Annie is going to have to find some way to get through this herself. And, in all honesty, the outlook isn't good. She hasn't finished high school, so getting a job will be next to impossible. Even if I could find her work that didn't pay starvation wages, who would take care of the baby while she was gone? Add to that food, medical care, someplace for them to live that's safe..." He heaved a sigh. "Well, you get the picture."

"Isn't there someplace for girls like Annie? Where there is child care and schooling, and—"

"There are some programs. I've been making calls. But most of them are full at the moment. I've been looking into starting one up myself in a great old turn-of-the-century house about ten miles out of the city. Zoning problems can be hell. Seems suburbia doesn't want a bunch of unwed mothers cluttering up their scenery."

"I know some people who might be able to help."

J.T. turned toward her. "Know what? I might take you up on it, princess."

"Please, J.T. Do. Let me help. I know you're wary of accepting contributions, but I won't get in your way. Say the word, and I can get enough funding for you to revamp that house from top to bottom. Get the girls out of the city."

"Out of the city? I've wanted to do that with all the kids—show them that there's a world out there beyond what they see. I've been working closely with a Wilderness Survival program, and have been able to filter a number of kids into that.''

''What about a lakefront cabin?'' Allison asked, suddenly eager. She crossed the room to J.T., her eyes shining as she caught his hand. ''I have a place on the northwest shore of Arawak Lake about a hundred miles from here. It's beautiful there, very private, with deer and forests, miles of trails winding through it.''

Arawak. J.T. chuckled. Even he had heard of the place—exclusive, expensive and impossible to get into unless you were a member. The idea of taking Ben and Sonny and Annie to hang out in one of those rich-but-roughing-it cottages was funny beyond words.

He shook his head with a grin. ''I bet your high-class neighbors would fall out of their hot tubs if they saw a parade of city kids traipsing all over their perfectly manicured wildflower beds. They'd probably toss you out of the co-op, your daddy's money be damned.''

The words stung just enough to be reflected in Allison's expression. ''I'm the one who bought the cottage. And if you think it's some pretentious showplace—''

J.T. cupped his palms around her face, tipping it up until he could look into her eyes. ''Ali, I'm not trying to be a bastard anymore, though God knows, it comes naturally enough to me, I suppose. It's just that I want the kids to see life-styles that are attainable for them. And I have serious doubts any of them are going to wake up as children of millionaires.''

Allison locked her gaze on the broad expanse of his chest. He was right, she supposed. She didn't understand what was happening here. She only knew that she'd never felt this way before.

It was as if the fierce intensity that radiated from every pore in J.T.'s body had somehow pierced her own, driving so deep she would never be the same again.

She closed her eyes, strangely daunted at the prospect of returning to her apartment, with hushed classical music drifting from the extravagant sound system, and the pristine easy chairs where she could curl up and read a book. Quiet, serene, nothing out of place in her rooms, or in her life. Why did it suddenly seem like the enchanted tower where Rapunzel had lived, cut off from the rest of the world?

The charity functions she had orchestrated were as sterile as the rest of her life, when men like J. T. James were elbow deep in battling drugs and crime and parents who threw their daughters out on to the street because the girls had made a mistake.

The tears were back again, welling up in her eyes, stinging her, burning her. She lowered her eyelashes, trying to hide them.

"Ali, I'm going to drive you home now."

"Drive me? But how will you get back here?"

"I can catch the train. No big deal. It's almost dark and, believe me, there's no way I'm letting you get back behind the wheel. You might tempt more of my Outreach Program kids into lives of crime."

"Those kids were yours?"

"Yeah. They're still living at home, but not in the best situations. They're not saints by any means, but they're not lost yet."

"Like Eli?"

"Yeah." There was a world of quiet despair in his voice. "Like Eli." He paused for a moment, then his gaze found hers, solemn, intent. "I want you to go back to your nice, safe life, Allison. Forget about all this."

"Forget?" The word was broken, incredulous.

J.T.'s gut clenched. He knew he should turn away, hustle this woman out of the door, out of his life. Take her back to her fairy-tale world, and obliterate her from his own completely. But his mind still whirled with images of

Allison Crawford, outraged when he let the muggers go. Allison Crawford, her stocking sliding in a whisper of silk between her long leg and his hands. And most devastating of all, the picture she had made in this very room—an angel cradling Annie's baby in her arms.

Allison's face had been as delicately beautiful as an antique cameo, her eyes as filled with compassion and pain as the eyes of the Madonna in the Catholic church where J.T. had slept a few nights as a kid.

The Madonna who had endured all things for her son, not thrown him away like a pair of shoes that pinched. Longing reverberated through J.T., down deep, past all his defenses, and he was rocked by the force of it.

With unsteady hands he threaded his fingers through the soft, candle-shine curls at Allison's temples. Her skin was like the petals of a gardenia, rich, elegant, her silky hair snagging on his own work-rough fingers.

With his thumbs he tipped her face up, and the sight of tears trickling down her cheeks made his voice go raw. "Shh," he soothed her. "Don't you know? Angels never cry."

"How can you say that?" she asked. "They must be crying, every time they see..." The words trailed off, her eyes flicking to the sleeping toddler.

Allison's lips were trembling, fragile, pink against her soft ivory skin. Her lashes were fanned in spikes of dark gold, arched over pools of green-gold as mysterious and alluring as the waters of some mystic sea.

J.T. drowned in them. Another tear trickled over his thumb, warm and wet. He wasn't a man given to tenderness, but he couldn't stop himself from dipping his head, brushing the tear away with his lips. The taste of Allison's sorrow filled him, and J.T. felt himself hovering on the brink of an abyss only he could see.

His heart thudded against his chest, and he stepped off the edge, lowering his mouth to hers. She tasted of strawberries warm from the sun, and dreams he'd never dared to have. Her scent—elusive, expensive—filled his nostrils, setting his senses reeling, the desires he had battled hard to bank inside him flaming to life like glowing embers scattered across a carpet of needles in a deep pine wood.

His arms closed around her, and he molded her against him, aware of everything—the give of her breasts, soft pillows against his chest, the warmth of her breath, ragged and astonished, the supple length of her body, trembling just a little in nervousness and anticipation.

He wanted to drive his fingers into the cloud of gold that wreathed her face like a holy aura, wanted to crush her lips with his, make her taste the pulsing, purely masculine drive of a man who had been without the pleasure of losing himself in a beautiful woman's body for far too long.

But she felt as if she might shatter in his hands—fine boned and blue-blooded, delicate and sensitive, with shadows of all she'd been through today etched in the skin beneath those huge, ocean-kissed eyes.

Regret tore, jagged, in his chest at the knowledge that he would have to let her go. And he rebelled against the certainty, his tongue easing out, gently parting her lips.

A tremulous moan whispered from her lips and was trapped by his own as she let him into the sweet, secret place he craved, let him taste impossibilities.

When her tongue came shyly to find his, the tip brushing delicately against J.T.'s own, spears of raw desire made him harden, ache. And he wanted to ease Allison down and cover her with his body, wanted to cradle his hips in those long, elegant legs and drive deep, losing himself for just a little while.

It was the most difficult thing he'd ever done to pull away. But J.T. had made tough choices before.

As he broke contact with Allison's mouth, she whimpered in protest and tried to recapture his kiss. His hands tightened on her shoulders, holding her away.

There was hurt in her eyes again, and confusion.

"Ali," he murmured, "this was a mistake."

Her mouth, reddened and damp from his kiss, crooked in an uncertain smile, but J.T. could tell she was worlds away from brushing this off as easily as she would like him to believe. "It wouldn't be the first mistake I made today. Don't tell me. It's against your moral code to kiss a millionaire's daughter?"

"I guess it's against my code to kiss anyone at all." He looked down at where her thin silk blouse caressed her breasts. Her hardened nipples pushed like delicate pearls against the fabric. His hands were burning to touch them, his tongue was burning to taste. "HomePlace is my life. It's all I have room for."

"It was one kiss. I was hardly expecting a marriage proposal."

The lady was tougher than she knew. J.T.'s attraction was one thing. The unwelcome sense of respect he had for this woman jumped up a notch, and was almost more dangerous.

"I know," he said. "I just—"

"Didn't want me to expect you to show up on my doorstep Saturday night in a suit and tie with a dozen roses in your hands?" She laughed just a little, her voice thin, shaky. "You don't have to explain, Jesse. I think I understand. But if you ever need anything—anything at all. For the kids, or for yourself..."

J.T. tortured himself by running his fingers, one more time, lightly over the halo of her hair.

"I'll know where to find you, princess."

In my dreams, when I'm lying in my bed, alone. Whenever I look at the child you held, or go into the infirmary, where I touched you, taunted you, saw you smile.

If you ever need anything...anything at all... Her words echoed through him.

He leaned his forehead against Allison's own, knowing that the one thing he needed from Allison Crawford could never be his to take.

Chapter 4

It was the kind of night J.T. dreaded. Cold and wet with a relentless drizzle seeping beneath garbage-bag ponchos. Every sheltered cubbyhole a bone of contention.

J.T. guided the battered HomePlace van in a slow path where the street kids usually congregated, ready to offer them rides back to the shelter. He'd swept through the area three times already tonight, and had managed to take two boys and a girl back to where Buck waited with hot soup, dry clothes and a bed far warmer than the space beneath an El-train overpass, or the vestibule of a cockroach-ridden housing project. And yet, he knew there were more kids out on this miserable night—hidden away, lonely and cold.

Nights like these he could feel them, unquiet spirits, slipping through his fingers like the chill mist that huddled in the glow of the few streetlights that hadn't been shattered by rocks or bricks or gunfire.

J.T. sagged against the van seat and grabbed up a tepid cup of coffee, brewed so strong it could dissolve nails. He slugged a gulp of the bitter stuff down and fought off waves of exhaustion.

It hadn't been his turn to work the streets tonight. Even now he should be up in his efficiency apartment on the top floor of the shelter. He should be lying in his narrow bed, asleep. Or, at least, as close to sleep as he ever got. God knew, he usually had a hard enough time getting through the night without waking up a half dozen times—a hold-over from the years when sleeping too soundly could mean a knife in the gut, or someone stealing the precious food tucked in his backpack.

But tonight it hadn't been his innate restlessness that had jabbed him until he couldn't find peace. It had been the picture of an angel with gold hair and wide, vulnerable eyes. A woman that was the living image of every unattainable dream J.T. had ever had.

In the end he'd dragged on his jeans and stumbled down the stairs, where he'd given the volunteer assigned to the van a night off. Hell, even driving around in the rain at three o'clock in the morning was preferable to tossing and turning alone in his bed, torturing himself with images of Allison Crawford.

He dragged his hand across gritty eyes, his mouth twisting in wry defeat. What he hadn't suspected was that she would follow him out onto the road, be waiting for him in the pools of light and in the echoing stillness.

Images of what he'd like to do to her, with her filled his mind. Visions of things that could never be. Because the only relationships J.T. dared to allow himself with women were the most surface kind—protected sex enjoyed by two people with the mutual understanding that there were no promises hidden between the sheets.

But even though he knew he would never be able to relegate Allison to the kind of casual fling he was comfortable with, it didn't keep his mind from spinning out fantasies tied up in those long, sleek legs in white lace garters.

Just the thought of them, so excruciatingly feminine with their touches of pink ribbon, was enough to make J.T. grind his teeth. In his years on the street J.T. had seen sex bottled and sold in every method imaginable. But the sexiest thing about Allison Crawford was that the lady didn't have a clue that she'd made his jeans hot enough to melt glass.

J.T. slowed the van, his eyes instinctively probing the shadows between two warehouses.

He'd had his share of women—especially in the days before he'd started HomePlace and gained some hard-won direction in his life. But never had one affected him the way Allison had.

He took another swig of the coffee, then shoved it back in the cup holder and muttered a low curse. The ache of arousal throbbed beneath the fly of his jeans in spite of the cold and the rain and the fact that he had passed exhaustion and made a lateral move to comatose a half hour ago.

Damn. This was crazy. He'd just met the woman the night before. And even then he'd known she was trouble in high heels.

He grimaced, remembering the phone call he had made the minute he'd gotten back from taking Allison home. He'd wanted someone to check on her, and Mike Flaherty had been the only one he could think of.

Mike, half crazed from packing for his impending wedding trip, had been less than thrilled with the interruption. And he'd gone ballistic when J.T. had recounted Allison's trip to HomePlace.

J.T. had waited by the phone until Mike had called back, more irate than ever. Allison hadn't been home. Obviously the lady had not been nearly as shaken as J.T. himself over what had almost happened in front of the Stop Mart. An incident that could've been far worse if it hadn't been three mixed-up kids who had attacked her.

There were plenty of serious criminals roaming the streets looking for an easy mark. Ones that wouldn't have hesitated to use a knife or a gun, not only to take Allison's purse, but to victimize her in far more personal, terrifying ways.

J.T. ground his teeth, trying to shove away the image of Allison, helpless, hurt. She was fine. Safe, back in her gilded cage with the security guards and the triple dead bolts on her doors. Goddamn Dirty Harry probably couldn't break in to her apartment.

Yet being brutally honest, J.T. had to admit that it wasn't the fact that she'd almost been attacked that was making him crazy. It was that damnable kiss that had made his blood sizzle with a hunger so fierce he could have laid Allison down on the floor and taken her, fast and hard, in ways that were far too primitive for a classy angel like her to understand. He cursed again.

He tried to put her out of his mind, forget about her and focus on things that really mattered. Sonny and Annie and the baby, whose fever had blessedly abated. The kids he'd processed into HomePlace tonight, and the zoning problems he was having with the new shelter he was trying to start up outside the city.

But Allison Crawford had gotten under his skin, and no matter how hard he tried, he couldn't shake free of her.

He felt his eyelids grow heavy, weighed down with the memory of Allison's mouth opening under his, letting his tongue steal in to taste the hot, wet, unbearably erotic secrets hidden beneath that angel's smile.

He'd felt the surprise in her, the astonishment. Thick enough that he was certain the society men she'd kept company with had never introduced her to the hotter side of her own sexuality. God, what J.T. wouldn't give to be the one to show her.

The hardness at his groin was a physical pain, almost as deep as the ache in his chest. God, what he needed was one hell of a cold shower. His eyes scanned the drizzle, his mouth twisting. What better place to walk off his sexual frustrations than in a downpour?

J.T. pulled the van over and parked it, turning off the key. He climbed out into the rain, the chilly moisture dampening his hair, his face. He jammed his hands into the pockets of the Long Rider coat that enveloped him from shoulders to past his knees, and started to walk.

It wasn't the first time he'd paced the streets on foot, looking for kids in hiding places not visible from the van. He knew the dangers, and accepted them as part of the price to be paid to find the kids, who were far more helpless and vulnerable than he was. J.T.'s only concession to the danger was that he never carried more than ten dollars in his pocket—a fact so well known on the streets that he was rarely bothered.

One more sweep of the area and he'd head back home and try one more time to get some rest. He passed a hooker, who offered him a helluva deal, and a wino down to his last shot of booze.

J.T. rummaged in his pocket for one of the plastic trash bags he always carried, and covered the old man with it, in an effort to protect him from the rain. Two teenagers were necking in a doorway, totally oblivious to a woman three stories up, who was sick of her man's freaking attitude.

J.T. raked his fingers through his hair and kept walking. The street sounds were familiar, strangely comforting as he continued block after block, nearing the outside edge of the area he was patrolling. He'd walk to the row of abandoned shops sixty yards ahead, then circle back and call it a night.

He was just quickening his step in anticipation when he heard something, muffled, out of sync with the other sounds. He froze, brows lowering as he tried to discern what the noise was, and where it was coming from.

"No! No, please!"

A girl's voice, pleading and terrified. It made the hairs at J.T.'s nape prickle. Every muscle tense, he turned, his gaze probing down an alley, the hulk of a trash hopper crouching in the shadows like a beast.

There was a thunk of something crashing into the metal, and a sob of pain.

Damn. It was times like these that tempted J.T. to carry some kind of weapon, but he'd learned early that violence only produced more violence on the streets, a vicious circle of escalating weapons and injuries. The only way to beat it was to use another defense—the street smarts he'd learned the hard way.

His boot hit something, and he looked down to see a bottle of wine with a little left in it. Thinking fast, he scooped it up, pouring the dregs down the front of his coat. He locked his fingers loosely around the neck of the bottle, and started weaving in a drunken path down the dark alley, wondering if he was walking straight into the barrel of a gun.

His eyes, half-hidden by his shaggy hair, were piercingly alert, taking in the sight of two burly men and a shadowy form that looked so small and delicate they could crush her with the palms of their hands.

"P-please. I don't . . . don't want to . . . I didn't see anything."

J.T.'s gut clenched. There was something in one of the guy's hands, black and shiny in the weak glow of a security light about twenty yards away. But even the gun wasn't as terrifying as what the other man was threatening her with.

"This isn't going to hurt a bit, kid. A little sting from the needle, and you'll be so high you won't even know you're dead."

The bastard had the girl by the wrist and was fighting to pin her against the wall, but small as she was, the kid was battling back, clawing and scratching. Even that wouldn't keep the needle out of her arm for long.

The gun-wielding son of a bitch laughed. "Hell, IceMan, can't you even handle that much woman? If you don't get this over with, I'm gonna have to blast a hole in her, and you know the boss doesn't like things to get messy. Too many questions.''

"Shut up, Earl. If I needed your advice I'd—oof!'' The girl's knee flashed up, driving into IceMan's groin. He doubled over, the syringe flying. The gunman roared with sadistic laughter.

In the next heartbeat J.T. catapulted over the trash hopper, diving headlong into Earl, cracking the glass bottle into the bastard's temple. Earl shouted in alarm, and crashed to the pavement, the weapon flying from his hand. The girl screamed.

"Run, damn it!'' J.T. yelled. "Get the hell out of here!''

But either the kid was very stupid or very brave. She flung herself on IceMan's back, fighting for her life and for J.T.'s.

Earl's fist slammed into J.T.'s jaw, and pain exploded in his head. The guy outweighed J.T. by a hundred pounds, easily. Again and again the man's fists slammed into J.T.'s ribs. His head swam, darkness threatening. If he lost it, the girl and he were both dead. J.T. sagged to his knees, the swirling dimness sucking him deeper. From what seemed a distance, the girl cried out. Had Ice gotten the gun yet?

No. They'd be dead if he had.

"Do it, Ice!'' Earl bellowed. "Get it the hell over with.''

The girl sobbed in terror. With his last ounce of strength J.T. shot upward, leveling Earl with a tremendous uppercut to the jaw. The man flew backward, cursing as he slammed into the concrete.

J.T. wheeled and lunged at IceMan, driving the toe of his boot into the bastard's head with all his strength. The killer shrieked with rage, falling back, the terrified girl scrabbling away from him.

In a heartbeat J.T. grabbed the girl's hand, yanking her to her feet. "Run!'' He squeezed out the command as he dragged her along with him.

His ribs were like points of a knife digging into his chest, and he could only hope none of them had been driven into his lungs. His head whirled, his gut so battered he felt ready to retch.

But he didn't dare stop. IceMan and Earl were probably already on their feet. He and the girl had to get the hell out of here. But where? He stumbled on, his breath rasping in his chest. He couldn't take this kid back to HomePlace—an action that would be tantamount to painting a target on the front of the shelter. Even the van was impossible to use; it had the shelter logo painted on the side.

Damn it, why the hell did Mike have to leave town now? He could take her to the police, and—

Gunfire shattered the night, a searing pain ripping through J.T.'s right side. He cried out, the impact driving him to his knees. He felt the warmth of his own blood dampening his shirt, his jeans. But he ignored it as the girl reached under his shoulder, shoring him up.

"Please, mister! You gotta keep going!" She was crying. And J.T. knew there were five more bullets in that police issue weapon with her name on them.

He staggered to his feet, knowing they'd never outrun them now. One arm locked over his wound, he stumbled into a labyrinth of alleys. In those dark, secret places were a hundred spots to hide. He should know. He'd flushed enough runaways from them.

He dared a glance over his shoulder. The two killers were barely sixty yards behind. Another shot rang out, slamming into a pile of boxes to J.T.'s left. The girl screamed, running faster.

J.T. swerved into another alley, then rounded a second bend, heading for a coal door in the ruins of a burned-out grocery store.

Raising up the door, he motioned the girl to slide down the chute. She did, without question. J.T. grasped his side and followed. The rusted coal door creaked on half-frozen hinges as he closed it, the sound like a cannon shot to J.T. His heart pounded, and he could only pray Earl and

IceMan hadn't heard. Grabbing a length of charred wood, he jammed it through the coal-door's lock.

He braced himself at the top, listening, waiting. What seemed only seconds later he heard the two bastards cursing each other out, the voices right on the opposite side of the rusted door. J.T. pressed his face to a crack in the iron, just able to see the killers in the streetlight filtering down the alley.

"Damn, this is going to get ugly if we don't find them."

"We're safe as hell." IceMan's voice, more muffled. "Cut a deal...cop. Hell, he'll have the whole precinct looking for them...then we can take 'em out."

J.T. looked toward where the girl was, sensed her huddled in the shadows, terrified. God, what had she stumbled into? It was clear this was not an instance of a young girl being assaulted. It was something even more ominous.

He tore off a piece of the T-shirt he'd worn beneath his sweater, and wadded it up against the wound. It had burned like fire after the initial impact, then had seemed blessedly numb for a few minutes. But now...now it felt as if someone was shoving a white-hot poker into his side.

He had to get this kid out of here. Fast. If nothing else, before he passed out and bled to death. He thought of Mike, his usual ally when things got tangled up like this. But Mike was in Vegas. Son of a bitch. J.T. had heard the creeps talking about cops—dirty cops. But which ones? The uncertainty made J.T. leery enough not to go to the station. He had to get the girl somewhere safe. Call Mike. Mike would know what to do. Who to trust in the department.

J.T. shifted, and shards of pain cut a vicious path through his side. He gritted his teeth against a groan.

Hell, what hotel did Mike say he was going to be in? He'd said they were going to pick one out when they got to Vegas. Knowing Mike, he might decide at the last minute that getting married in Guadalajara would be even more romantic.

No, he had to get the girl out of here, somewhere safe.

Safe... He had a fleeting image of Allison Crawford's towering high rise, with its security guards and visitor codes and enough locks to guard Fort Knox.

But he shoved the thought away. That was the last thing he could do, endanger Allison by tangling her up in a mess so down and dirty he didn't have a clue how it would shake out in the end.

But he was just about out of options. He had ten bucks on him, and no way to get them out of the city. And even if he did manage that much, where would he go? Even a fleabag hotel that rented by the hour would cost more than ten bucks. Not that they'd let someone who had a gunshot wound past the reception desk to begin with.

He had to go somewhere, far enough away to be safe, somewhere no one would suspect, just long enough to contact Mike or Buck and figure out what the hell he was going to do next.

"M-m-mister?" the girl asked in a shaky voice. "Are they...g-gone?"

"For now." J.T. let himself slide down the chute to where she was, a disembodied voice in the darkness.

"Th-they were going to k-kill me."

"Yeah. I figured that much out. The question is, why?"

He heard a scuffling sound, like the kid shrinking back. "I don't know."

J.T. forced his voice to be gentle, though his teeth were gritted with pain. "I'm J.T.—short for Jesse James." He used the name in hopes of getting the kid to relax a little. "Helluva name, isn't it?" He sensed her quieting.

"Like the outlaw?" the girl asked tentatively.

"Right. I run a shelter for kids about ten miles from here. I was looking around for anyone who wanted to get in out of the rain when I heard you were in trouble. What's your name, sweetheart?"

"Ah...I..."

The kid was going to lie through her teeth. He could tell.

"You can call me Raine."

Raine. Perfect. J.T. rubbed his face with his hand. Didn't anybody pick a fake name like Linda or Sue anymore? But he didn't have the energy to argue with the kid at the moment.

"Why were those men trying to kill you, Raine?"

"I told you, I don't know!" she cried, defiant.

"I think you do. And if I'm going to get us out of here, I have to know what this is all about."

"I can't tell."

"How about if I tell you what I know? IceMan and Earl are connected with drugs, considering that poison they were trying to pump into you. Not only that, but it sounded to me like they might have other connections. Connections with the police."

The kid whimpered. "No! Thank you for helping me. I'm grateful. Really. But this whole thing was just a mistake."

"Pretty dangerous mistake, then. Damn it, Raine, let me help you." J.T. took a step forward, and bit back a groan as pain unfolded in his side.

If he kept losing blood at this rate, he wouldn't be able to help an old lady cross the street, let alone make an escape with this kid. He had to get away from here, somewhere he could think what to do.

He closed his eyes. Allison Crawford's face rose up again, a shimmering angel face, through the red haze of his pain.

He grimaced. Apparently his libido was oblivious to gunshot wounds.

If you ever need anything... Her voice echoed in his mind.

J.T.'s mouth twisted as he envisioned dialing her number on a pay phone. *Allison, I've got a little problem here. I'm shot and need a getaway car because some possibly crooked cops linked in with a band of drug lords just tried to kill me. Mind if I come up to your lake house and take out the bullet?*

Suddenly J.T. froze, the solution hitting him with as much force as the bullet had fifteen minutes before.

What had Allison said about the place on Arawak Lake? Private, secluded, a cottage on the northwest shore. Hell, she'd all but offered an engraved invitation to him and the kids before he'd made her see how ridiculous it was.

He could be in and out of the place in a few days—however long it took to find Mike. And after it was all over, he'd let Allison know....

There was a sound out in the alley, and J.T.'s heart lodged in his throat. Silently he climbed to the coal door again and peeked out.

A skinny dog was rooting through the garbage, wagging its tail. But it didn't take a college education to figure out that IceMan and Earl would probably be doubling back soon with a party of their other friends.

"Raine, we need to get moving."

"Where? Where can we go? The police—" she started, then, obviously remembering her plea of ignorance, she stopped.

"I know somewhere safe. We just have to hot-wire a car."

"Steal a car? Won't you... well, get arrested?"

"Nah." J.T. couldn't help smiling just a little, in spite of the burning in his side. "I only steal cars from people I know."

His smile faded as he opened the coal door and slipped out into the night.

Hell, being arrested for grand theft auto was the least of his worries at the moment. The question was, would he be able to stay conscious long enough to drive the damn thing down the block, let alone a hundred miles to Rapunzel's lakeside castle?

Chapter 5

Arawak Lake spread in an endless sheet of liquid onyx, a ribbon of moonlight shimmering across its surface in a ghostly path. Allison sat in the darkness, curled up in the wicker rocker on the balcony that jutted out from the second story of the lake house, and listened as the birch trees on Sky Painter Point rustled in the soft breezes, the cry of a loon rippling out into the night.

She had wrapped herself in the familiarity of those sounds a thousand times, like the strains of a half-forgotten lullaby. But tonight the loon's plaintive call made her throat ache, and the warm kiss of the breeze only reminded her of the feel of J.T. James's hands against her skin. Lived-in hands that were scarred and callus roughened. So strong that she had wanted to lean her cheek against them, and sink deep into the sensation of being touched when she had been alone for so long.

The breeze whiffled the oversize white shirt that she wore, the thin material barely a whisper of cloth over her skin, and it was as if, in that delicate brush, she could feel

J.T.'s presence. That potent aura of danger and anger, wrapped up tight around a heart that was broken, bleeding because of the battles he fought every day.

A restlessness stirred inside Allison. In that brief time she had spent at HomePlace, J.T. had opened her eyes, shown her things she hadn't wanted to see. The frivolous bent of her life, the unimportance of parties and trust funds. The emptiness of going home night after night, with no one waiting for her.

The moment J.T. had dropped her off at her apartment this restlessness had torn through her, jagged, unrelenting. She had looked out the window onto the glittering city lights, but she had no longer seen beauty, but rather, faces, floating in the mist—lost children, frightened children, and children trapped in such hopelessness that they turned to the savagery they had lived with every day.

The walls had closed in on her—that nightmarish sensation that could carry her back in an instant to the cramped, dark trunk of the car where she'd been held prisoner. And she had taken the only cure that had ever worked to banish those ghosts.

Despite nerves still jangling from the encounters of the past day, she had flung a few necessities into a suitcase and called Ernie, asking him to drive her up to the lake.

The older man's face had been a thundercloud of suspicions when he had arrived a half hour later, and he had spent most of the drive trying to wheedle out of her what had precipitated this sudden trip.

Allison had been so emotionally exhausted she hadn't even felt guilty about lying to him.

She had told him that Leah Madsen had called and was going to be at the lake for a few weeks. They hadn't seen each other all winter, and Allison was anxious to see her best friend.

There was enough truth in the story that Ernie had bought it—almost. Though, crafty old demon that he was, he had insisted she call and notify Leah that she was there before he left. It wasn't safe, the older man had lectured, to be alone in the middle of nowhere, with no one nearby aware you were around. Heaven knew what could be lurking in all those damned woods Allison insisted on being buried in the middle of.

It had been a reprise of the broken-record warnings Ernie always gave her when he left her at the lake—an echo of the displeasure of Allison's father. She'd heard the warnings so often she barely noticed them anymore.

And though Allison had an aversion to being alone under most circumstances, she had never been able to explain, either to Ernie or to her father, that the lake was somehow different. Being alone here filled her with a feeling of peace, of security. A sense that was bolstered by the loaded rifle that always hung over the fieldstone fireplace.

Even though deception had never been one of Allison's strong suits, she had held a brief, fake conversation with Leah for Ernie's benefit, and then had all but shoved him out the door.

Yet once the older man had gone, she had felt the same throat-closing sensations that had haunted her in the city. Every nerve in her body felt exposed, and she had paced the lake house, not daring to flick on so much as a flashlight that might alert the other lake residents that she had arrived.

Most would give only cursory notice to the fact that someone had arrived at the cottage on the point. But Leah would hop in her Alumicraft and come zinging across the lake the moment she suspected something was stirring at Allison's place, anxious to catch up on a winter's worth of gossip.

Despite her longtime friendship with Leah, Allison couldn't bear answering any questions tonight. And one look at Allison's face, and Leah would have one heck of a lot of questions.

Allison buried her face in her hand. How could she begin to explain what she was feeling? How could she begin to describe a man like J.T. to Leah? Or the feeling of being all but mugged in front of a war-zone convenience store? How could she describe the surly, hate-filled eyes of the people she had seen on the streets? Or the smirk of triumph that had been on the face of a boy who had duped her out of two hundred dollars he would use as drug money?

It was a whole different world, as foreign as the set of any sci-fi movie. And Allison could still feel the despair in it, like a fine layer of silt over her skin. She could still taste the violence.

She shivered, suddenly cold, the darkness taking on a more sinister, brooding aura as the moon ghosted behind a raft of clouds.

She wrapped her arms around her ribs and listened, trying to recapture the soft, comforting sound of the breeze soughing through the trees, the almost tender touch of the night against her skin. The sense of security.

She was safe here. Nothing could hurt her.

Nothing...

At that instant an animal screamed. Allison jumped, her heart pounding as it was silenced, no doubt by some strong-jawed predator who was bigger and swifter.

She pressed her hand to her heart and listened, but the silence was even more ominous, the familiar night sounds stilled, as if something had reached out and slit their throats.

"Don't be ridiculous, Allison." She meant to say the words out loud, but no sound save a rasp came out. "There's absolutely nothing out there but— Oh, my God!"

The rattle of something scraping against the door downstairs made Allison's heart slam to a stop, her hands trembling. What in the name of heaven was it? Had she forgotten to wire down the garbage can lids and invited a family of racoons to a leftover feast? But no—she hadn't been here long enough to leave any leftovers.

More likely it was Clarence, the lakewide caretaker. He must have seen some sort of movement on this side of the lake, despite her best efforts to keep her arrival secret, and was now coming to check up on things.

She climbed to her feet and padded across the balcony, through the sliding glass doors, then, with one hand against the wall to guide her, she walked down the stairs to the pitch-black first floor.

She was just about to turn on the light when she heard a strange, high-pitched voice on the other side of the hewn-oak door.

"Hurry! Try the crowbar."

Raw terror jolted to the very tips of Allison's fingers, and she raced across the room to the fireplace. God, she hadn't been able to shoot a sick possum three years ago, how could she ever shoot another human being? Her hands closed on the rifle just as the door gave a horrible cracking sound and flew open. In the next breath the person on the other side staggered into the room, crashing into a table. A glass pitcher tumbled over and shattered.

Allison wheeled, the rifle ready. "Don't move. I'll shoot."

There was a beat of silence that seemed to stretch out an eternity. Then a husky voice, already achingly familiar, raked across Allison's nerves.

"Shooting me would be . . . redundant."

"Jesse?" Allison breathed in disbelief, gaping at the figure braced against the table.

"What the hell . . . you doing here, Legs? S'posed to be soaking in . . . Jacuzzi, getting dirt from . . . wrong side of town off you."

Another shadow flashed into the room, a girl's voice, terrified, breaking Allison's stunned silence.

"Please, lady, don't hurt him. He's bad off, and I . . ."

Allison lowered the gun and flicked on the light switch. One shadow took on the form of a skinny girl with hair tortured by a bad dye job. The other was indeed J.T. He stood braced with both palms on the heavy table, swathed in a Long Rider coat, his dark hair a damp tangle around features so ashen his eyes seemed to burn like hot coals.

"Jesse," Allison breathed again as those eyes captured hers. "What in God's name—" Tossing the rifle onto a couch, she raced over to him. His arms were shaking, his smile tight.

"How ya doin', Legs? Just thought I'd take you up on...the invitation for an...intimate little vacation. Hell, do I ever need . . . one."

"How did you ever find me?"

"Only cabin on the northwest side of lake."

His hands clenched convulsively in the checked table-cloth, and Allison looked down, horror clotting in her throat. A wadded-up rag lay on the table, stained with blood, while fresh red splotches spread across the fabric of the tablecloth.

"You're bleeding!" Allison said faintly.

"Yeah." J.T. stared down at the stain, affronted. "Who woulda thought a person could have...so damn much... blood. It's annoying the...hell out of..."

His knees started to buckle, and Allison cried out, try-ing to catch him, but he was too heavy. He crashed to the floor, biting back a low moan.

"J.T.? Jesse?" She flung herself down beside him, cra-dling his head in her lap. "Who did this?"

"The bad guys."

Panic electrified Allison as she ripped back J.T.'s coat, exposing the sweater beneath. It was sodden with blood.

The girl was next to him, her hands clutching J.T.'s bloodstained fingers. "It was my fault! Some men were trying to kill me, and he—he..."

A sob rent the girl's slight frame. "Oh, lady, you have to help him! He's been driving for two hours, and—"

"Damned car. Ran out of gas at the end of your... driveway. Pushed it behind your... shed. It was a real pain with hole in my side."

Pain? Allison thought wildly. It was a miracle J.T. had made it this far at all. Grabbing the tablecloth, she ripped it off, the things on top of it scattering as she balled it up and put it on the wound. "Here," she ordered the girl. "Put pressure on this. I'm going to call Doc Lewis."

"No!" J.T.'s hand closed on her wrist with amazing strength. "Can't...call doctor. Would have to report... gunshot wound."

"Good! They could start hunting the animals who hurt you."

"No. Raine not safe. Dirty...cops. Computers linked, would find...me." His eyes were silver flame, desperate. Allison could sense he was trying not to pass out.

"The police here could protect you. I know they—"

"Can't take risk. Find me. They find girl." His eyes filled with a terrible lucidity. "Kill her."

"But if you don't get help, you could die!"

"This...piece of cake. Had...lots worse. Want me to show you my scars?"

"This isn't funny!" Allison almost sobbed. "J.T., I don't know what to do. How to help. I—Leah!" She gasped out the name. "She'd know what to do. She had two years of med school, and—"

"Told you! No one...know. Danger."

"I'm not going to let you bleed to death all over my floor, damn you. Raine—is that your name? Hold him down." She escaped J.T.'s grasp and ran to the phone. She could only hope that Leah really was at the cottage. But the hollow buzz of the phone went on and on. And Allison's heart sank.

"Legs." J.T.'s voice was faint. "Have to tell you...what to do. Before pass out." There was the slightest hint of a smile at the corner of his mouth. "Don't like idea of bleeding to death on your floor, any more than you do."

Allison hung up the phone and stared down at him, so weak, so pale, the girl kneeling beside him half-hysterical.

"Have any...alcohol?"

"You want a drink?"

"No. For wound. Will...clean it...out."

Oh, God, Allison thought. She'd seen that cure in grade B Westerns. In this modern age of hospitals and anesthetics, antibiotics and laser surgery, it seemed almost profane.

"J.T., don't even think about it. I can't—"

"You have to. Do it, Allison."

"I have rubbing alcohol, would that work?"

"Yeah. And any antiseptic...have."

Allison ran to the bathroom, flinging the contents of the linen closet onto the floor until she found the first aid kit. She grabbed an armload of towels, soaking one in water, then she dragged them, along with the metal case, out into the living room, and started pawing through the first aid supplies.

The first thing was to get rid of his coat and sweater. She eased off the long coat, then grabbed a pair of scissors and went for the heather-blue knitted hem.

"Don't!" J.T. ordered. "Ruin my favorite...sweater."

"In case you hadn't noticed, you already got two holes in it yourself," Allison snapped.

"Embroider damn daisy over it if have to. Kid...made for me! Don't—"

The man was shot and he was worried about a blasted sweater? Allison almost laughed with hysteria. But he was so agitated she was afraid he'd do himself more harm. With a curse she started to work the garment over his head. She struggled long minutes, Raine lifting the wadded-up tablecloth just long enough to allow Allison to get the sweater off him.

She tossed it aside, the sight of J.T.'s bare chest making the nightmarish scene somehow agonizingly real. He was pale, the dark whorls of hair that gilded his chest a pattern of perfection that arrowed down to the waistband of his jeans. The muscles were chiseled, tense, but they were battered a sickening hue of purple, the skin stained with dark dried blood, and fresh blood, vividly red.

Allison pushed aside the wadded-up cloth so that she could see the wound. A ragged-edged hole the diameter of her thumb pierced J.T.'s right side, just below the lowest rib.

"Almost... clotted till broke open," J.T. complained.

"Is the bullet still in there?" Allison asked dubiously, certain she'd pass out herself if she had to dig something out of J.T.'s wound.

"Accommodating little sucker came out other side. Just have to clean hole."

"*Just?*" Allison repeated. The clear plastic bottle of alcohol was unopened. She wrenched off the bottle top with hands that shook.

"You can... handle it, Legs. Just think... what a bastard I was that... first night. Consider it... payback."

"How can you even say that?" Allison's fingers clenched on the bottle, and her eyes filled with tears. She saw J.T.'s face through them, his eyes such a rare hue of silver.

"You can... handle this, Ali. Stronger than... think."

She held the bottle over the wound for a long second, then upended it over the dark, deadly hole.

The liquid was ice-cold as it splashed over her hand, J.T.'s guttural cry fire hot, searing her ears. He arched back, twisting savagely, but keeping the wound beneath the stream of alcohol.

"Jesse... oh, God," Allison cried, cradling him in her lap, holding him tight. His whole body convulsed, then he lay deathly still.

Raine's voice came, timid, sick. "Is he... dead?"

"No." Allison's own hand was pressed to J.T.'s heart as if to convince herself. She drew strength from its steady beat. "We have to bandage this, then get him into bed."

She made quick work with gauze dressings, wrapping the strips around his chest, padding the areas of the bullet wounds. Then she cleaned up the blood on his chest and his hands. His skin was clammy, cold, and she couldn't help remembering how warm it had been when he'd touched her at HomePlace.

Oh, God. Don't let him die, she thought as she knotted one last loop of gauze around his middle. There are so many kids who need him. Kids like the girl who was even now sobbing quietly, terrified out of her wits.

A girl who had obviously crossed paths with the most frightening segment of criminals—those who pushed drugs, and those who hid behind badges.

"Come on, Raine. We'll put him in my room." It was the only bedroom on the first floor of the cottage. Allison took J.T.'s face in her hands, the light stubble abrading her palms. "J.T., listen to me. We have to get you to the bed. You're going to have to cooperate. Raine and I aren't strong enough to get you there on our own."

J.T. groaned in protest, curling his battered body onto his left side.

Allison tried to get leverage beneath his shoulder, but the man was deadweight, impossible to budge. Damn him, she couldn't just leave him lying in the middle of the floor. "J.T., get up. Now!" Nothing. Feigning anger, she tried another way. "Some tough-guy outlaw you are, James," she taunted. "A big baby, lying here. But then, wasn't Jesse James a—"

The name was like a cattle prod, even through his stupor. He rolled over, his eyelids fluttering. He made a heroic attempt to glare. "Don't . . . call me . . . that."

"I'll put it on every billboard in Chicago if you don't haul yourself into my bedroom right now."

He grumbled something, his eyes dark, but he made an attempt to lever himself up. It wasn't much, but it was enough. Between Allison and Raine they managed to get him to his feet, and half carry, half drag him into the room that had been Allison's whimsy. Battenburg lace dripped from windows and tabletops, and an antique brass bed filled the corner of the room, the textures a surprisingly lovely contrast to the rough-hewn bedroom walls.

Huffing and puffing, Allison shored J.T. up while Raine flung back the coverlets, then they eased J.T. down onto the bed. He swallowed a moan as he sank into the mattress and flung one bare arm up across his face.

Allison sagged against the wall, looking at him. Miraculously, the bandages hadn't slipped. He could almost have been sleeping there, if it hadn't been for the dirty, damp jeans that still encased his legs.

They were going to have to come off, too. The thought shouldn't have been as daunting as tending to a bullet wound, but it was. All Allison could think of was the image of his jean-covered lap in HomePlace, the rigid evidence of his arousal. He'd seduced her with those hot eyes, that flashing intensity. He'd infuriated her, teased her, yelled at her, and he had held her, kissed her, a heartbreaking sense of yearning in his lips.

She shook herself. She was being ridiculous. How could she even think about such things when the man was lying in her bed, half-dead?

She felt Raine's eyes on her, wary, uncertain, the girl hovering in the doorway. Allison's cheeks flushed. One thing she didn't need while she dragged off J.T.'s pants was a teenage girl watching her.

"Can you go into the living room and clean up some of the mess?" Allison fought to keep her voice steady. The girl nodded, then, with a last look at J.T., turned and went into the other room.

Allison walked to the side of the bed, and was horrified to see that J.T.'s face was pillowed on the wispy, feminine nightgown Allison had laid out on the bed when it was still light. There was something devastatingly sexy about the harsh, virile planes of that face against the silk. Her hands trembled more. She tugged off his worn boots and let them drop to the floor.

Steeling herself, she briskly unfastened a woven-leather belt, then unfastened the first steel button. She prayed for a nice zipper—a tab she could hold by the tips of her fingers and glide down in three seconds, keeping her knuckles studiously away from brushing J.T. But why should the man make anything easy? The jeans were the kind with a row of heavy metal buttons, tucked tightly into frayed buttonholes dotting the entire length of that bulge. Allison swallowed hard. It wasn't as if she had designs on the man, after all. She was just trying to make him more comfortable.

She worked the second button, then the third down, her fingers tingling, burning where they brushed the soft swell of J.T.'s private parts. The next button was agony, and she all but tore the rest free in her hurry to finish.

He was wearing an ancient pair of running shorts underneath, also bloodstained. Allison grabbed the waistbands of both garments, working them down over his hips, her eyes averted, locked on a wreath of dried flowers on the opposite wall.

J.T. gave a muffled curse. "Trying...kill me?" he asked groggily.

Allison glared at him, cheeks burning. "You've already done a good job of that yourself."

"Mmm. Some...angel of...mercy."

He was almost smiling, just a hint of gray visible through the thickness of his lashes.

"A man in your position can't afford to be overly particular." Tugging the jeans free, she threw them on the floor. Hastily she dragged the blankets over J.T.'s naked body. She tried not to look, but couldn't erase from her mind a fleeting image of long, muscular legs, a narrow waist, wide shoulders. Masculine perfection glossed over with intoxicating danger.

"J.T.?" she asked, her voice shaky.

"Yeah?"

"Don't you dare die in my bed."

"Lots of things...like to do...in your bed, sugar. But dying's not one of 'em."

She almost smiled. Nobody with that much of a smart-aleck attitude could be on the verge of checking out. "Just remember that if you do die, mister, I'll see to the inscription on your tombstone myself. Here lies Jesse James, dead of a gunshot wound—*again.*"

J.T. gave a raspy laugh that ended in a grimace of pain. "Come back to...haunt you forever if you did."

Allison stared down into his face, afraid that he already would.

His hand groped for hers, and Allison closed her fingers around his. "Legs...never would have come if thought you were here. Sorry dragged you into this."

"After you rescued me at the Stop Mart, I consider us even."

"Could get...dangerous. People after us not...country club variety. And they don't...give up easy."

Allison's blood ran cold. She released J.T.'s hand and tried to muster a bright smile. "I've got a rifle and I know how to use it, James."

"Yeah. You're a real tough lady. Can you...do something for me?"

Allison couldn't keep herself from reaching out to smooth the dark tangle of hair back from J.T.'s face. Her fingertips clung long seconds to the curve of his cheek. "I've already cleaned out your bullet wound and undressed you. What more could a guy ask for?"

"Call...Buck. He'll be worried. Van parked on corner of Danforth and Frayne. Tell Buck...tinker under hood before...picks it up. Make it look like broke down. Don't want crooks to...connect HomePlace to Raine and me."

Allison swallowed hard. The crooks would have to be brain dead not to figure out eventually who had rescued Raine. J.T. was notorious on the streets. In the jungle of the inner city, there would be someone who would sell him out, for enough money for food, or drugs. "I'll tell him," she said unsteadily.

"Oh, and...stole a car. Have Buck call Antone and say...thanks. Tone's gonna kill me when hears...got blood all over it."

A stolen car? That probably looked as if it had been involved in the St. Valentine's Day massacre? And it was parked behind her boat shed? If someone from the lake stumbled across it... Allison bit her lip. "I'll take care of it."

"And me?" His voice was groggy. He dragged the hand he held to his face and rubbed his mouth against it, breathing deeply. Her throat thickened.

"Go to sleep, Jesse," she said softly, wondering if he'd ever heard such words before. "I'll take care of you."

She watched him for long minutes as his eyelids fluttered shut, a kind of peace drifting over those pain-ravaged features.

But that sliver of peace was shattered in the next second. Raine came running in, her eyes huge, her face waxen.

"Lady—hey, lady," the girl gasped out. "I think someone's coming."

Chapter 6

Panic pumped through Allison, making her head spin. She grabbed the brass bedpost, fighting for balance.

Killers after us... not give up easy... J.T.'s words echoed in her mind filling with images of the wild race he and Raine must have made to the cottage. A race that could have ended with him bleeding to death. A race that might, even now, have been in vain, if the men who had tried to kill J.T. had tracked him to Sky Painter Point to finish the job.

No. Allison bolted out of the room, snatching up the rifle. Oh, God, if only she could call for help—Clarence, or some of the other men. If only J.T. had let her call the sheriff, or—

She dashed to the window, the sound of a vehicle coming up the winding road getting closer, closer. Was it possible the driver could glimpse J.T.'s broken-down car behind the shed?

Allison flicked on the back floodlights, determined to identify the vehicle as soon as possible. As the rusted-out

Land Rover spilled out of the shadows a fierce wave of relief all but sent Allison to her knees. Leah.

Yet in the next heartbeat, panic returned, full force. J.T.
had claimed no one must know he was here. That it would
be dangerous. And Leah's intuition was sharp enough to do
Magnum P.I. proud.

Allison raced to the fireplace to hang the rifle in place,
her gaze raking the room. Raine had made some progress,
thankfully. Only a few things still remained out of place.

"Get anything stained with blood out of here," she
snapped to the girl, "then run upstairs and hide. Don't
make a sound, Raine. No matter what."

"But who—"

"A friend," Allison said. Then she muttered to herself,
"A friend who's like a bloodhound on a scent whenever
anything's wrong."

Damn, Allison thought, grabbing up the bloody tablecloth and jamming it in the first place she could reach—the
refrigerator.

"Your shirt!" Raine cried. "It's covered with blood."

There was an ominous sound as the Rover's door
slammed, Leah no doubt walking with that annoying
briskness she had toward the back door.

Allison ran into her bedroom, stripping the shirt off just
as Leah knocked on the door. Allison grabbed the only
thing she could, the nightgown that lay on the pillow beneath J.T.'s head. He gave a mumble of protest as she
tugged it free, his eyelids fluttering half-open. But she
didn't even have time to be embarrassed as she dragged the
almost sheer garment over her head. She had started to root
around for her robe when she heard Leah's worried voice.

"Allison? My God—"

Allison had forgotten J.T. had been breaking in. The
door must be damaged.

Surrendering her search, she tore out of the bedroom and
slammed the door shut. "Lee?" she called out, praying

there wasn't any more evidence left where Leah's keen eyes could see it. "I'm coming."

But Leah was already shoving open the front door, the crowbar in her hand.

"Allison? Are you all right? My God, did someone break in?"

"I'm fine," Allison cut in, certain that she looked as guilty as sin. "I went out to take a walk after Ernie left and the door slammed shut and locked me out."

"You leave crowbars on your front porch in case of emergencies?"

"Of course not." Her mind raced, searching for some logical explanation. "The boat shed wasn't locked, and the crowbar was in there."

"Why didn't you take the Jeep to Clarence's house? Doesn't he have a key?"

"The Jeep's battery isn't charged enough to start it yet. And anyway, I forgot to give Clarence the key last winter. Besides, it doesn't really matter. I, ah, I wanted to replace the door, anyway," Allison lied desperately. "You know, something in oak with stained glass insets. Of—of birch trees and . . . loons. We talked about it last summer."

"I don't remember anything about it." Leah's brows drew together. "Ali, this is way too weird. Your door jimmied open, and there's a beat-up old car parked behind your boat shed."

Allison's heart lurched. It would be just like Leah to check the car out—and find it covered with blood.

"Oh, the car." Allison attempted to squeeze out a laugh. "It belongs to a friend of mine. Someone who—who was visiting, and . . . left."

"In what? A helicopter?"

"Someone, ah, picked him up. He'll get the car later."

"Him? You had a *him* up here?" Leah's eyes twinkled as if the gender of the car's owner had just sunk in. Her mouth tugged into a disbelieving grin. "Ernie dropped you off for a secret rendezvous with some guy?"

"Yes. I mean, no! Ernie didn't know..." Allison's voice trailed off, the lies tangling in her mind. She escaped the mess the only way possible, hurrying over to give Leah a hug, crowbar and all. After all, Leah could hardly notice the guilt in her face if she couldn't see it. "Leah, it's so good to see you. Winters seem to get longer and longer."

But Leah pulled back, her taffy brown eyes narrowed under a fall of light brown bangs. Allison tried not to panic. The great mystery buff, who second-guessed everyone from Hercule Poirot to Sherlock Holmes, wasn't buying Allison's act. The amusement had vanished from Leah's expression.

"Ali, what's going on here? You're shaking like a leaf. And this place..." Leah kicked a bit of shattered glass with the toe of her hiking boot. "Something's wrong."

"What could be wrong?" Allison gave a nervous laugh. "I just...bumped into the table, and a pitcher broke. I, ah, we got here after dark, and—"

"Cut the crap, Ali. I'm not leaving until you tell me what this is all about."

"I told you, it's nothing!" Allison said, a little too emphatically. Her cheeks heated. "You've been reading too much of that murder-and-mayhem stuff again. I'm just exhausted. I'd really rather be alone. I'll come over tomorrow, and—"

But before she could squeeze out another word the bedroom door swung open. Leah wheeled, and Allison gave a choked scream. Her jaw all but hit the floor as she saw J.T. lounging against the door frame.

What in God's name was the man doing? He looked for all the world as if he had just gotten up from a session of torrid lovemaking. His eyes were hooded, and the bed sheet was caught around his hips, just hiding the swathing of bandages. If Quasimodo had just done the Texas two-step out of Allison's bedroom, Leah couldn't have looked more stunned.

"Know what, sweet thing?" J.T. slurred. "You're a real rotten liar. Better just come clean, and—whoa!" He gave the crowbar in Leah's hand a pointed glance. "Hey, lady, want me to put my hands up? 'Course," he said with a woozy grin, suggestive enough to cause nuclear meltdown in any woman's knees, "I'd have to let go of the sheet."

"Allison, who—who is . . ."

"This is the man I told you about. Jesse. Jesse, uh, Tyler," Allison stammered.

"What's . . ." Leah's gaze was locked on J.T., and she seemed to be struggling to form a coherent sentence. "What's he doing—"

"In Ali's bedroom?" J.T. finished for her. "C'mon, babe, use your imagination. I bet you can figure it out."

Allison's cheeks flamed. Oh, great. Weren't things bad enough already? An injured man was in her house. A runaway kid being chased by drug lords was hiding upstairs. And now her best friend thought she'd been sleeping with a drunk lothario.

J.T. glanced down at her, and there was pure devilment in his face despite its pallor. Ali could almost believe he was drunk herself.

"'Course," J.T. continued, "Legs was pretty mad at me at first. I slugged down a few too many shots of tequila in town, an' she forgot her key an' I busted the door, an' then . . ." He swayed a little. "An' then I banged into the table an' broke her pitcher." J.T. staggered across the room toward them and Allison was afraid he was going to collapse. She ran to his side, looping her arm around him to give him something to lean on.

His skin was fire hot, his muscles rigid. She could feel the heroic effort it was taking J.T. just to stay on his feet. Damn the man, what was he trying to do? Break open his wound one more time? She had to get Leah out of here before he passed out.

He leaned down and nuzzled his face against Allison's neck. "I'm clumsy as hell when I get...wasted, aren't I, angel?"

Allison was sure her skin must be the hue of Rudolph the reindeer's nose, underneath the flimsy nightgown.

"Jesse, you'd better go back to bed. Now."

"Mmm. Bed." He slid his hand in an intimate caress along her ribs and gave a heartfelt groan. Then he blinked at Leah with bloodshot eyes. "That's where we made up, huh, Ali? Long and slow and hot."

Leah's eyes were round, her face red—and Leah Madsen didn't embarrass easily. Allison cringed at what her friend must be thinking.

"Say good-night to Leah, Jesse. I'm going to take you back to bed." Allison forced the words from her lips, then looked at Leah. "Listen, you really need to leave now. I'll call you—"

"G'bye, crowbar lady," J.T. began, but the words ended on a low groan. Allison looked up in alarm. His face was gray, sick, his whole body trembling.

"Jesse? Jesse?" Allison cried, bracing herself against his weight.

"I think," he stammered weakly, "I'm goin'...to be sick."

He tore himself away from her, staggering toward the bathroom's open door. Allison started after him, but he slammed the door behind him.

There was the sound of a dull thud, and then retching. She had to get Leah out of there, help him.

"Ali, where did you find this guy?" Leah's voice was faint, and there were shadows in her face—shadows, Allison knew, from a messy divorce eight years ago. Wounds that Leah had become skilled at hiding, but that had never quite healed. "Honey, I know he's great looking—I mean, he'd give Mel Gibson an inferiority complex. But there's more to a relationship than a great set of biceps. You know I don't usually butt in—"

"Then don't do it now. You've been telling me for years I should get out more."

"I was thinking more along the lines of someone like that business exec your dad introduced you to last year, or—or that nice senator's son. Not some burned-out biker who guzzles tequila and calls you sweet thing. I just don't think you know what you're getting into here."

Allison had a sudden urge to laugh hysterically. Oh, yeah. She knew exactly what she'd gotten into. Corrupt police and drug pushers, bullet wounds and stolen cars and a man who might be bleeding to death in her bathroom.

"Ali, it's just not safe to be picking up men like this Jesse person."

"I've spent my whole life being safe. Maybe I'm sick of it," Allison snapped. "Now, if you don't mind, I need to check on Jesse."

Hurt flooded Leah's face, but Allison didn't have time to soothe her. Leah walked to the table and laid the crowbar on the bare wood.

"Ali, this discussion is *not* over," Leah said.

"Yes, it is." Allison winced inwardly, knowing there was only one way to make certain that Leah stayed away until the danger was past. But the cruelty of it sickened her. "When it comes to men, Leah, I hardly think you're qualified to hand out advice. Now, do me a favor and let me have my sordid little fling without having to deal with your censure."

A stricken expression crossed Leah's face. "Have it your way, Allison. You know where to find me if you . . . if you need anything."

"I won't," Ali said briskly, desperate to know whether J.T. was all right on the other side of the bathroom door.

Leah turned and walked into the night.

Allison banged the door shut and wedged a chair under the handle in a makeshift lock, then she ran into the bathroom. J.T. was sprawled on the floor, his face the same chalky white as the tile. The sheet he'd looped around his hips was a pool of white just covering his lap, and his long, muscular legs moved, restless with pain.

Tears burned Allison's eyes as she slipped her arm around his bare back and struggled to help him up. "Oh, J.T. Why? Why did you do something so stupid?"

He wedged his feet beneath him, using the wall to brace himself as he battled to stand, the sheet abandoned on the floor. "Three more minutes of you . . . tryin' to lie, and the crowbar lady would have had the goddamn FBI crawling all over the place. Now—" he gave a hoarse laugh "—now she just thinks you're sleepin' with me."

He leaned heavily against her, his skin burning her through the wispy layer of her nightgown, and Allison was excruciatingly aware that he was naked as he looped his arm around her shoulders.

"My best friend thinks I'm having an affair with a drunk," Allison said, guiding him out of the room. "That's a huge improvement."

"You can straighten the whole thing out . . . later," J.T. sneered, stumbling just a little. "I'm sure it'll be a load off her mind when she knows you . . . haven't lowered your standards enough to . . . make it with a man like me." There was an edge to his voice that had nothing to do with his pain. "The senator's . . . son'll be so . . . relieved."

"Not everyone goes hopping from bed to bed. I haven't—I don't date much." Allison eased him back onto the mattress.

"Beautiful . . . woman like you? Wouldn't be able to keep my hands off you. Hell, I'd have you . . . in the back seat of my Porcshe before we even pulled out of the driveway. Oh, I forgot . . ." He gave a weak laugh. "I don't have a Porsche."

"My social life is none of your business. Besides, I—" Allison's breath hissed through her teeth as she saw fresh blood. "Damn you, Jesse! You're bleeding again! And you're burning up with fever."

"Wanna kiss it and make it better?" He shifted just a little on the sheets, and his face contorted. "Always did have rotten…luck. First time in…woman's bed in…three years, and…too broken up to…enjoy it."

She groped for something to say to this man who infuriated her, intrigued her, tugged at her heart in a way no one ever had. But even if she'd been able to form the perfect comeback, it was too late. J.T. had slipped into unconsciousness at last.

Allison refastened his bandages, and was pulling the coverlets over him again when she heard the soft sound of footsteps in the living room, the muted scrape of someone trying to open the door.

Raine.

Allison hurried soundlessly into the room. The girl was fumbling with the door, her coat fastened, the pockets bulging.

"Raine?"

The girl wheeled at the sound of Allison's voice, her pointed little face defiant, frightened. "I'm getting out of here, now. And you can't stop me."

Allison's hands knotted, and she searched for the right words to say to the girl. But her own relationships with kids this age were limited to Leah's daughter, Darcy, and her crowd here at the lake. Their greatest dilemma was whose mother was going to drive them to the nearest mall. The only thing Allison was certain about at the moment was this—if she started ordering the girl around, Raine would be gone in a heartbeat.

"I suppose you're right," Allison allowed. "I can hardly lock you in a closet."

"I have to keep moving. You heard J.T. They'll be looking for me. The cops and Earl and IceMan."

Allison paced over to the table and picked up the jagged bit of glass Leah had kicked earlier. "That's true. But if you leave now, they won't be the only ones looking for you. The instant J.T. wakes up he'll be tearing apart the state, searching for you."

"I'm sure." The girl gave a bitter laugh. "He won't be able to move for days. Besides, why should he bother? I'm nothing to him. Just some street kid he was stupid enough to help. Since all he got for his trouble was a bullet in his side, I'm sure he won't be trying it again."

"You're wrong, Raine. Helping kids out of trouble is J.T.'s life. It's what he does, who he is."

"Well, there's nothing he can do for me. Nothing anyone can do." Hopelessness weighed down the girl's face. "I didn't want anyone else to—to get hurt because of my mistake. I didn't want—" She stopped, as if aware she'd allowed Allison to see the chinks in her armor. Allison could almost feel the girl teetering on a blade's edge of indecision.

Allison took a deep breath, and pushed the only button she could think of.

"You have to do what you think best, Raine. But you might want to consider this. There's a man in the other room who got himself shot trying to help you. A man who cares about your safety so much that he refuses to go to the hospital. He's burning up with fever, and the truth is that I don't have the slightest idea how to help him. The only thing I do know is that I can't handle this by myself. I can't leave him alone while I drive to town to get supplies. I can barely even help him make it to the bathroom. And if he gets delirious, and starts thrashing around, I'm not strong enough to keep him from hurting himself."

Raine's eyes were bright, almost teary, but her jaw was clamped in an attitude of complete stubbornness. "It's not my problem."

"I suppose not. He's just some stranger who saved your life. But there are a lot of other people who care about J.T. Who need him. Love him. You said you didn't want anyone else to pay for your mistakes. Maybe you owe it to yourself to stay here, at least until he's out of danger."

Raine fretted her lower lip. "You don't understand. I'm scared."

"I'm scared, too. But of all the places J.T. could have brought you, this is the safest. It's remote and secluded, and I know everyone on the whole lake. In a week or so a friend of J.T.'s and mine will get back from his honeymoon. A policeman named Mike Flaherty."

Raine went ashen. "No police. I can't trust them. It was a cop who—" She stopped, clamping her mouth shut.

"You can trust Mike. With his help, and J.T.'s, you could get off the streets. Be safe. Or if you wanted to be on your own, at least you wouldn't have to keep searching every street corner for someone trying to kill you."

"No. No cops," Raine insisted, her voice quivering.

Allison could tell the girl was teetering on the brink of emotions so savage that they might shatter her.

"All right," Allison soothed her. "We'll leave it alone for now. I promise."

Raine rubbed her face with grimy hands, and Allison's heart twisted as she saw that the nails were bitten to the quick. "I don't know what to do. I want—I want to go home." Her voice broke. "I just want to go home. But if they find out who I am, they'll h-hurt—"

Tears trickled from between Raine's fingers, and in spite of the purple hair and clothes that were two steps away from a cheap hooker's she looked every inch a frightened child. A child who was obviously terrified for someone she cared about very much.

Allison wanted to go to her, draw her into her arms, but she knew the girl would reject any such comfort. Instead, Allison squeezed her own hands together. "Who will they hurt, Raine?"

"I c-can't tell. I can't. I don't know what to do."

"I do. You come on upstairs, take a nice hot shower, and I'll find you one of my nightgowns to wear. Then you curl up in the guest room and sleep, just sleep. You've got plenty of time to leave if you want to later on."

Raine nodded and scrubbed her sleeve against reddened eyes. Allison took her upstairs, and got out an armful of towels and a nightgown. Raine, her hands still shaking from the emotional turmoil of the past hours, tried to drag off her coat. It slipped from her fingers, and Raine gave a little cry, grabbing for it. She caught one sleeve, but the coat turned upside down, objects clattering onto the floor. Allison's billfold tumbled out, along with a gold-plated hairbrush and the gold bracelet she had left on the deck earlier.

Raine's face flooded with horror, and she clutched the coat to her chest.

Allison knelt, fingering the beautiful gold chain. Oh, God. If anything could get Raine to bolt, she feared this was it. Damn Jesse for being unconscious, now when he would know exactly what to say.

"My father gave this to me for my birthday last year," Allison said tentatively. "And this—" she touched the roses engraved on the back of the brush "—this was my mother's. She died when I was only two years old."

"I—I'm sorry. I just . . . I don't have any money. I didn't know how else to—to get some." Stricken, Raine scooped up the brush, and set it on the dressing table. "I took the first thing I saw that I thought I could sell."

She was quiet for a moment. "My mom's dead, too. I was ten. She got sick, and Dad and me, we had to sit and watch and there was nothing we could do. I never would have taken it if I'd known."

"I'd rather you had taken anything I had, than to think of you on the streets alone with no money." Allison took up the bills, and stood. Her mind filled with the memory of another kid—a boy with two hundred dollars in his hand and a smirk of triumph on his face. Please God, she thought desperately, don't let me be making another mistake.

"Raine, I'm going to take this downstairs and put it in that little box shaped like a unicorn. You and I will be the only two who know it's there. That way, if you need to leave, you'll be able to take care of yourself. At least, for a little while.''

The girl's eyes widened. They were hazel, a beautiful brown and green and gold, lost in gobs of smeared eye shadow. ''I don't understand.''

''There's only one condition. If you do decide to leave, you have to tell me. Up front.''

''Yeah, and *then* you'll lock me in the closet.''

''No. If you really want to leave, you can leave. It's like you said, I can't force you to stay.''

''Why are you being so nice to me? I got him shot, and I tried to steal stuff from you. Stuff that was your mom's. If I had anything of my mom's, I'd hate anyone who tried to take it.''

''Maybe I know what it's like to be scared. Besides—'' Allison mustered a half smile ''—think I want to get stuck lugging J.T. around by myself? The man must weigh a ton.''

Raine smiled a little herself. ''I'm hungry,'' she said.

Allison could see the lost little girl beneath Raine's tough facade. ''You get ready for bed, and I'll bring up something.''

''My mom—she used to give me cookies and milk right before bed. And—'' Raine fell silent, her eyes flicking to the gold-plated hairbrush with so much wistfulness Allison's throat closed.

''I'll see what I can do,'' she said, then turned and went downstairs. Who was this girl, so lost, so alone? Not some kid rejected by her family. Raine had said she wanted to go home, but was afraid. Afraid of whom?

J.T. would have been able to get more information from her, find out what had driven her to run. Maybe he already knew. But J.T. was lying unconscious in Allison's bed, fighting for his life.

While Raine was in the shower upstairs, Allison looked in on Jesse, then called Buck, giving him J.T.'s instructions about the van. Although the grizzled older man sounded worried, on the whole he seemed to take the fact that his friend had been gunned down with a level of calm that flabbergasted Allison. It was sobering, making her certain that this wasn't the first time they had dealt with a gunshot wound—or not reporting it to the police.

But even that was not as disconcerting as Buck's warnings. She was on her own until Mike could be reached. She couldn't even call HomePlace from the cottage again, in case someone tracked J.T. to the shelter, and put a tracer on the phone.

After she had hung up, Allison sagged against the wall, suddenly aware that she'd expected Buck, or one of J.T.'s other colleagues, to ride in like the cavalry and take the whole impossible situation out of her hands.

She unwrapped a couple of store-bought cupcakes left over from the drive, and arranged them on a plate, then poured out some lemonade. She could hear Raine moving around upstairs, out of the shower now. And when Allison mounted the stairs it was to find the girl at the window, staring out across the lake.

"It's real pretty out there. All the lights from the other places sparkling on the water. But something was crying a minute ago. It was the saddest thing I ever heard."

"The loons."

"You mean you got some crazy neighbors?"

"No. They're waterfowl. They always sound like they're looking for something they'll never find."

Raine turned and saw the cupcakes, and for an instant there was a bittersweet pain in her face. "Thanks," she said a little gruffly, then snatched the plate away and crammed half a cupcake into her mouth.

"There's plenty more food. Take anything you want. This can be your home for as long as you're here."

Raine laughed a little. "You know, our whole house could fit on the big wood porch out there? Yeah, with enough room left over to park my dad's truck." The girl's voice dropped low. "I miss him. I miss him so much."

"He must miss you, too."

The girl's face crumpled with guilt and anguish, then she crushed the feeling. "Bet he's glad I'm gone. I was nothin' but trouble after Mom died."

"Do you really believe that?"

"He's the one who said it. About me being trouble."

"Sometimes people say things in anger—things they don't really mean."

"Oh, he didn't mean it. But that doesn't change that it was true. He told me what'd happen, but I thought... thought he was being stupid, you know? That he didn't understand."

As if suddenly aware she'd revealed too much, Raine stopped speaking, and her eyes clouded over. Allison could feel that the girl was closing herself down. It was as if Raine could handle only a certain amount of emotional pain at a time, and she had pulled off as much as she could endure, held it in her hands and let herself feel it until it became too great to bear.

Raine went to the bed and climbed in. Allison wondered if the girl's mother had come to her at night and kissed her forehead, brushing away the bad dreams.

"Ma'am?" Raine's voice was tentative. "I don't even know your name."

"Allison."

"Allison. Listen, you can—can tell J.T. that I won't run, if you think that it'd make any difference to him."

"I think it would make a lot of difference."

Allison flicked out the lights and went downstairs. Her whole body ached with tension and exhaustion and a horrible sense of isolation, as frightening as the sensation she'd had when she'd been kidnapped so long ago.

She, who made certain she was always one call away from help, who never went out alone at night, who always had Ernie walk her to the door when he dropped her off at her apartment, was now stranded in an almost indefensible cottage, a lake away from the nearest neighbor, with a helpless girl and a wounded man dependent on Allison herself for everything.

Allison shivered. If the killers had managed to follow J.T. and Raine, wouldn't they make their move tonight, before anyone else could learn what had happened in the alley, or discover whatever secret they were willing to kill Raine to protect?

With great effort Allison replaced the chair at the door with a heavy bookshelf, blocking the entrance so thoroughly that no one could come in without alerting her. Then she took the rifle and a box of cartridges and carried them into the bedroom. She leaned the gun in the corner, and set the bullets next to it.

There was no way she could leave J.T. alone tonight, racked with fever, hurt. Ready to take up her vigil in the wicker chair beside the bed, she crossed to where J.T. slept. Light from the living room streamed across his face—a face flushed with fever.

Allison stared down into the features of this man who had shattered her well-ordered life in the space of two days, leaving chaos in his path, and an awareness so sharp, so relentless she couldn't be free of it.

His raw pain seemed to press itself into her chest like a jagged stone, every line and plane of his face like a physical scar left from the misery he'd seen, the agony he'd tried to heal. But Allison Crawford was no soldier in the battle J.T. fought every day. She was tired, so tired. And scared.

She sank into the chair, and tried to make her voice calm, soothing. "Jesse, Raine promised not to run away tonight. She wanted you to know, so you wouldn't worry. She's terrified. And lonely. And I tried to help her, but I don't know how. Not like you."

He groaned, an incoherent sound that wrenched Allison's heart. And she wondered if he understood what she was saying. Wondered if he was fighting, underneath the suffocating clouds of unconsciousness, to come back to her, to Raine, to help them.

She stroked back a strand of hair that straggled across his forehead. "Raine wants to go home," she went on, wanting him to remember how much he had to live for. "You have to get better, so you can help her do that. And Annie...Annie and little April, they need you, too. And all the other kids.

"Oh, God, Jesse," she breathed, her voice lost, frightened. "*I* need you. I'm so afraid."

Hot tears trickled down Allison's cheeks, dampening the pillow. A tiny sound came from J.T., his lips moving with grinding effort. And Allison's heart broke, as even wandering in unconsciousness, J.T. tried to offer comfort.

"Don't be . . .'fraid. Will be . . . all right. Promise . . . everything be . . . all right."

His hand groped toward her, then stilled on the coverlet. His palm was turned ceilingward, his fingers cupped—long fingers, tough and powerful and so very gentle.

She looked down at J.T. for a long minute, his face on her pillow, his lashes thick on his pale cheekbones. His nose had just the tiniest bump in the bridge, as if someone had broken it a long time ago, and there was a thin white scar just below his left eye. The slight imperfections made an already beautiful face knee-meltingly sexy. His lips were parted, full and firm over a jaw set at an angle so stubborn it seemed designed to make people want to take a whack at it.

Allison was certain plenty of people had tried.

She swallowed hard, as the need to be touched, held, swept through her. The need that she'd experienced when she was seven years old and at the mercy of hard-eyed men with guns. A nightmare that seemed far too real tonight.

Carefully, so as not to jar his wound, she eased herself down onto the bed beside J.T., wanting to feel the strength in him, the life.

Her fingers trembled as she reached across the narrow space of lace-iced sheets that separated them and closed her hand around his. His hand was hard and callused and hot, roughened by a hundred tasks every day that helped the kids J.T. loved.

Allison cradled it in hers like a treasure. For a heartbeat, just a heartbeat, she felt his fingers tighten on hers. And she wondered if, just this once, J.T. needed someone to hold on to, every bit as much as she did.

Chapter 7

Someone was hurting.

Allison could hear it through the veiling of sleep. Sounds—ragged, anguished, like some creature caught in a trap.

She wanted to stop up her ears, to block out the sounds, but they clawed at her, raked her, giving her no peace.

Her eyes felt as if someone had dumped a bucket of sand in them. Her whole body throbbed with exhaustion and a fine sheen of fear—fear that she couldn't put a name to, fear that she could still feel and taste and smell.

She whimpered and shrank to the far side of the bed, but something jabbed her in the ribs, the mattress rocking beneath the impact.

She rolled over, instinctively starting to lash out, but her hand froze in midair as a guttural cry jolted her awake. She bolted to a sitting position, the familiar cottage bedroom swirling before her eyes. Her gaze locked on the figure lying beside her, the whole night flooding back to her with a clarity that made her sick to her stomach.

J.T.

Oh, God, he was the one who was hurting!

She scrambled around to kneel beside him, her heart hammering. Had his wound broken open again? Had his condition gotten worse?

She reached over, flicking on the light on the bedside table. His hair was tangled in a dark cloud on the pillow, sweat dampening the sheets where he lay. His eyes were clenched shut, his long limbs thrashing. The tortured sounds that had awakened her were coming from low in his throat as fever raged through him, his lips parched as they struggled to form broken sentences.

"Help her . . . have to let me . . . help her . . ."

Was he thinking of Raine?

"She's all right, Jesse." Allison tried to soothe him. "Everything is fine." She smoothed a hand over his forehead.

"Love her! Melissa . . ."

The words were like a knife to Allison's heart. And she tried to picture who had wrung that tormented cry from this man who was so strong. "Melissa?" she echoed.

"Can't she see . . . want to . . . take care of . . . her? Won't let me . . . doesn't want . . . me."

Allison swiped a hand across her eyes, certain now that J.T. wasn't speaking of the girl who slept upstairs. He was delirious, caught in some half world of pain that had been deeply buried.

"Don't understand!" His voice shattered on a sob, his fingers clutching her nightgown. "My fault . . . Everything because of . . . me. Have to . . . take care of . . . her."

His hands closed on hers, crushing them until they throbbed, but it didn't matter, nothing mattered but the agony tearing through him. What had happened? Who was Melissa? Some woman he had loved with the same fierce intensity that he loved his kids?

Allison was surprised by the stab of naked pain she felt at the thought.

Had the woman left J.T.? Torn herself out of his soul, leaving a gaping hole that could never be filled?

Oh, God, Allison thought, to be loved by a man like J.T., the very thought was so terrifying, so wonderful, so impossible it made her hurt inside.

"J.T., it's not your fault. Whatever happened. I know it's not your fault."

"They... can't keep me away, Melissa. I'll... find you. Promise I'll... find you." He buried his face against her breasts, the heat of his fever burning her.

Allison felt something hot and wet soak through her nightgown to dampen her skin. Tears. Tears from J.T. James.

"I'm here, sweetheart. I'm here."

"Never...called that before." He groaned, low, a sound of disbelief shuddering through him. "Did just like...said I would. Found you, Melissa. I—" His voice splintered into raw anguish. "No. You can't...mean it. Can't want...me out of your life. Want to take care of you."

The harsh sounds died, suddenly, terribly. For an instant terror jolted through Allison, and she checked to see if he was still breathing.

In the next moment she wished he'd remained silent.

"Money—that's all you care...about, isn't it?" His voice was flat, dead, and she could see a yawning chasm inside J.T., filled with darkness.

She felt the fight drain out of him, seeping away like the blood he had lost hours before, leaving him empty. Slowly the hands that had clutched at hers loosened, let her go.

Allison put her arms around him, tight, wanting to be his anchor in the sea of agony that had him in its grasp.

Now she knew the secret hidden behind those compelling wolf gray eyes. Rejection. So painful and terrible she could feel it still pulsing just beneath his skin. Whoever Melissa was, he must have loved her very much.

Allison clenched her teeth against her tears, instinctively hating the woman who had done this to him. Oh, God, what had really happened?

He had blamed himself—for what? The breakup of the relationship? Or something more? He said he had wanted to take care of her. Had the woman been hurt in J.T.'s sometimes violent world? Or had he loved Melissa, lost her even before he went into the streets?

All Allison knew for certain was that he had struggled to find this woman again, wanting only to take care of her.

But she hadn't wanted him.

Allison closed her eyes, pierced through by the poignant imaginings of what it would be like to be loved by this man with his searing intensity, to see him smile without the hard edge of cynicism, to hear him laugh without the shades of bitterness. To see his eyes shine with not only resolve, but with a kind of serenity she sensed he'd never known.

Allison stroked J.T.'s hair, savage protectiveness surging through her.

Money—that's all you care about... The words echoed in Allison's mind, blending with the memory of the first night she had met J.T. Scorn had dripped from his gaze as he had scanned the glittering array of guests at the charity event; his voice had been edged with bitterness when he'd told them to keep their money, and had demanded that they give nothing less than their time.

Even when he had dealt with Allison herself at the event, and later, at the Stop Mart, there had been such immediate hostility she'd been angry and stunned and oddly hurt.

Now she cringed inwardly, thinking about the image he must have seen—a millionaire's daughter playing hostess to a gala dinner, with a price per plate that would feed the kids in HomePlace for a month.

A tangible reminder of a rejection that had been far more personal—a woman casting him aside because he hadn't had what? A credit card with a limit high enough to suit her?

Had the woman been insane?

Allison looked down into J.T.'s face, wondering what kind of price tag someone could put on a man like J.T. What would it have cost a man so strong, so proud, to be traded away in favor of a bank balance?

It was little wonder he'd looked at Allison with contempt, when he matched her life-style against that of a frightened teenage mother, unable to provide even the crudest care for her sick child.

A simple bottle of medicine to take down the fever.

The fever.

"Oh, Lord!" she breathed aloud, her mind suddenly flashing back three weeks. She'd had a sore throat, and had gone to her doctor. Concerned that it might be strep, he'd started her on medication. But when the throat culture had come back negative, she'd just stopped taking the pills...and, as always, had left the bottle in the bottomless pit that was her purse.

If they were still there she could give them to J.T., see if they might help him.

She raced out to the living room, dumping the contents of her purse onto the couch. Prescription bottle and glass of water in hand, she returned to his bedside.

"J.T.?" Allison said firmly. "I have medicine here. You have to take it. Wake up, right now."

J.T. mumbled something, turning his face away from her.

"I mean it, J.T. It'll make you feel better."

"Right...and I've got a...seaside resort to sell you in...Arizona."

The voice was no longer tortured. Instead it was weary, faint. But Allison took some comfort from the fact that it was somewhat more lucid.

"J.T., listen to me. Are you allergic to any penicillin derivatives?"

His eyelids fluttered. "Only...thing allergic to...is bullets."

Once, Allison would have smiled at his attempt at humor. But now it made her eyes burn with tears. Tenderly she got him propped up, then coaxed him to take the medicine. He swallowed convulsively, choking a little. Laying him back down, she got a cool cloth and bathed him, cleansing away the sweat, wishing it was as easy to sweep away his bitterness.

She was tired, so tired, and raw inside.

"Who was she, J.T.?" Allison whispered, running her fingertips down his beard-stubbled jaw. "Who hurt you this way?"

"Some...ugly son of a bitch named...Earl," he murmured, his head lolling to the side, his mouth going slack. She leaned down, pressing her lips to J.T.'s forehead, certain that, even once this was all over, he would never really tell her who Melissa was.

J.T. lay perfectly still on the mattress, afraid that if he moved he'd blast apart. His side throbbed, his stomach churned and he felt as if one of the boys had stuffed a week's worth of gym socks into his mouth. Worst of all, his chest hurt—with that battered, hollow sensation that always came after the dream.

Furious with himself, J.T. gritted his teeth, blotting away the horrible aftershocks of betrayal that still reverberated through him. Hell, he should be tougher than this. Should be able to fight it.

But the dream was one thing J.T. had never been able to defeat. It had always lurked just beyond the edge of his consciousness, like a bottomless pit, waiting for him, mocking him, leaving him feeling as if he was battling ghosts that he couldn't catch, hold, or drive away from him.

Damn.

He shifted against sheets that were soft, fresh, and sucked in a breath, something sweet and flowery tantalizing his nostrils. Where the hell was he, a damned garden? Or was it his own funeral?

He pried his eyelids open one lash at a time, the effort almost killing him. The glare of sunlight pouring through the windows lit everything in a golden glow. Lace curtains made shadow patterns on the downy comforter that covered a huge bed, a bed that was a fantasy iced in white. Rainbows danced through a tear-shaped prism that was suspended by a thread in the window, while floppy, old-fashioned hats with dried flowers around the band decorated one wall. A dressing table in one corner was cluttered with woman things. Cut-glass bottles and silver brushes and a delicate china rose.

The door to the room was open just a crack, and a nightgown sexy enough to make a man's eyes ache was draped on a hook.

Maybe he had died, J.T. thought numbly. If this was heaven, he couldn't wait to see his own personal angel decked out in that thing.

An angel with candle-shine hair and wide green-gold eyes.

Allison.

Awareness slammed into his gut with a force that left him gasping, spilling out images of what had happened like pictures from a broken photo album.

Raine, terrified, battling Earl and IceMan, the horrible drive to the Crawford cottage, Allison's huge, terrified eyes fixed on him over the barrel of a gun. And then, nothing but emptiness, bleak and blank, that and the dream....

How many days had passed since he'd first staggered into the cottage? Two? Three? Days that were a blur of fever and pain and the terrifying knowledge that he was too weak to fight off Earl and IceMan if they should come bursting through the door. Days when J.T. had been floating in and out of reality, catching glimpses of Allison's worried face and Raine's rebellious one. Faces that would shift into Earl's ugly mug, or the drug-deadened eyes of IceMan.

Or Melissa . . .

J.T. raised his hand to his forehead, crushing that thought ruthlessly, completely.

He should be thanking God, or whoever protected idiots like him, that he'd made it through. He had been lucky this time. The bullet must have missed anything vital, and the jerks who had drilled him must be getting their asses kicked by whoever their boss was, for losing their quarry.

That thought gave J.T. a twinge of pleasure.

The soft creak of the door made him look up, his stomach almost revolted at the motion.

From the first moment he'd seen Allison Crawford he had thought she was beautiful—untouchable, ethereal, as far beyond his reach as the moon.

But as he looked at her now, with her hair a tousled halo, her legs encased in faded jeans, and a sweatshirt two sizes too large skimming her dainty breasts, J.T. was struck with the knowledge that this woman had a far deeper loveliness than he'd given her credit for. The kind of inner beauty that made a man want to fall into the heaven of her eyes, and stay there. The kind of strength and courage and sensitivity that reached out and touched all the soft places in a man's soul, places J.T. had never admitted existed inside him, even to himself.

He tried to draw breath, but the air seared his lungs with helpless yearning and fierce regret that swelled into a desperate need to bolt out of this bed, out of her life as fast as he could.

And he would do it, he promised himself. The minute he could move without feeling as if he'd been hit by a truck.

She hesitated in the doorway, her mouth curved in a tentative smile. "You're awake."

"In a manner of speaking. I doubt it's a permanent condition. How long have I been out?"

"Three days."

"Three days?" He swore, trying to lever himself upright. A groan tore from his throat, and he sagged back. "Anything could have happened in that time."

"But nothing did. Raine and I hid your car, kept watch and . . . took care of you." Those incredible eyes flashed away from his, and her cheeks colored.

Her embarrassment seemed to flood over J.T., and he was suddenly aware that he was stark naked against the sheets. Instinctively he grabbed the white-lace edge and drew the pool of cloth higher on his bare chest.

God knew, he'd never been particularly modest, but there was something about the thought of Allison undressing him that left him feeling vulnerable in ways that he didn't even want to consider.

"The girl—Raine. She's still here? I thought she'd be halfway to California by now."

"She's upstairs poking around in my books. She wants to run—badly. But I told her you'd hurt yourself looking for her if she did. She decided she owed it to you to stay until you could talk. J.T.," Allison said, hesitating, "I don't know what made her run, but she's afraid."

J.T. grimaced. "Having someone try to jam a syringe filled with enough drugs to OD half of Cincinnati into your arm tends to make one a little jumpy."

Allison flinched, and J.T. felt like a bastard. "What I'm trying to say is that I can't guarantee how long she'll stay, now that you're awake."

"She'll stay, all right, if I have to chain her to the wall," J.T. growled. "Animals like Earl and IceMan run in packs. Packs that could slit her throat and use the same knife at a five-course meal three minutes later." He shifted in bed, ever so slowly, and welcomed the physical pain that kept his mind off the more illusive hurt just looking at Allison was causing him. "Has there been any news coverage yet? Any sign of a search? Do you even have a TV here?"

"There hasn't been anything on the news, or in the local paper, but I can't be sure what's happening in the city."

"Buck'll know. Help me out of this damn bed, so I can call him."

"He said not to call HomePlace from the cottage. If there are corrupt policemen involved, he's afraid they might try to trace it."

"Corrupt policemen?" J.T. snorted. "*Corrupt policemen?* It's bad cops. Don't you even watch detective shows on TV?"

"No, I don't." He'd struck a nerve with that one. "Watching criminals terrorize their victims doesn't have any entertainment value to me. As for Buck, he said to tell you he'd do everything possible to contact Michael. While you've been unconscious I've even made some calls of my own to try to reach him. Unfortunately, it doesn't look like Michael and Danielle went to Vegas."

"Perfect. Just perfect. Well, Buck can go straight to hell if he thinks I'm going to sit on my hands up here with the beautiful people while he plays Magnum P.I. The scum that want Raine dead aren't going to take a vacation from searching for her until Mike gets back. This isn't a game of hide-and-seek."

"I know it's frustrating, J.T., but the more disturbance you cause, the more likely these criminals will be able to trace you and Raine to the cottage. If they had any leads, they would have come here two days ago and tried to kill us all before we could tell anyone else what had happened."

"Yeah, and maybe they're just outside right now, setting up a hell of a party for the three of us."

"I don't think so, and neither do you." Allison's chin lifted a notch. "I know you're hurting and angry and feeling, well, helpless. And I know it's a lot easier for you to play the hero when you're dodging blasts of gunfire and taking on drug pushers and pimps, but right now the best thing you can do for Raine is to just...keep your head down, and not draw attention to yourself."

A wisp of memory flitted through J.T.'s mind. Allison facing off with her friend—Leah? Was that her name?—

while J.T. played the role of drunken lecher with the finesse of an Olivier.

"Seems to me I drew plenty of attention before I passed out that first night. Your friend has probably broadcast the fact that you're having an affair with some low-life biker halfway around the lake by now. After all, don't you rich types thrive on scandal?"

"Not all of us are like that." Allison paled a little, but her eyes didn't fire with the anger he'd hoped would build a barrier between them. Instead, they clouded with something that tied J.T.'s stomach in knots. Sympathy.

His breath froze in his lungs. He'd drifted in and out of delirium for three days. Oh, God, he hadn't...couldn't have talked?

But that was how Buck had found out about J.T.'s past. J.T. had been a scared sixteen-year-old who had taken to breaking into Buck's motorcycle shop every night in the dead of winter, to get out of the cold. The dream had been so terrible that night, and J.T. had been so exhausted, he hadn't awakened before the older man came to open the shop. In fact, J.T. had been so deep in the dream, his survival instinct hadn't kicked in and warned him, even when Buck was standing over him with a warm blanket in his hands.

Buck had heard J.T. babbling in his sleep, and had caught enough of what he'd said to piece together the whole sordid story.

He was the only person who had ever known.

Until now?

Humiliation rushed through his veins, the sensation unbearable.

"J.T.?" Allison's voice was soft, aching, the brush of her fingertips feather light against his jaw. "I know this is hard for you—"

He jerked away as if she were poison, pain jolting through him so savagely he almost passed out. His gaze slashed to hers, and her face swam before him. "Don't kid yourself, princess. You don't know a damn thing about me. If you did, you couldn't take the truth. The bottom line is, I don't need any of your bleeding-heart sympathy, Miss Crawford. I'm gonna get the hell out of here, if I have to... walk."

Her fingers curled into her palms, and she swallowed hard. Was she going to cry? J.T. wondered a little wildly. Son of a bitch, he didn't think he could take it if she did.

He expected tears, or anger, anything except what Allison Crawford gave him.

There was something in her face more than a little ornery. "So you're going to walk, are you, Mr. Tough Guy? It's thirty-some miles to town. I'd love to see you try it." She stood aside, as if clearing a path for him. J.T. would've sold his soul to the devil to be able to walk out of that room. But it seemed even the devil didn't want to bargain with J.T. James.

He glared balefully at Allison as she added insult to injury, the soft indentation at the corner of her lips deepening into a smile.

"You're so hardheaded, you probably would try it," she said, tsking. "And if I've learned nothing else the last few days, I have learned that you weigh a ton—though how someone as lean as you are can be so heavy, I can't begin to guess. Anyway, weighing the choices of locking you in the bedroom, retrieving you when you pass out at the end of the driveway, or listening to you throw a tantrum, I suppose I'll just have to take you into town myself."

She left the room and returned a few minutes later with his jeans—soft and freshly washed—and a shirt that obviously belonged to some other man. It was a white oxford, with one of those stupid little horses embroidered on the front, to show everybody it cost an obscene amount of money.

Even though he was feeling like garbage, J.T. felt a swift wave of jealousy. For a woman who claimed she didn't date much, it was a little coincidental that she had a man's shirt tucked away in a closet.

When she tossed the shirt toward him, he knocked it aside. "Where's my sweater? I'm not running around looking like a damn Yuppie."

"In case you forgot, you got a couple of holes in your sweater. Suspicious-looking holes, especially with your bandages visible through them. If Earl and IceMan have people looking for you, it would seem pretty stupid to run around advertising the fact that you'd been shot. Of course, we could always say you'd been bitten by a very large snake."

"You think this is funny, do you, princess? Let me remind you that those were real bullets the bad guys were shooting at Raine and me, and now that you got tangled up in this mess, they wouldn't be averse to putting a few holes in you, either."

"I've been at gunpoint before, Mr. James. I can assure you, I didn't think it was funny at all." Her voice frosted with that high-class ice that could burn hotter than any raging temper.

"Where'd you learn to freeze people with a single glare, sugar?" he drawled, a nasty curl to his lips. "Boarding school?"

"No. I learned it by being forced to deal with men who have disgusting misogynistic attitudes."

J.T. stiffened as if she'd whacked him. "I don't have a thing against women!" he snapped. "Fact is, if they'd been running the world for the past hundred years, I figure things would be a helluva lot better than they are."

"You mean you don't have anything against poor women, or middle-class women. But anyone who can shop at Neiman Marcus is a different story, isn't that right?"

"Son of a—" He slammed his fist against the mattress. The agony reverberating from his wound nearly sent him off to la-la land again.

The only thing that pulled him back from the brink was the knowledge that Allison Crawford would like nothing better than to keep him flat on his back here at this cottage.

He mentally shoved away the waves of darkness. Grabbing the Yuppie shirt, he tried to maneuver himself into it. Hell, he'd wear Ronald Reagan's damn shirt if it meant he could get the hell out of here.

Allison watched his struggles for a few moments, a hard, determined light in her eyes, as if it was taking all her willpower to keep from helping him.

At last she muttered a word under her breath J.T. *knew* hadn't come from boarding school. And she grabbed the collar of the shirt, helping him get it on.

The bullet wound hurt badly enough, but somehow, the brush of her fingers cool against his bare skin hurt more. Hurt in ways that made him certain it would be safer to run straight into the barrel of IceMan's gun than to stay within fifty miles of Allison Crawford.

She buttoned the shirt, her fingertips stirring the light gilding of hair on J.T.'s chest, her knuckles brushing against his nipples, sensitizing them beyond bearing.

J.T. gritted his teeth, forcing himself to concentrate on his need to get out of her life, away from her hands, her smiles, those eyes that made him want to sink in, deep. He thought about Earl and IceMan and Raine. But he wanted to close his hand around Allison's slender wrist and flatten her soft palm against his skin.

When she was finished with the last button she made a move to grab his jeans. The thought of her fingers sliding the denim into place was pure torture. Hell, he never said he was a saint. Besides, any arousal on his part would probably send him right back to where he'd spent the past three days. Unconscious. He was already more than a little dizzy.

His fist knotted in the jeans. "Unless you want a replay of the reaction I had to you at HomePlace, sweet thing, you'd better go. Put on some of that expensive perfume you wear, or dust off your designer jacket, or some such. And make sure Raine comes with us. I don't want her taking off for God knows where.''

Allison smiled with acid sweetness. "Anything else I can do for you, oh great high king?"

"Oh, yeah," J.T. muttered, more to himself. "There's plenty more I'd like you to do for me."

But she'd already turned and left the room.

Chapter 8

Twenty minutes later the jeans were in place, the shirt that had looked so starched and perfect was crumpled and wilted, and J.T.'s whole body was covered with a sheen of sweat. He'd taken the brush from Allison's dressing table and raked it haphazardly through his hair, then knotted it back with a rubber band.

His boots were at the foot of the bed, and were a son of a bitch to get on. But the next time he faced Allison he wanted it to be on his own terms, dressed and standing—or should he say wobbling—on his own two feet.

When he did edge his way out of the bedroom, what he saw nearly kicked his legs out from under him.

A girl—totally unrecognizable as the runaway he'd rescued three days ago—sat at the kitchen table. The hair that had been tinted such an ungodly color had washed clean to a soft wheat-blonde. The preprostitute fashion statement had been toned down to a pair of baggy khaki shorts and a pink-and-white candy-striped T-shirt that was just a little too big. There wasn't so much as lip-gloss on a face that was almost elfin, with its tip-tilted eyes and pointed chin. But the familiar trapped-animal fear was still in the girl's eyes, so strong, J.T. half expected her to take one look at him and make a lunge for the door.

Protectiveness surged, thick and hot in his veins, blessedly dulling the confusing emotions Allison had stirred in him.

"Raine?"

She turned, color flooding her cheeks. She bit at the nail on her index finger. "Hi. Mr.... James."

"J.T. Just call me J.T." He made his way to the table and sank onto the chair that was between Raine and the door.

"I thought you were gonna die," the girl confided. "I mean, it was pretty bad when you were yelling and stuff. It scared me. Scared Allison, too."

J.T. winced inwardly. Yelling? Please, God, let him have been yelling about IceMan or about Earl, or anything but the dream.

"I was pretty scared myself," J.T. admitted. "I thought you'd be gone when I woke up."

"First I stayed because Allison said I owed you that much. She said you'd come after me, even though you were hurt."

J.T. squirmed at the fact that the woman already knew him so well.

"Then I stayed because..." The girl hesitated, shrugged. "I figured she was right. This is the safest place right now. 'Course, if I want to, I can be out of here in a minute. She even stuck some money in a jar, in case I wanted to leave. Said she didn't want me out there without any way to take care of myself."

"You don't have to worry, Raine. You and I will be out of here before nightfall. But if I'm going to help you, I need to know how you ended up at the point of Earl's gun."

"It's no big mystery." The girl grimaced. "A drug deal gone bad."

"Right." J.T. looked into the girl's features, saw the classic symptoms of adolescent denial, the glitter of defiance in her eyes.

"Problem is, there's always more to it than that, isn't there? I mean, the pushers don't materialize out of thin air, and neither do the kids who get messed up by them." J.T. had broken through the defenses of countless kids. Carefully he began to work on Raine's emotional walls.

"You know what, Raine?" he said. "The funny thing is, you don't look like the kind of kid who gets mixed up with druggies."

Raine tugged at the shirt she'd borrowed from Allison, and gave a scornful laugh. "Maybe not in Princess Di's clothes. I mean, a first grader could wear this stuff."

"I suppose. But what I can't figure out is why you look so much more comfortable in them than you did in your street clothes."

"Maybe you just feel more comfortable with me dressed this way, and you're imagining things."

"I've known so many street kids, you could parade around in a circus tent and it wouldn't even faze me. I've learned not to look at clothes, to make judgments about who kids are. I look in their eyes. And the more I look in yours, the more certain I am that the whole hooker getup was just that—a disguise."

"I looked great in those clothes," Raine started to protest.

"Yeah. You looked terrific. I bet your mom would've been real proud to see you." It was one of J.T.'s most tried-and-true weapons. He could see it hit the mark.

The hard attitude Raine had adopted cracked visibly. She winced. "My mom's dead."

J.T. knew a moment of regret as hurt and bitterness and grief welled up in the runaway's eyes—necessary pain, but it never made the hurt any easier to bear. "I'm sorry."

"Yeah. Well, not as sorry as me."

"You want to tell me about it?"

"Cancer." Raine looked away. "It's a real ugly way to die. The doctors couldn't help her, so Dad and I just had to watch her get sicker and sicker."

"That must have been hard. It sounds like you loved her very much."

"I did." She hesitated, fidgeting with the edge of the tablecloth. "We tried to take care of her, me and Dad, but things just kept getting worse. Dad had to take so much time off work that he lost his job, and there wasn't any insurance. While Mom was sick, we couldn't think of anything but her. But after she died, everything caved in. Dad and I used to be real close. All of us were. But after Mom died, he was different. He was mad all the time."

J.T. closed his eyes, and was stunned by a fleeting image of Allison's face, fragile, so fragile. What would it be like to stand by, helpless, watching the woman you loved die?

"My dad had always taken care of Mom and me." Raine twisted a lock of her hair around one finger. "We weren't rich, or anything, but he worked hard. Only this time the bills were so bad he couldn't fix it. We lost the house three weeks after Mom's funeral."

J.T. saw a shadow of guilt, regret chase across the girl's face. "That must've been rough."

"It was awful. But what was worse was that I blamed my dad for what had happened. I thought he should've been able to find some way to keep me with my friends, in my same school. I'd already lost Mom, and Dad was so different it was like I didn't even know him anymore."

"He must've been hurting. And so were you. You both needed time."

"I didn't care what he needed by then. I hated it at Dalton, I didn't know anyone. I wanted to make my dad as miserable as I thought he was making me. So, I started dressing different, doing stuff to my hair that he hated. He barely even noticed. Then I met Dirk. Back then, I thought Dirk was wonderful. He understood, you know? About not getting along with parents. His mom was drunk all the

time, and his dad traveled alot. The best thing was, Dirk
always had time for me. And my dad, well, he noticed me
when I was with Dirk.''

''Noticed you?''

''It would've been hard not to notice a kid that age driving a Porsche. Specially when Dirk's parents didn't have
tons of money. Anyway, my dad hated Dirk, real bad. We
got in tons of fights about it, but I wouldn't listen. Dad was
working three jobs, and wasn't ever home. There was
nothing he could do to stop me from going out with Dirk.
He said Dirk was bad. But I'd spent my whole life being
good, you know? And what did I get for it? My mom dead,
my dad . . . he might as well have been dead.''

Her voice trailed off. J.T. waited. ''I was hurting so
bad,'' she went on at last. ''And Dirk made me feel special. Kids at school started talking to me, treating me like I
was somebody.''

She hesitated for a minute. ''I heard rumors, you know
how kids talk. They said Dirk was dealing drugs. But I
didn't believe them. I guess I didn't want to think about it
too hard, 'cause it made sense. I mean, where else'd a kid
his age get that much money?''

''Yeah. Kind of hard to maintain a Porsche working in
a fast-food restaraunt.''

''Yeah. Well, my dad and I had a terrible fight one night,
and I went to Dirk's. I wanted to get away from that stinking apartment where Dad and I were. I wanted...I wanted
to be anywhere else, be anyone but me. I wanted . . . my life
back.''

Tears welled at her lashes and trickled free.

''Dirk said he could set me up on my own somewhere—
if I'd be his . . . I mean, if I'd let him, ah . . .'' she stammered, flushed.

''Have sex with you?'' J.T. supplied evenly.

''Yeah. I don't know why I wouldn't let him. It wasn't
like I cared about anything anymore. Just, every time I almost gave in, I'd remember my mom telling me how I

should wait, and not rush into something I didn't want just because some guy was pressuring me. I know it sounds wierd, but it was like she was watching me, or something. But I think I was so desperate that night, I would've agreed to anything to get out of the house for good."

"So you left with Dirk, and . . . ?"

"He had some business to take care of, first, he said. People he had to meet. We drove to this real deserted place, and waited. As long as I was going to be his woman—he called me that, his woman. I hated it. Anyway, he said I should know about what he did. Where he got his money and stuff."

"Drugs."

"I didn't know!" Raine choked out. "When he told me, I was so scared. All I could think of was my dad, telling me that Dirk was bad. Dad had been so angry, but scared, too. I was glad when I saw he was scared over me. I was glad that he was hurting. But I . . . oh, God, I never really thought . . ." She lowered her face into her hands.

"What happened next?" J.T. prodded gently.

"I tried to make Dirk take me home, but he laughed at me. I got out of the car, and started to run away just as another car pulled up. I hid, too scared to move. There were three men in the car. That Earl and IceMan, and . . . and another guy who I recognized from school. Dirk had talked to him lots of times, sometimes when I was around. First I thought Dirk was in trouble, that he was going to get busted. The guy was a narc. Everybody knew it. But he was in on the whole drug thing—one of Dirk's suppliers, I guess. The cop said that Dirk was getting too careless, that he'd been bragging or something, made some kind of mistake. And then . . . then he grabbed Dirk, and that IceMan guy . . . shot something into him. Some kind of drug. He was screaming, and I tried to help him. But when they saw me—"

J.T. put his arm around the girl. She was shaking, her breath ragged.

"I don't even know how I got away, but it didn't matter. The narc knew who I was. If he ever caught me, well, I knew he'd kill me. And if I went to the police—well, who would believe me?"

"Why didn't you go home? To your dad? Even with all that had happened, you have to know he loves you, would help you."

"They would have hurt him, don't you see? I knew that. And Dad had tried to warn me about Dirk, tell me what would happen. I just ran. I had the money Dirk had given me, and the things I'd packed to run away. I just ran, and tried to hide."

"How long were you on the streets?"

"Five weeks, maybe six. I almost thought things had calmed down. But they found me, and, well, you know what happened after that."

J.T. gritted his teeth at the thought of this girl, terrified, alone on the street. And her father—the poor man must be insane with fear. At that moment J.T. would have sold his soul to be able to pick up the phone and call the man, relieve him of the agony of waiting, not knowing what had happened to his little girl. But there was no doubt that this bad cop knew Raine's real identity, and her father would be watched for any contact. That single mercy call could easily sign the kid's death warrant.

"I'm going to get those bastards who tried to hurt you, Raine," J.T. assured her. "And after I do, I guarantee, they won't be hurting anyone else, ever again."

"Who are you? The Lone Ranger, or something? These guys are bad—really bad. And they'd do anything to knock me out of the way. Truth is, probably the best thing I could have done was to run away again, so they won't come after you. That's the thing that scares me the most. That they'll hurt someone else trying to get to me."

There was the tiniest catch in her voice. J.T. reached over, and closed his hand over hers. "What happened to me wasn't your fault, Raine. It was Earl's fault, and Ice-Man's. And whoever the hell is holding their leashes."

"You don't know. You don't understand."

"I think I do. Maybe more than you give me credit for."

"You mean people have gotten in trouble because of you? Because you were stupid and wouldn't listen when—" She stopped, her eyes searching his. "Is that—that what you were yelling about when you were so sick?"

J.T. felt as if she'd plunged a fist into his gut. "I don't know. But I've done plenty of things I'm not proud of."

"J.T.?" Raine asked, her eyes seeking his, pleading, almost childlike. "Did you do something to hurt...Melissa?"

The name was a jagged blade raking through his chest, the pain honed even more savagely by the sound of the screen door slamming shut.

The tragedy of the girl's story was washed away in a rush of J.T.'s own anguish as he turned to see Allison standing there. It was as if his own past had betrayed him while he'd tossed in that mind-numbing delirium. Some unfeeling god had ripped out the deepest secrets of his soul and dragged them into the light.

He tried to fight out of waves of blind panic, his eyes locked on Allison.

Her cheeks were deep pink, her fingers fidgeting with her keys, while beneath her thick lashes were pooled a hundred questions.

Once J.T. had taken a dozen kids to a horse ranch in Montana. The rancher had captured a renegade stallion, had him penned in a corral with rails two feet over the horse's head. J.T. had sensed the desperation in the magnificent animal, the wild, pulsing power.

The first time someone had tried to ride him, the stallion had flung himself at the fence in an effort to escape. He'd broken his leg, and had to be put down.

As J.T. sat there he knew what the animal had felt. And J.T. would have been almost grateful for the feel of cold lead deadening the emotions raging through him.

"Raine." There was a gentle warning in Allison's voice as she gave her head the slightest shake. "Everyone has a right to a little privacy. I'd hate to think what I'd talk about in my sleep. Falling off cliffs, being chased by gorillas on motorcycles." She gave a forced smile that quivered just a little. "We'd better get going."

J.T. should have been grateful to her for deflecting the girl's question. Instead, it only made him feel more vulnerable. And vulnerable was the one thing he couldn't afford to feel around Allison Crawford.

Getting to his feet, he stormed past Allison and staggered down the steps to where an almost-pristine Jeep Cherokee was parked. He hauled himself into the passenger's seat, then sagged back against the cushions, and closed his eyes.

He was aware of the doors opening quietly a few moments later, as Raine and Allison got in the car. The engine purred to life, and the vehicle began to navigate the rutted cottage road. J.T. tensed against the jarring, concentrating on staying alert. Still, every muscle in his body ached by the time the gravel shifted to the smoother ride of concrete. She didn't even have the radio on to mask the silence.

Wasn't it bad enough that he had to live with what had happened? J.T. thought, furious. Wasn't it bad enough that he had to carry it around like a cancer eating inside him, forever? Why the hell did it have to come spewing out like poison whenever he was sick, or hurt, or exhausted? Why did he have to keep living it over and over again?

Showing his weakness in front of Buck had been devastating enough. Knowing he'd done so in front of Allison was the most horrifying thing he'd ever endured.

How long they had traveled, he couldn't be sure. Forty-five minutes, an hour? The sound of a couple of cars passing the Jeep made him open his eyes to see a cluster of buildings that ostentatiously called itself a town.

Allison pulled up near a phone booth outside the tiny postal station, and J.T. started to get out. She reached over to stop him, and handed him a fistful of change. He grimaced. He didn't want to take anything from her, but hell, he couldn't even buy himself a cup of coffee right now without her.

When he reached the phone he punched the number to HomePlace with a vengeance. Relief flooded through him when he heard Buck's familiar voice.

"Buck, you have to get me out of here. Now," J.T. snapped.

The older man chuckled. "God, boy. I knew nothin' would keep you down, but I didn't expect to hear you spittin' nails quite so soon. You aren't goin' nowhere, mister. Not for a while, anyway. There's nothin' you can do here but get in trouble, and that damn Flaherty might as well have vanished from the planet. Until I get ahold of him, you're gonna have to stay put."

"Like hell! Either you come get me, or I'll hitch back to the city. I can't stay here. I've got the kids to think about, and that zoning meeting, and—"

"Already took care of postponing the zoning thing. Told the city fathers you were sick and would reschedule it once you weren't puking your guts out."

"Perfect," J.T. growled.

"There wasn't much else I could do, J.T. If you come back here, you might as well draw a target on Home-Place's roof, you bullheaded idiot. You don't think those scum have been nosing around, looking for whoever helped that girl? You don't think they're gonna figure out it was you?"

"I don't give a damn if they put my face on a blasted billboard with a million-dollar reward. I'm—"

"You're what? Going to take them on single-handed? Shoot-out at the O.K. Corral? I've always thought that damn name of yours gave you a rotten attitude. Whoever these creeps are, they're not going to be overly particular about who gets in the cross fire if they find you. Half the kids here would just jump in front of an Uzi for you, and gladly. Is that what you want?''

"You know I don't! Damn it, old man. Listen to me. I—"

"For once in your life, you can listen to me. What's gonna happen to these kids you say you love so much if you get your head blown off? You think the zoning committee is going to deal with a dead man? Quit being so damn selfish, for once in your life, J.T. Think about somebody else for a change."

J.T. started to swear, banging his fist against the phonebooth wall. "Buck, you don't understand. I'll go underground if I have to. I can't stay here."

"Because you've got it bad for Allison Crawford?"

J.T. swore. "I've had women before."

Buck only chuckled. "Not like this one. She's prime, J.T. Prime. Tougher than you'd think, too, under all that highclass polish." The respect in Buck's voice was the last straw.

"I'm coming back to the city, Buck. Be there before nightfall. The hell with—"

"Don't bother with the threats, boy. You know I'm right, and it's making you madder than the devil. Well, tough. The bottom line is, you're stuck until Mike Flaherty decides to surface. Who knows, maybe the lady will manage to civilize you a little before you come home."

Buck hesitated for a minute. "I'm not asking you to stay there forever, boy. Just for a little while."

"Easy for you to say, old man. Fine. Have it your way."

J.T. slammed down the phone. He leaned his head against the warm plastic of the receiver, unable to face the prospect of being locked in the same building with Allison for God only knew how long. Unable to face the questions that remained in her eyes. Questions she'd never ask. Questions he'd never answer if she did.

She didn't say a word when he finally returned to the car. She just put the Jeep into Drive, and headed back to the cottage.

Couldn't she even say "I told you so"? Couldn't she turn on some annoying New Age music, or something, so he could yell at her? Anything to push him over the edge, let him blow off some of this frustration building inside him?

No, she had to sit there quietly, her eyes fixed on the road without a hint of triumph, her lips full and moist, her face a little sad.

For him? J.T. couldn't even stand the possibility.

It burrowed into the raw places in his soul, spilling out a nameless yearning. A yearning he knew he'd better kill before it got out of control.

"One thing we'd better get cleared up right now, princess." The words were a weapon. He aimed them with the precision of a marksman. "As long as I'm stuck here, we're going to do things *my* way. I'm in charge. *Me.* Got it?"

Something flashed in her eyes, so briefly he thought he'd imagined it. When she spoke he was certain he had.

"If being *in charge* will keep you from doing something stupid to endanger Raine or yourself, I suppose I have no choice," Allison said evenly. "Do I?"

J.T.'s hands fisted against his thighs. She was making him feel like a stubborn fifteen-year-old, stuck in one of those give-him-enough-rope-and-he'll-hang-himself scenarios.

Well, it was too late. J.T. had already been hung by a generous heart, a soft, sensitive mouth and an old man who had left him no way to escape them.

J.T. turned his face toward the woodland that was rushing by, but instead of the green and gold of the forest, he saw all the colors of Allison's eyes.

Just for a little while, Buck had said. *I'm not asking you to stay forever.*

Did the old man have any idea what he *was* asking? J.T. wondered.

The man who hadn't flinched at gunfire or switchblades or the most notorious drug dealers on the streets felt something like fear coil in his gut.

The question wasn't how long he'd have to stay at Arawak Lake.

The question was, when this was all over and he was finally able to go back to HomePlace, how many pieces of himself would Allison Crawford force him to leave behind?

Chapter 9

Allison gripped the lemonade glass in two hands, barely resisting the urge to shatter it against the table.

J.T. was at it again—beating some innocent nail into oblivion with a hammer somewhere around the cottage.

In the five days since the trip to town, he'd graduated from semi-invalid to crazed carpenter, until now he was attacking home repairs as if it was a mission from God—fixing the door, repairing the boat dock, replacing loose boards on the deck. She wouldn't have been surprised to find him sneaking out at night, dismantling things, just so he'd have something to fix in the morning.

Anything so he wouldn't have to have a civil conversation with something besides a piece of plywood. He'd made simple things like eating dinner or watching late-night T.V. an ordeal, sitting there, surly as a caged grizzly, just waiting for a chance to escape.

She supposed she should be glad he was taking out his frustrations in such a constructive manner, considering the fact that he was abusing the nails because he'd like to throttle someone else.

The trouble was, Allison couldn't figure out who he wanted to strangle the most—Earl and IceMan for getting him into this mess, Buck for forcing him to stay at Arawak, or her for having the gall to be visiting at her own cottage when he wanted to use it as a safe house.

In a moment of total frustration she had even offered to leave. But he'd only scowled at her. "What if that friend of yours comes snooping around again? She'd probably think I knocked you off and had you buried out behind the shed, or something. Besides," he'd admitted grudgingly, "Raine likes it that you're here."

Yeah, Allison was tempted to fling back, and you hate it that I'm here. Believe me, mister, you're not half as eager to get rid of me as I am to get rid of you. But the truth was that from the moment J. T. James had careened into her life she'd been dancing on the edge he loved so much—she'd been restless and angry, wild racing sensations pulsing through her. Sensations that frightened her, seduced her. Sensations she was struggling with all her being to crush.

A particularly loud thump resounded from somewhere in the vicinity of the boat shed, and Allison jumped.

"Geez!" Raine's sullen voice came from the corner, where she had her nose stuffed into the copy of *A Tale of Two Cities* that was never far from her hand. "How long do you think he's going to keep banging on stuff? Sydney Carton's about to get guillotined, and I can't even concentrate enough to cry."

Allison turned toward the girl, still amazed that the kid who had appeared so street tough was a literary classics junkie. Raine's insatiable appetite for reading had made it easier to keep her entertained, but even so, the girl was starting to get restless. And the amount of freedom Raine was to be allowed was fast becoming a major sore spot between Allison and J.T. He had insisted the girl stay inside, out of sight. But after five days with no sign of trouble,

Allison couldn't see any harm in Raine lying out on the deck while she read, or taking a dip in the lake after dark.

God knew, the teenager was so pale she could use a little sunshine.

Amazingly enough, Raine had taken J.T.'s dictates meekly so far, but the fact that she was trying so hard to cooperate with Jesse only made Allison angrier on her behalf.

"He's going to keep pounding for an eternity," Allison groaned. "Though, with that wound of his, I don't have a clue how he's managing to do it."

"It must hurt a lot, huh?" Raine asked.

"Not nearly enough," Allison said through gritted teeth. "If it did, he'd have to give us some peace."

A crash of gargantuan proportions made Allison leap to her feet. "That's it. I've had it." She slammed her glass down. "I'm going to take that hammer and—"

She caught Raine's gaze and bit off the end of the sentence. The girl didn't need to be dragged into the argument. After all, she and J.T. were the adults here, weren't they?

"And throw it in the lake," she finished lamely.

Raine gave a heartfelt sigh. "He'd just go in after it. And probably find something even noisier to fix."

There was something about the girl that got to Allison, something vulnerable and sweet, helpless, afraid. She remembered what it was like to be a teenager—trying so hard to be grown up half the time, wishing she could still play with teddy bears the rest. To be caught in that adolescent limbo and also be confronted with life at its most ruthless must be horrible beyond imagining.

Allison forced herself to wink at the girl. "If J.T. tries to get the hammer back, I'll drown him. Then our problems will be over."

Raine laughed, looking longingly at the sweep of lake visible through the window. "Drown me," she said. "Please!"

It was the closest thing to a complaint Allison had heard
from her. Allison grimaced. If she'd been Raine she'd have
been in the grip of a full-blown tantrum by now.

It was a perfect day for swimming, warm and sunny. The
sound of boats droned on the lake, while kids on water skis
shouted and laughed, and tried to impress each other.

How many times had Allison seen Raine press her nose
wistfully against the window, watching the other kids?
Though the girl's past was still a mystery, Allison would bet
her father's stock portfolio that Raine had never experienced a lakeside summer.

Maybe Raine couldn't race around on water skis or party
at the clubhouse with the other kids, but half an hour on
the deck or a cooling dip in the lake weren't too much for
the girl to ask, in spite of circumstances, were they?

Allison's jaw tightened. Of course, it was no problem for
J.T. to hand out his orders. He didn't stick around long
enough to see the effect they had. Well, maybe it was time
that she opened his eyes—with a blow from a two-by-four,
if necessary.

Fighting to calm the ragged ends of her nerves, Allison
grabbed her lemonade and went out into the sunshine.

The pebble pathway crunched beneath her sandals, the
sound of J.T.'s working making her grit her teeth.

He was up on a ladder, doing something to the boat
shed's gutters, every blow of his hammer reverberating
down the length of curved metal. His T-shirt stuck to the
taut muscles of his back, his running shorts clinging like a
second skin to lean hips and muscular thighs. He was every
woman's fantasy—sexy, sweaty and dangerous.

Allison was tempted to kick the ladder out from under
him.

She knew a moment's amazement that he could affect her
so strangely—breaking her heart one moment, inciting her
to homicide the next.

All she knew for certain was that she'd never felt this way before—experienced emotions that ran so deep, so swift she was overwhelmed by their power.

At the moment he was murdering a nail right beneath the eave. She stopped to glare at him. For a man who kept insisting he was worried about killers sneaking up on them, he was pretty doggone oblivious to what was going on around him. Earl and IceMan could have set up a bazooka and blasted him into kingdom come by now, and J.T. wouldn't have known a thing.

Not to mention the fact, Allison thought suddenly, that if they did get some hostile guests, J.T. would have to run fifty yards across the clearing to the house in order to reach Raine or the rifle.

Her mouth tightened. Obviously that danger was less important than keeping the two of them under house arrest, while J.T. stayed as far away from them as he could get.

The thought infuriated her.

"Jesse?" She called his name loudly, just beneath the ladder, taking fiendish delight in the way he jumped.

"That's a good way to get a hammer dropped on your head, princess," he snapped, wiping away the sweat from his forehead with one sinewy forearm. "It's not smart to sneak up on someone who's expecting felons to pay a visit."

Allison gave an unladylike snort. "Earl and IceMan could have driven a tank up the driveway and you wouldn't have noticed, Mr. Outlaw."

"Like hell."

"Oh, right. I'm sure you were alert, ready, whatever. Listening to every movement in the forest to protect your womenfolk."

"My *womenfolk?*"

Allison's cheeks burned. "I may not have watched many detective shows, but I sure as heck saw plenty of grade B Westerns in my day. And I never saw any trail bosses or scouts or wagon masters acting the way you are when they were waiting to be attacked by Indians."

He was laughing at her, his lips curled in a mocking smile, his eyes glittering. "I'm an outlaw, remember? Bad news in cowboy boots. If you expect me to act like the hero, you can forget it, babe."

"You know what I think, Jesse James? I think you're full of it. You don't think the crooks are coming anymore. You don't give a damn how much noise you make."

"Nobody can hear me anyway with all the damn ski boats tearing up the lake!"

"You know what I think? I think this whole campaign to keep Raine and me inside is just because you don't want to deal with either one of us. You're ticked off because you can't just run off and do whatever stupid testosterone-driven macho Clint Eastwood stunt you've cooked up at the moment. And you're taking it out on the two of us."

J.T. came down the ladder as if she'd built a fire under it. "That's the most air-brained, ridiculous accusation—"

"Is it?" Allison went nose-to-nose with him—not an easy feat with a man five inches taller than she was. "Then why do you barely speak to either of us anymore? Why do you leave the house before we get up, and drag yourself in when you're so exhausted you fall asleep at the dinner table? Why don't you ever even look at me anymore?"

She stiffened in shock at the words that had slipped out, her face burning with humiliation and a strange sense of hurt she hadn't even realized was chafing at her until this moment. Instinctively she took a step backward, and collided with the boat-shed wall.

J.T.'s eyes went dark as he stepped close to her, bracing his hands on either side of her head. Her breath caught in her throat, as if she'd just felt the jaws of a trap close around her.

"What's the matter, sugar?" he drawled. "You one of those women who can't stand it unless every man they meet can't keep his eyes off you?"

There was a deliberate cruelty in his voice that Allison sensed was as foreign to J.T. as lounging in a deck chair at a pool party would be.

"All right, babe, I'll feed your ego. I look at you, sugar. Hell, yes, I look at you. Problem is, when I'm on the ragged edge like this, I don't have a lot of self-control. If I let myself get too close, looking isn't going to be near enough."

Hunger. Primitive, raw. It fired beneath his thick lashes, clung about lips so sensual they made Allison feel as if she were melting.

Her mouth went dry at the memory of those hard, callused hands on her skin, that full, sensitive mouth on hers, hinting at mysteries that she longed to explore.

She was shaking inside, way down deep. She vowed she wouldn't let him see it.

"Fortunately for you, I've got enough self-control for both of us," Allison lied. "And I'm sure I'll be able to find a way to cool you off, if I need to. I'll have no problem resisting your..."

His what? she wondered wildly, gripping her glass of lemonade. His raw animal magnetism? His intoxicating sense of danger? Or, worse yet, the tenderness? The sensitivity? The vulnerability that slid like the pieces of a kaleidoscope behind those incredible eyes?

She couldn't tear her gaze away from his face, every tiny bead of sweat glistening on his skin, the shadowy stubble along his square jaw, the odd twist to his mouth almost as if he were in some kind of pain.

He was close, so close, and so still.

Allison's tongue flicked out to moisten lips that were suddenly parched.

J.T. made a sound that was half snarl, half groan. "You think it would be so easy for you, sweet thing? If I wanted to, I could make you beg—"

Fear pulsed deep and wild in Allison. Fear of something intangible, some unseen calamity that she sensed she was already too late to escape.

Her fingers tightened instinctively on the glass.

"Go ahead, babe. Cool me off. If you think you can," he growled, lowering his mouth toward hers.

In raw terror Allison used the only weapon she had, flinging the icy lemonade into J.T.'s face. It splashed those high cheekbones, dripped down the rigid muscles of his neck, wetting his shirt.

She expected him to jerk away from her, furious, or laughing that laugh that made fun not only of the world but of himself.

But J.T. only stared down at her a long minute, then he closed his mouth over hers.

Allison tensed as if he'd just jolted her with a hundred volts of electricity, zapping to excruciating awareness every nerve ending in her body.

Hot, tasting of salt and sweat, lemons and anger, J.T.'s lips moved over hers, fierce and demanding, leaving no room for petty lies or excuses.

His tongue pressed against the crease of Allison's lips, forcing them open, giving her all the rage, the need, the helpless fury that he'd been trying to drive away with his sweat and aching muscles and exhaustion.

He held her captive with nothing but his kiss, and Allison sagged against the wall, weak and needy as his tongue thrust into her mouth in a rhythm that left no doubt what he really wanted.

Suddenly he jerked away from her, turning until his back was braced against the wall. He sank onto the ground, his head bent, his arms on his raised knees.

Allison pressed trembling fingers to her lips. She knew she should think of something to say—some sharp, witty exchange to show him how strong she was. But she couldn't squeeze enough air past the pounding of her heart.

She just stood there, looking down at the riotous mass of J.T.'s hair, the slump in those broad shoulders that was something like defeat.

Slowly she reached out, wanting to touch him, but she curled her fingers into her palm and drew back. She'd been right that J.T.'s motives for keeping her and Raine inside hadn't been solely for their safety. But she'd discovered he had other motives that were far more unnerving than simple frustration or anger. She wanted to flee up the gravel walk, back to the cottage, and never come out again.

But that was just what J.T. wanted her to do.

She stared out toward the lake as a red ski boat zipped by, one of the Ostrom boys skimming over the water behind it on a pair of trick skis.

She closed her eyes, thinking again of Raine, alone in the house. And she knew that, uncomfortable and embarrassing as it might be, she and Jesse had to work this out.

She sank onto the warm grass in front of him, and drew circles with her finger in the condensation on the side of her glass.

"Jesse, I'm sorry you're so miserable here," she said, feeling as if she were walking through a verbal mine field. "I know it's difficult. But there's no reason to make things worse than they have to be."

"You think that's possible?" J.T. sneered.

"Yes, I do. For Raine, anyway. She's stuck in that house all day, with nothing to do but watch TV or read."

"It's better than walking the streets."

"Maybe. But if you allowed her to get out a little bit she might remember what life is like off the streets, and never want to go back. If she could just take a walk once in a while, go for a swim—"

"No. Absolutely not," J.T. cut in. "What if someone finds out she's here and starts asking questions? What if someone recognizes her, or something? We can't be sure what's in the city papers. They might have printed a picture."

"Even if they had, no one would recognize her. You barely knew her yourself the first day you saw her in my clothes, with that purple stuff washed out of her hair. She looks like a totally different girl from the one who staggered in here with you the night you were shot."

"Are you willing to bet her life on that?"

Allison's chest tightened, and she experienced the weight of responsibility J.T. always carried with him—making decisions that could affect a child for the rest of their life. Was she making a mistake? Taking a foolhardy risk? Or were her instincts about Raine right?

She looked at J.T.'s features, so harsh and tough and angry. His eyes were lost in shadow, every line and crease on his face seeming to reflect the ugliness that he had seen, the cruelty, the indifference. Street life, which trapped children in a cage of violence and poverty, fear and hopelessness. But there were other kinds of cages…gilded ones, filled with everything your heart could desire, except the one thing you really wanted, needed. Freedom.

Allison turned the glass in her hand, trying to form the words to explain to him. "When you were Raine's age I bet you wouldn't have lasted five minutes cooped up in that house," she said quietly.

J.T. frowned. "When I was Raine's age I would've been too damn stupid to stay there. That doesn't change what's best for her."

"What's best for her." Allison repeated the words. "Do you know how many times my father said those words to me? I'm doing this because it's best for you, Allison. So you'll be safe. You can't drive alone, you'd be in danger. Play in the park without bodyguards? Absolutely not! Do you want to be kidnapped again? Do you want those bad men, or others like them, to lock you up in the trunk of a car? Hurt you? Maybe kill you? You have to be careful—it's best for you. I'm only doing this because I love you." There was age-old pain in her voice. She could hear it. And it made J.T.'s muscles tense.

"He was probably right," J.T. admitted. "I mean, hell, you were hurt once. Must've scared the devil out of your father. And you," he added softly.

"You know what, Jesse? What those men did to me wasn't half as bad as what my father did after he got me back. I was so frightened I was looking for kidnappers in every shadow, outside my window at night, under my bed. Every repairman that came to the house seemed dangerous to me. He wouldn't even let me go out on the grounds of our house to play with my dog without somebody hovering over me."

"It made you safe."

"It made me terrified. It stripped away any self-confidence that I'd managed to cling to through that whole ordeal. It made me feel incompetent, Jesse. Like I needed to be protected, sheltered. I was totally dependent, and that was exactly the way my father wanted it. Because then he felt that I was safe."

"You're a big girl, Allison. Whatever happened before, you seem to have managed to come up swinging."

"But it's been hard, Jesse. Harder than you can imagine. It would've been much easier to stay in the glass bubble my father wanted to keep me in. Rapunzel in the tower, locked away from anything ugly or dangerous. The only thing was, it was all an illusion. I wasn't really safe, Jesse. Something could still have happened to me. But waiting, watching for the bad guys to materialize out of the mist crippled me in ways you can't even imagine."

"I doubt there's much chance Raine's dad could afford to hire bodyguards, even if he wanted to."

"Maybe not. But I know that the most important gift we can give Raine now is a feeling of confidence. Strength. What happened to her was horrible. But if we make her afraid to step outside the cottage we're going to do her even greater harm."

"I'm not talking about locking her in her room for the rest of her life. A few weeks at most—"

"And every minute she stays in that cottage it will get harder and harder for her to take that first step outside. I'm not asking you to let her set off fireworks on the dock. One of us can be with her every moment. We can go outside only after it's dark. We can even keep the rifle with us if it would make you feel better. I just think it's important that she starts to get over her fear. At least a little bit. If you could just let her take that first step. Don't you remember what it was like to be that age, J.T.? Restless and gawky, lost somewhere between being a child and being a grown-up?"

"No." J.T.'s mouth twisted, and he looked away. "I was never a child."

He'd let her stray into a tiny corner inside him. And she wondered if he would ever let her probe deeper. She had a flashing image of his face when Raine had mentioned Melissa's name, and she wondered how much of his anger was tapped into whatever memory that had triggered.

"Surely it wouldn't hurt to let Raine get out a little bit. Arawak is a private club. The caretaker keeps an eye out for strangers, and so does everyone else."

One of Jesse's brows shot up. "Right. You've got a regular Fort Knox here. Security to rival the Pentagon. I just got lucky when I came strolling in here, gut shot, breaking into your cottage—"

"All right, all right. You managed to get in here without any trouble. But it's been eight days since your run-in with the killers, Jesse. And I don't notice you staying inside."

"Your friend already knows that I'm here. Raine is different. What if someone sees her? How are you going to explain a kid who has suddenly appeared on your doorstep?"

"I don't know. We'd think of something. We could say she's your daughter, or—"

J.T. gave a surly laugh. "Terrific. Why don't we just pretend to be Mr. and Mrs. Suburbia, and let Raine go out and play with the rest of the kiddies. After all, this is a private club, and so damned secure. I'm sure the Yuppies on the other side of the lake would be thrilled to discover that their kids were running around with a girl who was two steps away from a body bag a week ago."

The words hurt. Allison curled inside herself. "Of course I wouldn't want to involve the other kids in this. I may not be as streetwise as you are, but I'm not stupid. I wouldn't put anyone at risk—"

"Oh, yeah, you're a regular poster child for Safe Living. You didn't think twice about the danger you were in when Raine and I came barging into your cottage. For all you knew, Earl and IceMan could've been three steps behind us, and you just ushered us inside and—"

"The next time you turn up on my doorstep bleeding to death, I'll just hand you a bandage through the mail slot," Allison said, aching, exasperated. "From the first time we met, you've made it absolutely clear exactly what you think of me. But this isn't my fault, Jesse. I don't expect you to be grateful—God knows, it would probably choke you to say thank you. But I don't think I deserve to have you mock me and yell at me and—and act like an arrogant jerk."

Muttering an oath, J.T. jammed himself to his feet and stalked a few steps away. He stopped, kicking at a clump of moss. His shoulders stiffened, his head arched back, and she could sense the struggle inside him.

He was swearing under his breath, and Allison was glad she couldn't make out most of what he was muttering. Suddenly he turned, his eyes snapping with something like anger. "I hate it when you're right," he growled.

"What?"

"Can't you understand plain English? I'm saying thank you—sort of." She could see him struggle manfully against a smile. He lost. "And just to keep the record straight, I have been acting like a jerk. In fact, I deserve to be called a helluva lot worse, but I bet Swearing 101 was neglected where you went to school. If you want, I could teach you some great insults."

She had expected him to be angry, maybe even to stalk away, or to fling her words back at her with his accustomed edge of sarcasm. Instead, that beguilingly handsome face fell into lines of self-disgust.

Allison lost herself in those regret-filled eyes. "I'll let you fill in the blanks yourself," she said. "Jesse, do you really think that she's in danger here? Honestly?"

"She could be. I don't know. Lowlifes like IceMan and Earl can be damned resourceful. Until they're behind bars none of us can sleep too easy at night. Not that I can sleep, anyway, with you in the next room."

Allison's cheeks burned.

"But," J.T. went on almost sheepishly, "you are right about one thing. If I really believed they could've tracked us here, you can bet those terrific legs of yours I would be sitting in that cabin with the two of you, that rifle two inches from my hand."

Allison smiled, her chest tightening as she looked into the face of this man who was beginning to mean far too much to her.

J.T. chuckled, but it was a sad sound. "You want to know what I think of you, Allison? I think you're one helluva woman. You've been a real trouper about all this. I mean, I know this isn't exactly what you had in mind when you came up here the other day—taking care of a burned-out hard case with an attitude and a runaway kid one step away from the barrel of a gun. You were probably heading up here to work on your tan and drink martinis."

"I drink lemonade." Allison couldn't help but smile a little.

"Drink it, throw it." J.T. shrugged. "I was thirsty, you know. You could've had better aim."

Allison sucked in a deep breath. "Do *you* want the truth, Jesse? About why *I* came up here?"

His eyes searched hers for a moment. His smile faded. His expression said he'd already read too much in her face. "I don't think I do."

"It was because of you."

"Allison—"

"I was so confused. Scared. Because of what you made me feel."

"Forget about it. God knows, I'm trying to. It's impossible for there to be anything between us, Allison. I won't let you believe any differently. We might as well be from different worlds. Hell, we're from different planets."

"Not right now. We're both here."

"And the minute I get word from Buck, I'm leaving. I'll be glad to leave, Allison. You understand that?"

"I know," she said in a small voice. "But would it be so terrible to have a truce while you're here? To just . . . *be* instead of worrying about a million things we can't control."

"Like the way I want you?" The words were ragged, harsh, determined. "I can't be in the same room with you for five minutes without imagining what it would be like to make love with you. Every time I close my eyes I taste you on my mouth, smell that damn perfume you wear—sexy, subtle, just enough to make a man crazy to touch you. But I'm not going to slip into some casual affair that will hurt you, Allison. I may be a bastard, but there are some places even I have to draw the line."

"I'm not asking you to go to bed with me." She tried to keep her voice steady, even though the very words conjured images of him—long, lean, tan and sinewy—silhouetted against the sheets. "And I'm not asking you to let Raine run wild. Let's just . . . take the time we have, and enjoy it. Let's not waste it being angry."

She held her breath as he seemed to consider. Then he reached out, one long-fingered hand skimming her cheek. "I think I've been angry forever, princess. I don't know if I can stop. Even for you."

She wondered what had made him the way he was, what had triggered the fury that was always just beneath the surface. She wondered if anything, anyone, could ever wipe it away.

She knew that, even if she wanted to, she wasn't the woman who should try. She wasn't the woman he needed.

For a moment panic fluttered in her chest, and she wondered how much pain she was setting herself up for, when this was over and he and Raine walked out of her life.

She wanted J.T. to kiss her again, kiss her until she couldn't think about criminals and runaways and the loneliness that was waiting for her on the other side of this tiny island of time.

There was need in J.T.'s eyes, a muscle ticking in his jaw, betraying the desire he felt, as well, the desire he was fighting so hard to keep under control. She held her breath and ghosted a kiss along his chin.

"Damn it, Allison," he growled, threading his fingers back into her hair. "Don't you understand? I'm trying to protect you. Don't tempt me to start something we're both going to regret." The words died in his throat as a sound like gunfire came from the region of the lake. They sprang apart, running for the cottage. They hadn't reached the door before they heard some kids laughing hysterically over some antics with fireworks. But the relief Allison felt shifted to dismay as she and J.T. hurried into the cottage.

Raine was cowering behind the couch, sobbing, shaking.

"It's okay, honey." Allison rushed over, putting her arms around the girl. "It was just some kids messing around."

"I thought—thought it was someone trying to—to shoot my head off. I've been waiting and waiting, thinking they might be in the woods...." Raine's voice broke, and she gave a laugh edged with hysteria. "It's hard to read Dickens without a head."

Allison tried to take the girl into her arms. Raine tore away. "Raine, it'll be all right." She tried to soothe her. "This will all be over soon."

"It'll never be over! I'll be locked up here, forever. Scared and—"

"Hey, now, easy." J.T.'s voice came, low, steadying. "Truth is, you don't have to be so scared anymore. I think you're pretty safe here."

"Right. That's why I can't even stick my nose out the door."

J.T. grimaced. "If I still thought it was that dangerous, you can bet I wouldn't have been out back, banging on nails."

"Then why can't I go out?" Raine demanded, frowning.

"You can. Under certain conditions. With Allison or me, after dark, when no one can see you." J.T. caught Allison's eye, his mouth twisting wryly. "It's going to be okay, Raine. I promise, it's going to be okay."

"How do you know? For sure, I mean? How—"

"Call it gut instinct, just like the one I had when I knew you were in trouble. Now, how about you go upstairs and take a nap, then the minute it's dark we'll head for the lake, take a swim or something."

Raine eyed him warily. "I might be too busy reading. I might not feel like it."

"Okay. We'll wait and see."

Raine grabbed her book and went up the stairs.

Allison watched her, still buzzing from the panic of moments ago. She heard J.T.'s footsteps coming toward her, felt his hand close on her shoulder, warm and bracing.

"Ali, you should have hit me with a goddamn two-by-four to make me listen. You were right. About Raine."

J.T. turned Allison to face him. He mustered a formidable frown that was softened by a gentle light in his eyes. "Of course, letting Raine out of this house—even with the two of us guarding her—is probably going to be the biggest mistake I've ever made," he insisted.

But as he looked at Allison's face he knew that he was wrong.

The worst mistake he'd ever made was the night he'd staggered through the cottage door and ended up in her arms.

It was an error he knew was going to cost him.

Cost him big.

He had a sick feeling that the payoff just might be his heart.

Chapter 10

A gentle breeze stirred the surface of the lake, icing the night-dark waves with foam. J.T. leaned against one of the dock's support posts and stared out across the water, his mouth twisting in a grimace.

Wasn't that just like a kid? he thought wryly. Typical. Just typical. After the blowup with Allison, the scene with Raine and J.T.'s agonizing decision to let her out of the house, the girl had exercised the perversity of her age group and decided that nothing except several tons of dynamite was going to blast her out of her room.

It shouldn't have bothered him so much. He'd done everything possible to stay out of the girl's way up to now, and Allison . . . well, he couldn't have made his feelings about her any clearer if he'd put them in lights over Wrigley Field.

But tonight, with the crickets singing and the leaves rustling, tonight with the lights glittering on the other side of the lake and the breeze skimming over his skin, J.T. would've given anything for a little meaningless conversa-

tion to take his mind off other things. Thoughts that were
as dangerous as Earl's bullets, as oddly heart wrenching as
one of Allison's smiles.

He tensed as the distant sound of laughter carried from
the other side of the lake. There was a bonfire just visible
through the trees. He wondered if it was a bunch of those
rowdy kids that kept tearing around the lake on skis, or
whether it was just a family, roasting hot dogs and telling
ghost stories. Making memories that sisters and brothers
would still laugh over on long-distance calls twenty years
from now when they were grown and gone.

The thought left J.T. with an unaccustomed sense of
melancholy. A sensation of emptiness that had been sur-
facing with more and more frequency ever since he'd
stormed across the charity ballroom and glared down into
Allison Crawford's green-gold eyes.

He sighed. Hell, he'd give anything for a little distrac-
tion, something to pull him away from thoughts of the five-
year-old he'd seen with her daddy in a flat-bottom boat the
other day—fishing with a cane pole and a bobber, her orange life jacket making her look like a plump little pump-
kin.

J.T. had been hammering away on a loose piece of
board, but he'd been unable to keep from watching them.
He hadn't been able to help listening to the moppet's cries
of delight as she pulled her first sunfish out of the water, a
wriggling, rainbow mass of silver and green and gold.

He'd never had much time to wish for anything except
favorable zoning regulations for his shelters, or getting
runaways to finish their GEDs. God knew, he'd never have
believed he would be stupid enough to picture himself in a
Norman Rockwell summer scene like the one captured in
the tiny girl and her father.

He winced at a vague memory of when he'd been a kid
himself, being tossed high in the air by a laughing man with
shaggy dark hair, believing that the man would always be

there to catch him when he fell. But life wasn't like that. Sometimes you crashed and burned. Badly. Really badly.

And those memories had ended up the same place as the rest of his childhood dreams had.

Other kids had to run into the harsh reality that there was no Santa Claus, after years of believing in the magic.

J.T. had escaped that traditional disillusionment.

He'd never believed at all.

He'd wanted to. God, how he'd wanted to. In the same way he had wanted to believe in happily-ever-afters. But in the end, he'd had to face the fact that Santa Claus was just as ridiculously impossible as J.T. picturing himself in a boat, helping a little girl with a gap-toothed smile and Allison's gold curls to put a wriggling worm on a hook.

He swore at the pain the thought caused him, the yearning that settled heavily, deep in his chest.

How many times had Buck told him he needed a life outside HomePlace? How many times had the older man warned that the bitterness, the anger would eat J.T. alive if he didn't give himself something to hold on to? Some kind of haven to recharge himself with hope?

J.T. had always dismissed it as a bunch of garbage—he needed to keep his edge, stay focused. Devote every waking moment to the kids. What woman would be crazy enough to want to share his life, anyway?

He jammed his hand back through his hair, imagining Allison in the cramped apartment above the shelter—three rooms that would fit inside her closet. Mismatched furniture, threadbare rugs and plumbing that was questionable at best. Not to mention the intercom that buzzed with exhausting regularity throughout the night whenever there was an emergency at the front desk.

For an instant J.T. allowed himself the luxury of imagining the apartment with little feminine touches, imagined himself sinking into sheets like the ones in Allison's bed—crisp, white, edged with lace. He imagined her curled up beside him on the porch swing, watching the kids play basketball, her hand threading through his hair.

His fist clenched, and he forced the thought away, overlaying it with another image—Allison, crumpled on the asphalt in front of the Stop Mart, terrified, bleeding. Allison—the perfect target for the enemies J.T. had made on the street. Men like Earl and IceMan, and so many others J.T. couldn't even name them all.

Allison had asked him to enjoy this time they had together, as if it were a gift. But as J.T. stared out into the bleakness that was the rest of his life, he knew that this time was a curse. A ruthless, merciless hand, tearing off the blindfold he'd put on himself all these years, showing him everything he could never have.

Why was it, then, that watching Allison, listening to her voice, seeing her smile was like a drug to him, intoxicating, addicting? Why was it that instead of wanting to block her out of his life now, he wanted to drink her in, every moment, every gesture, to save up like pretty shells in a jar that he could take out and hold when she was gone?

"Jesse?"

The sound of her voice made J.T. turn, and he gritted his teeth against how beautiful she was.

She hovered where the dock met the shore, an uncertain angel bathed in moonlight. Her legs were long and bare and sleek, her feet in sandals that were no more than a delicate lattice of rose ribbons that tied at her ankles. A thigh-length wisp of gauze misted the rose swimsuit that clung to her breasts and swooped high on her hips, while her fingers plucked at the white towel she had looped over one arm.

For a moment J.T. forgot to breathe.

"I just checked on Raine, and she's asleep," Allison said tentatively. "I thought I might go for a swim. But if I'm intruding... I mean, I don't want to disturb you."

Disturb him? Just looking at her made him crazy. He felt like a teenager himself—a ball of raging hormones, a voice he couldn't trust and needs that were like a brushfire, far beyond his power to control.

"No, it's fine," he heard himself saying. "It's a perfect night for it." Trouble was, he didn't define *it*. A perfect night for stripping away that bathing suit, tasting every inch of that ivory skin with his tongue. A perfect night to sink into her sweetness, her strength, and bury his bitterness in the silky caress of her hands.

He felt a stab of guilt, as if just by his thoughts he were defiling her, somehow.

Hell, she was a grown woman, she'd probably had lovers before. But there was something so innocent about her, so *good,* that it made him feel jaded and tired and old all of a sudden. So damn old.

She padded down the dock and sat beside him, the expensive, subtle scent of her feeding the red haze of his desire.

He knew he should get the hell out of there—fast. But he couldn't take his eyes off her long, elegant fingers as she slipped the ties of her sandals free and set them on the rough wood of the dock.

Hell, he'd never known he was a masochist. But this was a torture so sweet he couldn't stop himself from diving into it, reveling in it.

He wanted her to slip into the water so that he wouldn't have to talk past the knot that was fast forming in his throat. Instead she dangled her legs over the side of the dock, dipping her feet into pools of moonlit water.

After a moment he spoke. "You don't have to sit out here with me," he said. "You must have had something you wanted to do up here before Raine and I came barging in."

"I did," Allison said with a tentative smile. "I wanted to sit on the dock at night and dangle my feet in the water. And I wanted to think . . . about you."

J.T. had thought fantasy was painful, but it was nothing compared with the reality of the breeze wisping Allison's loose hair against his shoulder, the slow, excruciatingly sensual swirl of her toes stirring the water. "Some things are better left alone, princess," he said, tearing his gaze away from her. "If you looked too close at me, you wouldn't find the hometown hero in the magazines or news articles. Truth is, you wouldn't even find the man you saw at Home-Place."

"What would I see?"

"Just . . . anger. A helluva lot of anger. Bitterness."

"And pain."

J.T. winced at Allison's hushed words.

"Some of it for the kids you help. The rest . . . from somewhere inside you." Silence fell for a heartbeat. Then that soft, probing voice lanced through him again.

"Where does it come from, Jesse?"

As long as he could remember he had hated the sound of his name. On Allison's tongue it sounded beautiful. He stiffened, his jaw clenching. As if he could tell her where his pain came from. As if he could tell anyone.

"Does it matter?" He tried to evade her question.

"It matters to me. I feel like I know you better than anyone in my life—there's this strange closeness. Like we're kindred spirits, or . . . I know it sounds crazy."

J.T. crushed a hundred things he'd kill to be able to say to her. Instead, his mouth curled in mockery—not of her, but of himself. "What we feel is called lust, angel. I want you, and you think that you want me. It's simple."

"It doesn't feel simple. It feels . . ."

"Dangerous?" J.T.'s voice was harsher than he'd wanted it to be. "It would be dangerous for you."

"Why?" As if the gentle question wasn't bad enough, she took hold of the hem of her cover-up. J.T.'s mouth went dry at the thrust of her breasts as she pulled the gauzy garment over her tousled curls, then tossed it aside.

"You're not the kind of woman who could fall into bed with a man one night, and forget it the next," he rasped, his hands aching to touch her. "You'd want promises, Allison. You'd deserve them. And you should have a man who can give back to you at least some measure of what you would give him. Everything I have belongs to the kids at HomePlace. It has to, Allison, don't you see?''

He'd wanted to erect walls between them, make her see reason. Instead, she braced her arms behind her, leaning back, her eyes growing even more luminous in the moonlight.

"So you're saying it would it be dangerous for you, too?"

Oh, God, J.T. thought, ravenous with his hunger to touch her. If you only knew...

"Let's just say I'm probably going to be irritable as hell until I get out of here."

"Irritable? You? I don't believe it," she said in mock astonishment. J.T. couldn't keep his lips from tugging reluctantly upward at the corners.

"You're getting to be a card-carrying smart mouth, Miss Crawford. You've been hanging around with the wrong kind of man for too long."

"Maybe..." Allison caught her breath. "Maybe I was seeing the wrong kind of man before."

She could see J.T.'s jaw tighten, as if she'd touched a place that was sore and raw. The kinship that had existed moments before vanished in the harsh lines that settled about that beautifully formed mouth.

"I suppose your friend Leah thinks the senator's son is just great," he said with sudden bitterness. "Italian loafers, Armani suit, a family tree stretching back to the Mayflower."

It was the bitterness that put the lie to the harsh words J.T. had said before. Lust couldn't have brought that shading of hopelessness to that strong face, wouldn't have made his fist knot unconsciously on the dock post.

She remembered J.T.'s reaction to Mrs. Alexander the night of the charity ball, the way he had reacted when the woman had mentioned her son. Had J.T. had some kind of run-in with the senator? Budget cutbacks? Social programs gutted? Some sort of legislation about kids that had been cut down by Alexander?

All Allison knew was that she wanted to drive that pain from J.T.'s face—drive away the pain and find what lay beneath. Beneath his hard words, beneath his dismissal of the currents of emotions that had raged between Allison and J.T. from the moment they met.

"I dated Peter once or twice," she allowed, sliding from the dock into the waist-deep water, feeling J.T.'s eyes on the wetness that made her suit cling to nipples that were tingling beneath his gaze. She dipped lower into the waves, shaking back her hair until it floated out behind her. "It was all incredibly civilized. I don't think he swore at me a single time."

"Give the boy a gold star."

"He didn't make me angry, he didn't mock me, he didn't—"

"I get the picture."

She was pushing him—toward what, she didn't have the slightest idea. "Peter didn't make me laugh, or cry, or want to... to kick ladders out from underneath him."

J.T. slipped his own legs over the edge of the dock, as if he hoped the water would cool the heat shimmering in his eyes. "What? Throwing lemonade wasn't enough?" Allison knew he was trying to keep things light, but there was something far darker in the planes of his face, something just visible in the dancing shadows.

She swallowed hard and waded toward him, feeling him tense as she leaned against his knee. She reached up to touch the taut curve of his bottom lip. "And Jesse... he never kissed me like you do—so hot and sweet until I feel like I'm melting inside, and I want to—"

"Damn it, Allison!" He grabbed her shoulders, glaring down at her, suddenly savage. "Did you hear a word I said? I'm not going to make any stupid mistakes and hurt you. I'm not going to send you back to the senator's son or some man like him after I've held you, touched you."

"Why?" A heavy ache throbbed in Allison's breasts where they pressed against J.T.'s sinewy leg. "Why should it matter? If it's only...lust?"

"It would matter to Alexander, damn it. To anyone like him to know that a man like me had taken you."

"No one could blame you for taking anything from me, Jesse. Not when I want to give it. Freely."

Scarcely believing her own daring, Allison curved her wet hands behind J.T.'s ankles and slid her palms up the hair-roughened muscles of his legs—muscles that were clenched, iron hard, as if in pain.

She moved into the space between his knees and looked up—past the rigid evidence of his arousal thrusting against the soft material of his running shorts, past the swathe of bandages around his midsection to the broad wall of his chest. She could see the effort it was costing him to drag air in and out of his lungs, and she let her hand travel up to where his pulse was trying to beat its way out of his throat.

"Don't. Allison, my God, please..."

He might have been able to resist her if she hadn't leaned forward at that instant, her fingertips touching a scar on his chest that he'd gotten in a knife fight years ago.

She made a tiny sound in her throat and leaned toward him, her breath hot, sweet as she whispered against his skin, "Oh, Jesse. So much pain."

The soft kiss seared through him, to places he hadn't even known existed in his weary soul. And any thought of being noble, saving her from his touch, vanished in a white-hot flood of need.

With a curse of surrender he lifted her out of the water, the twinge of pain in his side paling to insignificance as his body skimmed the sleek wetness of hers. His hand knotted in the towel, and he flung it over his shoulder, then he turned back to Allison and scooped her into his arms. The silky swimsuit she wore did nothing to disguise the hard eagerness of her nipples, the swelling of her breasts as he carried her to the soft sand of the shore.

She was trembling just a little as he eased her to her feet, but then, so was he. His hands were as awkward, as eager as if it was his first time.

Maybe it was. . . .

He spread out the towel that was so large it could almost have been a blanket.

Then, with a groan, J.T. dragged Allison up against him, hard, leaving no doubt how much he wanted her. His mouth came down on hers, open and hungry, and her lips parted to invite him in.

J.T. groaned, his hands devouring her, sliding restlessly down her back, her buttocks, up the curve of her waist as his tongue traced her lips, danced with her own in the sweet, welcoming haven of her mouth.

She pressed herself against him, eager little sounds coming from her throat as she tangled her fingers in the hair at his nape, pulling him harder, deeper into the kiss.

When he couldn't bear waiting a moment longer he rained kisses down her cheek, the slender column of her throat, the vulnerable curve of her shoulder, his fingers snagging the thin straps of her suit, dragging them down. The rose silk cups that held her breasts clung to her wet skin, and J.T. kissed a path down to the edge of fabric, tugged it away from the delicate globes with his teeth.

A groan tore from his chest as he drew far enough away to see them, pale, beautiful, the dark disc of her nipple dainty, begging for the tip of his tongue.

As if she were some priceless treasure, he cupped her in one hand, gliding his thumb over the crest again and again, until she whimpered with need.

"My God, Ali, you're beautiful. So. . . beautiful," he moaned. Then he dipped his head to taste her.

Time spiraled out, stood still, as he drew her into his mouth, suckled her. In all his life J.T. had never tasted anything so sweet.

Restless, she arched her breast against him, her damp hair tossing. One elegant leg skimmed up the outside of his thigh, and J.T. thrust his arousal against the silk V of swimsuit that was hiding the place he was burning to claim as his own.

He eased her down onto the towel, and lay beside her. His hand slid down to her thigh, his fingers insinuating themselves between the suit and her skin. Allison gasped, a breathy, bone-meltingly sexy sound that almost threw him over the edge.

"Oh . . . oh, it feels so . . . so good . . . J.T. . . ."

He gave a guttural moan as he found the satiny-soft petals. "No. Call me . . . Jesse."

She drew back for an instant, her eyes wide, confused. "But you hate—"

"I love the sound of it on your tongue. Say it."

"Jesse." Her voice was warm brandy, trickling down his spine, spilling through his veins. "Jesse . . ." Her splayed fingers explored his shoulders, his chest, her palm gliding over his own nipples, making them throb with pleasure. "Jesse . . . Jesse . . . Jesse . . ."

His finger dipped, circled, worshiped. He drank in the feel of her, the sight of her, the sounds of her pleasure. And something inside him cracked—a dark shell that had been there forever, blocking out the light.

Jagged slivers of brightness pierced through him, painful, yet more brilliant, more beautiful than anything he'd ever dreamed. And for a heartbeat he wanted to tear away the last of the walls inside him, spill everything he was, everything he could ever be into her hands.

Todays, tomorrows . . . even the yesterdays he'd fought so hard to bury forever.

He loved her.

The knowledge slammed into his heart with a force that made him want to jam himself to his feet, run. Love, that most merciless emotion. Love, the one thing that could destroy him.

He loosened his hold on her, started to draw away, but at that moment Allison's hand dipped beneath the waistband of his shorts, grazing his shaft.

There was something almost shy, heartbreakingly beautiful in that caress. And he knew if he paid for this night forever, he would do it and gladly, just for the feel of those soft angel's hands touching him, trying to heal wounds inside him far too deep and jagged to ever disappear.

"God, I want you," he breathed, kissing her as he felt her writhe against his hand. He urged her closer, closer to the edge. "Ah, babe, I want you so much."

As if she couldn't get enough of him, her hands tugged at his shorts, a soft, frustrated sound coming from low in her throat.

"I need you, Jesse," she pleaded, trying desperately to touch him. "I need you inside me. Oh, please, I—"

Her words were heaven, hell.

J.T.'s hands went to rip down his shorts, but reality slammed into him with the force of a blow as his fingers tangled in the empty back pocket of the shorts. His wallet with the condom he needed to protect her. Damn it, it was up in the cottage....

In that moment, he knew he could never take what she offered. But the thought of stopping was beyond bearing. The knowledge that this wasn't a chance they'd ever have again made him steel himself with resolve. No, they'd both have something to remember years from now, when they were alone.

"Jesse," she breathed, "Jesse, please..."

With a curse he grabbed her hand and dragged it away from his burning arousal. He pinned her arm over her head, leaving her helpless, protesting.

He blocked out the sound, his jaw stone hard as he buried his face against her breasts, every inch of his being straining to bring her to climax. A sob tore from her throat and she arched, with a low, keening cry.

He felt the waves of sensation take her, hurl her higher, higher, until she plunged into a release he could only imagine.

Gently he let go of her wrist. She crumpled against him, drained, her breathing ragged against the thundering of his heart.

Ever so carefully he eased her suit back in place, then drew her close again.

She was quiet, too quiet.

When she raised her face to look into his eyes, J.T.'s heart broke a little. There was a wounded quality to her eyes, and her lips trembled.

"Did I do something wrong?"

"God, no!"

"Then, why...why didn't you...I wanted you to..." She let the question trail off.

J.T. braced himself on one elbow and cradled her face in his palm. "Oh, God, Ali. I wanted it, too. More than you'll ever know. But..." He sucked in a steadying breath, willing away the need inside him that only throbbed harder, deeper, burned brighter after the beauty of her climax.

"Let's just say, my wallet is still up in the cottage."

"What?"

"I didn't have any way to protect you."

He couldn't see the blush that flooded her cheeks, but he knew it was there.

"Allison, I care about you too much to take a risk."

"Oh." She pulled away from him and climbed to her feet. Walking to the dock, she grabbed up her cover-up, drying herself off with jerky movements.

She was shivering, and J.T. had a sick suspicion that all of the dampness on her cheeks wasn't lake water. "I suppose that I should say thank you. I mean, I suppose it makes sense to be prepared in case you, uh, run across anyone you want to have sex with."

"Not just anyone, Allison." He stood, his side burning, but not half as painfully as the regret eating inside him.

"Be Prepared." Allison bent over and tossed her hair over her face, drying the strands with fierce energy. "Isn't that a motto or something?"

He grabbed her wrists, dragging the soaking gauze away from her face. "Damn it, Allison! Stop this." She snapped to almost rigid attention, glaring at him, but he didn't let her go.

"Allison, I carry protection in my wallet because that's what I teach my kids to do. Be responsible. I can hardly expect seventeen-year-olds to use their heads and have safe sex if I don't set a good example."

She winced. "I'm sure you're a sterling example, J.T."

"I hope so! Do you know how much pain one mistake can cause?" He saw the hurt, the confusion in her face, and suddenly knew where it came from.

"Allison, I didn't say I keep the condoms in my wallet because I use them. I said I keep them there to show the kids how important I think it is to be safe."

She regarded him warily.

"Sugar," he whispered, feathering his hand along her cheek, "I haven't been with a lady since... I can't even remember when, it's been so long. I don't even have time to take a shower half the time, let alone make love to a woman. Even if I was tempted to." His thumb skimmed her lips. "And I haven't been, Allison. Not even close. Until the first time I saw you."

She watched him for a moment, the glare softening until she gave a quavery laugh. "I'm sorry. Not sorry that you haven't been... tempted. I'm glad about that. And I'm sure that you've had your chances."

J.T. was stunned to feel his mouth tick up in a smile. "I've had a few. But I found out a long time ago that sex only makes you feel more isolated, alone, unless you... care about the woman you're with."

"Do you care, Jesse?"

J.T. turned away from her, wondering if she knew that her soft question was twisting a knife blade in his heart. "How can you even ask?"

There was a soft shushing sound of her bare feet against the dock as she came to stand behind him. She linked her arms around his waist and leaned into him, her cheek velvety and warm against his back.

"Then I guess there's only one thing to do. Make sure you never leave the house again without your wallet."

Her words should have made him smile. Instead they forced him to see that he could never allow himself the heaven of making love to her completely.

"I don't think it would be fair, to either of us, to . . . slip again. It'll already be hell to leave you, lady."

"Maybe you wouldn't have to, Jesse. Maybe—"

He closed his eyes against the impossibilities her plea taunted him with.

J.T. turned, pressing his fingertips against her lips to stop her words. He couldn't speak, so he shook his head, a silent plea for her to stop.

She looked up at him, so beautiful, so vulnerable, an angel with candle-shine hair and soft, healing fingers. But no man, especially a man like him, could hope to hold on to an angel for very long.

"Oh, Jesse," she whispered, her eyes shining with tears in the moonlight. "What are we going to do?"

He drew her into his arms, knowing he could never dare to touch her again. "We're both gonna do what we have to do, Ali," he said softly.

Even if it breaks our hearts.

Chapter 11

Allison lay in her huge, empty bed, listening to the sound of Jesse in the room beyond. He was spending the night tossing and turning on the couch, the same way he'd spent every night since that first infuriating drive into town. From the moment he'd became fully conscious, he'd refused the comfort of Allison's bed, even though she'd been more than willing to take one of the rooms upstairs or sleep on the couch herself.

Allison had thought he was just being stubborn—a mule-headed man determined to get his own way, even if that meant he'd be miserable the whole time he was getting it.

But now, as she lay in sheets that still held the faint scent of J.T., Allison knew why he had been in such a hurry to quit the room.

Every time she closed her eyes in this bed, her head filled with wildly erotic visions of the two of them beneath the lacy icing of sheets. And after the tortured sound of Jesse's voice on the dock tonight, after the desperation she had felt in his hands, she knew that he had suffered the torment of imagining her with him in this bed, too. The two of them, together in the way Allison was certain J.T. would never allow them to be now.

It'll be hell to leave you, he had rasped earlier that night. And he was right.

But as Allison lay in bed, listening to J.T. kick out restlessly in slumber, she was certain that no hell could be worse than the one she was in right now.

The hell of knowing that all she had to do was get out of bed and open the door. All she had to do was kneel beside the couch and reach out to caress those strong shoulders that seemed to carry the weight of the whole world.

All she had to do was lower her mouth to his, and kiss him.

Half-asleep, he surely wouldn't be able to hold on to his resolve not to touch her. If she told him how her body burned every time she looked at him. If she told him how it had felt when he had hurtled her into heaven on the lakeshore, and how much she wanted to give that same gift to him, too. If she told him how empty she felt inside and how desperately she needed him to fill her.

And yet, was it possible that breaking his resolve might be the cruelest thing she could possibly do to this man who had already endured so much?

He'd told her from the beginning that everything he was belonged to the kids at HomePlace. There would never be rainy summer nights making love together in ways that were familiar and yet forever new. There would never be Christmas presents hidden in her closet for him, or nights she sat up worrying where he was, what he was doing. There would never be walks at sunset, or babies with J.T.'s devilish smile.

Because J.T. would never let it happen. No matter how much the man wanted it, the internationally known child advocate could never belong to any one person.

Allison supposed if she was a truly selfless person she would accept that. But her head was too full of images—

Jesse's hand on her stomach, feeling their baby kick. Jesse bringing home medicine and a squeaky frog for his own little son. Jesse learning to laugh, without the bitterness in those glorious eyes.

No. It was crazy even to think about such things. Jesse had never even hinted that he wanted the kind of life Allison had always dreamed of.

He had told her he cared for her. He hadn't said he loved her. Maybe it wasn't lust, the way he had wanted her to believe at first. But it wasn't the forever kind of love, either. Because there was no room for her in Jesse's world.

These days in the cottage were the only time she and Jesse would have together. Days that were slipping away like droplets of lake water cupped in a toddler's hands. And J.T. wouldn't even allow himself to fully enjoy this time, because he was already tallying up the amount of pain they would both feel when it was over.

A loon called, like a ghost from the lake beyond, and Allison sat up in bed. The cooling breeze from the open window ruffled the Victorian-style nightgown she wore, the delicate lace teasing her breasts where Jesse had kissed her, touched her.

Oh, God, why couldn't things have been simple? Why couldn't J.T. be a simpler man? Why couldn't one of the business execs, the entrepreneurs, or the senator's son she'd dated have been like J.T.?

Because there was only one J.T. James. After she had fallen in love with him, how could there ever be anyone else?

In love.

She raised trembling fingers to her face.

How could she have been so reckless? So foolish?

How could she have done anything else?

The nagging hopelessness pooled around her, making her eyes sting. Unable to stop herself, she went to the door, opened it.

She wouldn't wake him. She just wanted to look at him, memorize every line of his face, every contour of his body.

The moonlight streamed in from a skylight above the place where he lay, limning him in silver. A renaissance sculptor might have frozen the perfection of his frame—the aquiline nose just a little off center, the sleekly defined muscles of his chest. One arm was flung over his head and lay pillowed on the midnight waves of his hair. The tiny gold loop in his ear gave off a mellow glow and his lips were parted, as if he were seeking something sweet to taste.

Allison's mouth went dry, her gaze skating down the shadowed cords of his neck to the dusting of dark hair that spanned his chest. The sheet he used to cover himself was draped low beneath his navel, while one long leg was bare, half off the narrow couch.

Allison crept toward him quietly, and carefully slipped his leg onto the padded surface, draping the sheet over it again. Then she drew the white fabric up over his chest, tucking it around him.

Shadows were pooled beneath his cheekbones, his hair straggling across his forehead. Allison reached up to smooth it away. She'd barely touched him when she froze, suddenly aware that he was watching her from beneath the thickness of his lashes.

"Jesse!" She felt as if he'd caught her peeking underneath the sheet, instead of putting it back in place. "I was just going to get a drink, and I saw that you needed to be tucked in."

Tucked in! Allison winced. What a ridiculous term to use with a man like Jesse. She might as well have said she'd come out to rock a panther to sleep.

But there was something almost boyish in the way J.T. reached down to feel the covers. "I've never been tucked in before. It's nice."

His voice was groggy. Allison sank onto the edge of the couch. Never been tucked in? Her heart ached as she thought how little she really knew about J.T.

"Probably wouldn't have done any good for your mother to tuck you in, anyway, Mr. James. You're the most restless sleeper I've ever seen. You'd just kick the covers right off."

"I suppose." There was something in his voice, hidden deep.

Allison curved a hand around his cheek. "Try to sleep now. I didn't mean to wake you."

It was impulse, born in the silent yearning in his eyes. She leaned down and pressed a soft kiss where she had brushed his hair away.

Even with the various and sundry nannies Allison had had in the years before she'd been trucked off to boarding school, there had been bedtime rituals to keep bad dreams away. But J.T. looked stunned, confused.

"What's the matter, Jesse? Don't tell me you've never been kissed good-night."

He hesitated for a heartbeat. "Sure. Don't all mothers do that?" She flinched at the biting sarcasm in his tone, and for a moment she considered pressing him about it. But as if he sensed what she was about to ask, J.T. defeated the whole purpose of the tucking-in ceremony by swinging his legs over the edge of the couch and sitting up.

His eyes traveled up and down the nightgown with such burning intensity that Allison looked down and was dismayed to see that the light from above was silhouetting her body against the filmy fabric.

If she'd been dressed in nothing but moonlight he wouldn't have been able to see her more clearly.

She backed away and bumped into the table. "I'm just going to get my—my drink." She flicked on a light switch and started for the kitchen. She could hear J.T. get up and pace across the room. "Jesse, do you want any—"

The sudden shrill of the telephone ringing made Allison cry out. J.T. regarded the telephone as if it might explode.

He was closest, and he grabbed the phone.

"Hello?"

"Who the blazes is this?" The dictatorial voice would have done Hitler proud. Whoever this guy was, he didn't have a clue he was throwing matches at a stockpile of dynamite.

"Where'd you learn phone etiquette, mister?" J.T. asked in a silky voice that would've made anyone who knew him run for cover.

"I said—"

J.T. cut him off. "I know exactly what you said. Tell you what, you tell me who the blazes you are, and I might consider answering your question. That is, if you ask me again, real nice."

"I don't know who you are, or what you're doing at that cottage, but you get Allison Crawford on this phone immediately, or I'll—"

"You'll what? Reach through the phone cord and punch me out? I'd love to go a couple rounds with you. Now, Allison Crawford is much too classy a lady to have to put up with your mouth, so you can just take your attitude and stick it, whoever you are."

"Whoever I am?" If a voice could do deadly damage, J.T. would have been ready for an undertaker. "I'm Allison's father."

"Her . . . father?"

J.T. felt as if he'd been gut kicked. His hand knotted on the phone.

Oh, Christ. As if he hadn't already screwed things up enough for Allison by alienating her best friend. Now he had to come at her father with all the subtlety of a wounded bear.

He heard Allison's gasp as she raced from the kitchen and snatched away the phone.

"Daddy?" she choked out. "Why on earth are you calling at such an early hour? Is everything all right?"

J.T. sagged against the wall, calling himself every name in the book as he listened to Allison try to smooth things over.

"There was no reason for Ernie to alarm you this way. I can't imagine how he heard— His name is J.T. James. Yes. The man from the shelter. Of course I wasn't hurt. It was just some boys who—no, it wasn't a mugging exactly, it was just—"

J.T. drove his hand back through his hair. The old man had found out about what had happened at the Stop Mart? Terrific. Crawford had scoped J.T. James out at his best. Undoubtedly he was exactly the kind of guy Crawford had hoped his daughter would bring home someday.

"No, Daddy," Allison continued. "We aren't exactly seeing each other socially. Something happened, and he had to— No! It's not like that. There was an emergency, and I invited him to—Daddy, I *would* explain myself if you'd give me three seconds to talk," she said with an edge of exasperation.

"Ali." J.T.'s face was on fire with embarrassment as he reached for the phone. "Why don't you let me explain—"

She glared at him and wheeled away, snatching the receiver out of his reach. Doubtless she figured he'd only make things worse. As if that was possible.

"J.T. isn't the kind of man who would take advantage of me," she insisted. But J.T. figured she must be thinking of what had happened by the lake, because her voice choked up just a bit.

"I understand that you're worried about me. But I'm not— Dad, I'm not twelve years old."

No, J.T. thought grimly. You're old enough to get in a helluva lot of trouble on a moonlit strip of lakeshore.

"Of course he knows who I am. We met at the benefit I gave." She laughed with a suddenness that made J.T. grit his teeth. "Money? Daddy, if there's one thing I'm sure of it's that J.T. isn't after my money."

No, J.T. thought wryly. He didn't want her money. He wanted something that would make Crawford even more alarmed. Her love.

"This is my cottage, Daddy," Allison said firmly. "I'll have anyone I want here as a guest. Now I'd suggest that you quit worrying about me, and go out on the Champs Elysées with Renée and Lizette. Have a *beignet* for me. This conversation is over. I love you."

She hung up the receiver and collapsed into a chair, burying her face in one hand.

"Allison," J.T. began, "God, I'm sorry I lost my temper like that. I shouldn't—"

"Oh, J.T." She raised her head to give him a look of acid sweetness. "For a minute I didn't recognize you without your foot in your mouth."

He gave a self-deprecating smile. "I can understand why. I keep screwing up with people you care about. What was it you asked me that first night we met? Anyone else I wanted to alienate?"

He slid into the chair beside her. "I'm really sorry. I just wish you would've let me talk to him again, so I could've straightened things out."

Allison laughed. "I don't think my father was in a particularly reasonable mood. If he'd been king, Mr. James, you would've been hung, drawn and quartered, boiled in oil, or something equally entertaining. My father has a pretty explosive temper."

"Terrific. Some common ground to build on. Truth is, I wouldn't have blamed him for letting loose on me. I have nothing but respect for parents who care about their kids enough to try to protect them."

"But I'm not a child, Jesse."

"Yeah, well." He shrugged. God knew, she didn't look like a child, sitting there in the light. The nightgown he'd seen on the back of the bedroom door that first night he'd regained consciousness was draped around her slender body, setting it off to perfection. Her nipples were a sweet rose blush through the material, the thin cotton bodice caught up in dozens of tiny tucks beneath her breasts. Sky blue ribbons tied the thing together where it dipped into the soft shadows of her cleavage, and a hundred tiny mother-of-pearl buttons ran down the front, to the flounce that skimmed the delicate instep of her bare foot.

Hell, he should be apologizing to Andrew Crawford, J.T. thought. He shouldn't be imagining the excruciating pleasure of unfastening each of the man's daughter's tiny buttons, leaving her naked under J.T.'s hands.

The buzz of the phone was as effective as a jolt from a cattle prod, shattering J.T.'s erotic thoughts. Crawford from Paris again? Obviously the man was smart enough not to be satisfied with Allison's lame explanations. J.T. dove for the phone before Allison could reach it, determined to make things right with her father.

"I'm glad you called back," J.T. said the instant he had the receiver to his ear. "I want to apologize for—"

"Apologize? For what? That bullet must've hit you in the head." Mike Flaherty's jovial voice made J.T. all but drop the phone.

"Mike?"

"Yeah. You remember me. Irish cop, a helluva good one. The guy who drags your butt out of trouble all the time."

"God, Mike. It's good to hear your voice."

"Whoa, it always makes me nervous when you aren't biting people's heads off. What's the matter, buddy?"

What's the matter? J.T. thought hopelessly. Besides the fact that I've fallen in love with Allison Crawford?

"Let's just say the time since your honeymoon hasn't been boring."

"What honeymoon? We had one terrific wedding night and then Buck called. I've been working on this blasted case for the past week. I told Buck to keep quiet about it, even to you. I hated to keep you in the dark, but with someone in the department involved, I figured it'd be best for all concerned if the rest of the world still thought I was in Tahiti, or something. Anyway, Buck gave me the girl's descriptions of the perpetrators. A couple of guys I can trust have them under surveillance. And I'm going in with Tony Manoletti to get Jack Standish."

"Standish?"

"The guy on the force. Never liked the SOB, anyway. But then, he's half-English. Listen, J.T. We're going to make the bust tonight."

"It'll be all over after tonight?" J.T. should have felt elation, relief, but he looked at Allison and felt only despair. The emotion was mirrored in Allison's face as she stood and hastily crossed the room. She opened the sliding glass door and stepped onto the deck.

"Yep, they're history, man," Flaherty told him. "You can kick up your feet and relax."

"That's great, Mike," J.T. said, struggling to concentrate on Flaherty's words, while he was wondering what Allison was thinking, feeling. "Nail 'em for me. They've got a rotten way of treating little girls, you know?"

"I know. We'll be up to pick up our star witness as soon as we get things finished up here. Day after tomorrow. Or is it already tomorrow? What time is it?"

"Five in the morning."

"Time flies when you're havin' fun. Anyway, you've only got one more day and night to get through and it'll all be over. Bet you'll be glad to get back. It must have driven you nuts, being stuck up there."

"Yeah."

"But it was great of Allison to help out. I told you she's an angel." Flaherty's cavalier tossing out of J.T.'s own term for her made him wince.

"She's the most generous person I ever knew," J.T. said.

There was a beat of silence on the other end of the phone. Then Mike gave a nervous laugh. "If I didn't know any better, I'd think you were falling for her."

J.T. looked out onto the deck. He could just make Allison out, a vision in white, leaning against the rail. The wind was toying with her hair. He wanted to bury his hands in it.

"I'm not the kind of man Allison needs," he said to Mike.

The brightness went out of Flaherty's voice, and he let fly a low whistle. "I wish I could tell you you're wrong, man. You know I love you like a brother. There's nobody I respect more. But Allison...she's not cut out for the rough edge of life, J.T. She always reminded me of one of those flowers in hothouses, you know? The ones that wilt if you touch them?"

J.T.'s eyes burned. "You don't know her at all, Mike. She met me at the door with a rifle, and took care of a gunshot wound like a pro. She kept guard while I was out of it, and she handled the runaway better than anyone on my staff could've. And she..."

He closed his eyes, remembering her going head-on against his temper—a temper that even Flaherty had had the sense to back away from.

But for J.T. the most painful of all was the image of her on the lakeshore—loving him in spite of the bitterness that ate him up inside. Once, just once, he had to say it out loud. "Mike, I love her."

There was nothing but dead silence on the other end of the phone.

"Don't worry. I love her too much to tangle her up in a relationship with a man like me."

"Damn, J.T." Mike sighed. "I'm sorry as hell."

"I'm not." J.T.'s gaze clung to Allison's silhouette. "I'm not sorry for one minute I've had with her, no matter what happens now."

He said goodbye to Mike and hung up the phone, then turned and looked at Allison. She looked so alone, silhouetted against the darkness, the breeze toying with her thin gown. She'd wrapped her arms around herself, as if she were cold.

J.T. went into her room and grabbed the coverlet from her bed. Walking quietly up behind her, he draped the lacy thickness around her shoulders. They were trembling. And J.T. wondered if it was from the cold, or something else.

"Ali?" He turned her around and touched her cheek. His fingers came away wet. The thought that she was crying made J.T.'s chest ache.

"I suppose we should be celebrating," she said with a catch in her voice. "The good guys win again. Raine will be able to go home to her father, you'll be able to go back to HomePlace and I'll... I'll be able to..." Her voice broke, and she turned away from him. "Funny, I can't remember what it is I'm going back to."

"Your life, Allison. Planning benefits, raising people's consciousness about all the pain outside their front doors."

"Oh, yes. Getting people to try and out-donate their neighbors. Deciding whether or not to serve caviar or lobster pâté at a luncheon to raise awareness on the homeless."

"Don't dismiss what you do as unimportant. It matters, Ali. Knowing you the way I do, I bet there are plenty of social services that are able to keep their doors open solely because of your work."

"But money doesn't matter, remember? Isn't that what you told me that night at the benefit?"

J.T. had the grace to blush. "It doesn't matter to me, Ali. I'm not used to depending on anybody. I made sure that I could keep HomePlace open myself."

"That's a pretty amazing facility to keep open on one man's salary, and I hardly think you have a day job. What are you? The son of a millionaire hiding behind some secret identity in the inner city? Or are you really an outlaw, robbing banks in your spare time?"

There were only three people who knew the truth—it wasn't something J.T. had ever advertised. In a way he was strangely shy about what he did outside the shelter. "I'm kind of, well, I'm good with motorcycles. Engines."

"You work in a motorcycle shop to keep the shelter open?"

"No. I design parts for the engines. I get patents. I've been able to make a pretty decent chunk of change from companies that want to use them. I'm not rich, Ali. But I'm able to keep things going."

"You're an inventor?" She couldn't have said "you're an astronaut" in any more stunned tones.

"Yeah. After Buck took me in, I studied everything I could get my hands on. I'd mess around with things—I guess it was my way of trying to pay him back for the roof over my head. When he found the part I'd been working on, he was stunned. Told me that what I'd done was special. From that time on, I've been able to take care of myself. And the kids."

She was looking up at him with eyes that shone. "You're amazing, Jesse James. You see pain and you try to heal it. Wrong and you try to right it. I just wish : . . wish you'd let me..." She put her arms around him, pressing close against his chest.

He held her tight, stroked her hair.

"I love you, Jesse," she murmured against his skin.

J.T. thought he'd waited an eternity to hear those words. He locked them away in the secret places of his heart, knowing that they'd be just as miraculously beautiful when he remembered them a dozen years from now. He wanted to tell her he loved her, too, wanted to give her that gift.

But if he did, she'd cling to those words, remember them when some other man—a better man—came into her life to give her a home and a family. Everything she deserved.

He buried his lips against her hair, mouthing the words. *I love you.*

Oh, God, J.T. thought. It hurt. It hurt so damn bad.

"Jesse, I know that you don't—don't love me. I know that you're going away, and . . . just, please, let me hold on to you today. Just until Mike comes and . . . and you leave."

He took her in his arms and settled them both in a lounge chair, wrapping the coverlet around them. She curled up against his chest, silent as they watched the sun inch over the horizon. A drop of red, it spilled into the lake and spread rosy fingers across the water. It touched the crumpled towel they'd left on the sand. The impossible dreams J.T. was trying to forget.

He'd been strong before, made sacrifices. Tough ones. But he'd never made one that tore his heart out of his chest and left him aching, empty.

It was nearly eight when Allison slept, her face nuzzled against him. As stiff as he felt, he wouldn't have moved for the world.

That was where Raine found them. The teenager's eyes were wide with curiosity, confusion as she peered at J.T. through the glass door. "Uh, excuse me. I didn't know I was—was interrupting—"

"It's okay," J.T. said, trying not to wake Allison. "We've just had a long night. Mike Flaherty called, that friend of mine who's a cop. You don't have to be afraid anymore, Raine. He's going to arrest Earl and IceMan. And the cop who's at the bottom of all this. By tonight they'll be in jail, and Mike will be coming up to get us."

"You mean they'll be arrested? They won't be able to hurt me?"

"Not you or anyone else."

The girl fidgeted with the collar of the oversize T-shirt she wore as a nightgown. "I've been thinking about it a lot. Do you think I could call my dad when we get back to the city?"

"You bet."

"Maybe he won't want to talk to me. I mean, I did a lot of stuff to make him mad even before I left."

"Do you think your dad loves you, Raine?"

"I know he does."

"Love doesn't change just because you make one mistake, sweetheart. No matter how big that mistake might seem at the time. I can't guarantee anything. But if I was taking bets, kid, I'd put my money on you." J.T. winked at her.

The girl nibbled her lower lip. "We were real close before my mom died, you know. Then things got bad. Maybe we could start over."

"You might not be able to go home right away. There's a possibility Mike will want to keep you in witness protection for a while, but I'm sure we can get your dad in to see you."

The girl grinned at him and ran into the cottage. J.T. sighed. Sometimes the good guys won. He had a gut instinct that when all this was over, Raine was going home.

Going home.

J.T. closed his eyes, thinking for just a moment what it would have meant to him when he was a kid—to have somewhere to go back to. Somewhere he belonged.

He'd spent his life making sure other kids had a place. A home. But for him...

He allowed himself one poignant moment of imagining his arms around Allison as he carried her over the threshold of his apartment. He imagined kissing her there, saying the words he'd sell his soul to be able to say.

Ali, I love you. We're home.

As if she'd somehow heard his thoughts, Allison's lashes fluttered on her cheeks. Her eyes opened, pools of luminous green. He knew the exact moment she remembered he would be leaving.

One day. Was that too much to ask? Just one day to spend with her before he had to give her up.

"Ali," he said, stroking her cheek, "I want you to show me everything today—everything you love about this place. Can you do that?"

Her lips curled into a tremulous smile. "Of course I'll show you."

J.T. wondered if she knew how much she already had shown him. An inner goodness, a faith, a sense of trust he'd doubted the existence of before. Laughter and acceptance and courage.

She got up from the lounge chair, her hair tousled, dark smudges under her eyes. A certain sadness clung about her lips. She could have been a child, trailing around wrapped in the blanket.

J.T. thought she'd never looked more beautiful.

Then she reached out and took his hand.

Chapter 12

The afternoon sun was suspended like a golden medallion in a china blue sky, the wind whipping at the orange-and-red sail of the two-person catamaran. They'd tipped over three times, laughing and splashing in the water like a couple of kids. Twice J.T. figured the lady had flipped the thing on purpose, just to see him take a dive.

If she only knew that she had only to point a finger and he'd dive headfirst into hell for her.

He pulled the line that held the sail tighter—what the devil was the thing called?—and felt the breeze sweep the little boat faster along the silvery water. He was rewarded by Allison's laugh.

"Just don't get cocky, Mr. James, and run us into the island. We could get shipwrecked, you know, and never get back to civilization."

J.T. felt a sudden urge to run the boat smack into the little oasis of land in one of the lake's three bays. He winked at her. "It'd be rough, Legs. But at least we wouldn't starve."

She'd spent part of the morning filling a dented tin pitcher with wild blueberries that grew along the shoreline. He'd insisted he didn't like berries, until she crammed one between his lips. After that he'd eaten until he was almost sick on them.

They'd tried to drag Raine out onto the sailboat, but the kid had insisted she wanted to finish her book. He suspected Raine knew they wanted to be alone, and he felt like a bastard because he hadn't made the slightest effort to change her mind.

Selfish as it might be, he didn't want to share Allison with anyone today.

He grinned and waved as the ubiquitous red ski boat skimmed by twenty yards away. The nut-ball Ostrom boy with glasses and a grin that must've been breaking hearts from one end of the lake to another held up the canoe paddle he'd just been slaloming on.

J.T. laughed with the boatload of boys, wishing that he could bottle their enthusiasm and confidence to take back to the kids at HomePlace.

J.T. came about, tacking the sailboat as flawlessly as if he'd been captaining one since the day he was born, and Allison scooted to the other side of the boat as it caught wind. Her sunglasses were perched on a nose that needed sunscreen. Her hair was wet from their last dunking. There was a blueberry stain on her cheek, and he wanted to kiss her so badly he felt it as a physical pain.

Instead, he smiled at her. "I've about got this puppy whipped, wouldn't you say, Miss Crawford? What's next? Tightrope walking on the clubhouse roof? A few rounds of golf?"

That sent her into gales of laughter. "The thought of you at the local country club is the stuff nightmares are made of. We could fish if you wanted."

J.T.'s grin faded, and he looked away. "No, thanks, sweet thing. I'm a city boy. I don't mind taking down drug pushers, but I draw the line at taking fish *off* hooks."

"There's one more thing I could show you. Of course, we'd have to walk a ways."

"I suppose a sidewalk is too much to hope for?"

"Dream on. Take us back to port, skipper. We'd better change."

He did as she asked, and managed to take down the sail and tie the boat to the buoy on the far side of the dock. By the time he'd dragged on his jeans and his clean but somewhat holey T-shirt, Allison had changed into hot pink shorts and a white blouse that bared her midriff and tied under her breasts.

She ran upstairs for a moment to check on Raine, then went into the kitchen and grabbed a bottle of wine and some stuff from the refrigerator.

Then she caught J.T.'s hand and took him out to her Jeep. She hopped in the driver's seat. He eyed her askance.

"Where are we going?"

"You'll see."

She jammed the thing into gear and hit the gas. The road to the cottage was a glorified path of gravel. But it was a five-lane interstate compared to the place she took him. An overgrown path, with grass and wildflowers growing in the tire tracks, it dove straight into the Wisconsin woods. Slender white birch trees swayed like Indian dancers against a curtain of pines. Granite boulders left by glaciers centuries ago sprinkled the woods, like impromptu seating for the warriors who had once roamed the land. And three smaller lakes were hidden like jewels in the rolling hills, the only sign of life on them a rickety fishing boat with oars at the ready.

A doe leaped across the road a dozen feet in front of them, and they had to slow to almost a stop and wait patiently until a lazy skunk waddled across their path.

It was beautiful, peaceful. J.T. leaned back in the vehicle's seat and sucked in a deep breath, wishing this road could go on forever.

Allison pulled the Jeep to a stop at the foot of the largest hill they'd come across, and J.T. could see a clearing ahead, some kind of rickety structure at the top.

"What the blazes is that?" he demanded, shielding his eyes with his hand as he looked up at what looked like a tiny ramshackle house on hellaciously tall stilts.

"It's the old fire tower," Allison told him, putting the Jeep into Park. "I never had the guts to climb it before. I thought maybe we could try it."

J.T. climbed out of the Jeep, and went over to where a small ladder went up one of the supports. About twenty feet above his head it was enclosed by a tunnel of metal strips to protect people from falling, but it didn't look any too sturdy.

"Don't you think Smokey the Bear or whoever's in charge of this thing might, uh, not appreciate us poking around?"

"It hasn't been used for years." She dimpled. "At least, not for looking for forest fires."

J.T.'s eyes narrowed and he saw a fresh carving on one of the wooden poles, blending in with a dozen other messages. C.O. + C.D.

Allison laughed. "Looks as if Craig has himself another conquest. Must be that Duren girl. Cathy."

J.T. grinned. "You mean this is the lake version of the back seat at a drive-in?"

"C'mon and see the show." Allison took up the bag with the supplies she'd gathered in the kitchen, and stuffed in a blanket from the back seat of the car, then she slung the whole thing over her shoulder. "I'll race you."

"You go first," he said, taking the bag from her. "I'll follow behind you so I can break your fall. And my neck, when this whole thing comes down on top of us."

"Not likely. The kids keep it in pretty good repair."

"I'll bet."

J.T. watched as Allison climbed ahead of him, her derriere a tempting curve, her long legs flashing just out of his reach. She was laughing, teasing him, and for an instant he wished that he was sixteen again, and he'd just carved her initials on the post. He wished that he could have his first kiss here, in the woods, with the wind blowing away any memory of the city streets and hunger and fear.

When they reached the platform he leaned on the rail for a long time, looking out across a sea of treetops. Far away he could see Arawak, so small in the distance it looked as if he could hold it in his hand.

"It's beautiful here," he said, and meant it. "Like another world."

"That's why I love it so much."

He looked down. She'd spread out the blanket, and laid out crackers and cheese, strawberries and wine.

"I come here to recharge. Everybody needs a place like Arawak."

J.T. gave a soft laugh. "You sound like Buck. He's always harping at me to take a break from it all, catch my breath. But I run on pure adrenaline. Adrenaline and anger."

"And look at the charming things they do for your personality. Make you bite the heads off unsuspecting women at benefit dinners. You know, I get physically ill when I have to give speeches, Mr. James. There could've been some pretty unattractive consequences to our little altercation. Though it might have taught you some manners, mister."

J.T. grimaced. "Forget about playing the delicate flower with me, Crawford. I've see the way you handle a rifle. I'm probably lucky I came out of that ballroom with all my body parts still intact."

She laughed and patted the blanket beside her. J.T. sat down. He dangled his legs over the edge of the platform, and opened the bottle of wine.

"I forgot glasses." Allison shrugged. "We'll have to share."

"Wine out of the bottle? Now we're on my home turf."
J.T. held the bottle out to her and she took a sip, then gave
it back to him. He put his mouth on the place still warm
from where her lips had touched it and was intoxicated by
the taste of her on his tongue.

"I never had a place like this when I was growing up, either," Allison admitted. "We had a couple of houses, but
they were both more like armed camps, after the kidnapping. And as hard as my father tried to stay around, he was
gone a lot. Business and such."

"Your...mother, too?" J.T. was opening dangerous
ground, but he couldn't stop himself.

"She died when I was two. I used to claim that I remembered her, that she wore a lavender dress that fluffed out in
hoopskirts. But I'd really only seen a picture of her at some
costume ball she and Daddy had gone to once. People say
I look a lot like her."

"Then she must have been beautiful." J.T.'s voice was
low. He tasted a strawberry, knowing that the burst of
juices wasn't half as sweet as Allison's mouth would be.

"What about you, Jesse? You must have had a family."

"There's a big difference between a family and biologi-
cal parents, sweetheart. It's nothing I talk about."

She'd pulled her knees up and looped her arms around
them. She leaned her chin against one arm. "Do you talk
about Melissa?"

J.T. almost dropped the wine bottle. His jaw clenched
and he looked away. "I've never told anyone about...my
past, Allison. It's too damn painful."

"I don't want to hurt you."

He would have been able to brush away her question,
change the subject, any of the hundreds of ways he'd
learned since he was a kid to evade talking about his life.
But at that moment he looked into Allison's face, and fell
deep into those sensitive angel's eyes.

Maybe he couldn't share his future with her. But he could
share his past.

"Melissa was my mother's name. I never called her anything else. She was a diamond-studded debutante who fell for a kid who couldn't afford to give her a ring out of a gum-ball machine. He was the bad boy, you know? The leader-of-the-pack kind of guy that girls that age fight over. I was the surprise package that came out of too many nights steaming up the car windows at the local drive-in."

Allison looked into J.T.'s ruggedly handsome face, and wondered if his father had been half as wonderful as J.T. was. If so, she could understand the debutante following him anywhere.

"They ran away together. Melissa and my dad. Before anyone knew about me. I know he loved her. Maybe she loved him, as much as she was capable of. He was just a kid himself when I was born. Seventeen. And he died when I was eight. I remember things about him, though. Little things. He had this great old motorcycle, and he'd hold me in front of him. No helmet, just me and him and the wind whipping in our faces. We'd ride for hours." J.T.'s voice dropped, and he looked away.

"Most kids remember lullabies, you know? Or being tucked in at night. The thing I remember is how his leather jacket smelled, and the way he'd take me everywhere with him. Pool halls, motorcycle shop. It wasn't exactly Mr. Rogers's neighborhood, but, God, I loved that man."

Allison reached out and took J.T.'s hand. "It must have been wonderful."

"I wouldn't go that far. As great as things were with my father and me, there were always problems between me and my mother. I didn't understand it then. Figured the distance was all my fault, somehow. Now I know that Melissa was used to having center stage. She wasn't thrilled to be sharing it, even with her own son. She also was less than thrilled with the fact that the apartment needed to be cleaned, and I needed to be fed. I don't think she could even open a can of soup without help. That's the only time

I remember my dad losing his temper with her. When he found out I was hungry..."

Allison watched the shadows of memory skim across J.T.'s face, remembered his anguish when he'd been delirious. He'd been so desperate, so broken. But he hadn't been calling out for the father who adored him. He'd been begging, pleading with his mother.

"I started taking care of my mother after that. You know, so my dad wouldn't get angry. Melissa said that if he got mad enough he'd leave us. I don't think I really believed even then that my dad ever would have left me. The weird thing was that I remember thinking my mother might. I was scared. So scared. And then—" J.T. sucked in a deep breath "—then my father did leave, even though he didn't want to. A panel truck turned in front of him, and he couldn't avoid it. End of story."

Allison imagined the devastation J.T. must have felt.

"I was a kid. I thought my dad was like a superhero, or something. I remember screaming at my mother that he'd come back. That we had to stay at the apartment, wait for him. He was—he was coming back."

J.T.'s voice stumbled over the memory. "She slapped me to shut me up. I think she was half-crazy with grief herself. She loved my father in her way. Not only that, but we were barely scraping by, as it was. With my father dead... Well, let's just say that a job at the Burger Heaven wasn't Melissa's style. So she went back home to her mommy and daddy. I remember them bad-mouthing my father. I remember Melissa just taking it. Even agreeing with them. I was so mad. I mean, this was my father, and they were acting like he was dirt to be swept out of their lives. It was like they were glad he was dead. I lost it. I remember kicking my grandfather in the shins and calling him the names I'd learned in all those pool halls."

"Oh, Jesse." Allison's voice trembled.

"Yeah. It was a real touching homecoming, let me tell you. In the end they told my mother she could stay. But it would be better for all concerned if they sent me off somewhere to be civilized. Melissa wasn't much of a mother, but she was all I had left. I remember clinging to her, crying. I begged her to tell them to go to hell, told her I'd take care of her. She could get a job and we could stay together.''

Rage balled in Allison's chest. She had heard that little boy plead, felt those clutching hands in the cottage bedroom after J.T. had been shot. In that instant she hated the mother who had hurt him so badly.

"What happened then?"

"Oh, she cried a little and told me that this was best for both of us. I'd only be gone a little while. If I was real good she would come and get me. They found a couple in another state that would take me. They were decent enough people. They tried to make me part of their family, but I wouldn't have anything to do with them. See, I was only going to be there for a little while. Melissa was coming to get me."

The sick certainty of where his story was going lay in Allison's stomach like a stone. "She never did?"

"After a couple of years she didn't even visit anymore. I thought that her parents were like—like the Wicked Witch of the West, or something. That they wouldn't let her come. I tried to run away a couple of times, got mean as hell. Managed to alienate the family I'd been staying with. I just . . . just wanted to find Melissa, you know? I was older now. I could take care of her. I thought if I could see her, then—I don't know. We could live happily ever after, or something. Be a family."

J.T. picked at a splinter in the rail, peeling it back. The place he exposed was raw, like a scar on the wood. Allison knew it was just a reflection of the scars that his mother had left on his heart.

"What happened then?" she asked softly.

"I finally made it. Yep, all the way to my grandparents' fancy house. I was thirteen, filthy. Been eating out of garbage cans for weeks. I wouldn't steal anything from the people I'd lived with. When Melissa saw me she looked as if I was a rat running across her carpet. All those years I'd thought it was my grandparents who didn't want me. But they were both dead by then. Melissa had moved back into her old life without missing a beat. It was as if my father and I had never existed.''

Allison stared at J.T.'s rigid back. How could a woman forget a man that she loved? How could a mother forget her son?

"I suppose I should've congratulated her. She was getting married to some rich guy. The trouble was, he didn't have a clue about me. When she'd run away her parents had even fabricated some crazy story about her studying in Paris or something, so the family wouldn't be shamed by the fact that their daughter had been living in sin with Tyler James.''

J.T. levered himself to his feet, paced restlessly down the narrow walkway. "She stuffed a thousand dollars in my hand and told me to go back to the Adamses. She said she'd send money for me every month when she sent them their check for taking care of me. Said she'd pay whatever I wanted, as long as I stayed out of her life.''

Tears were streaming down Allison's face. Oh, God, why had she forced Jesse to open up these old wounds? He'd tried to stop her, but she hadn't let him. She'd been so certain it would be good for him to share his pain. Now she was certain she'd been wrong. It was crushing her until she couldn't breathe.

She'd wanted to know what had made J.T. James the man he was. She hadn't known her heart would lie in ribbons when he was finished, that her mind would be haunted forever by images of the boy he had been.

His mother had thrown him away, with no more thought than a stained dress or a broken glass. She'd lied and lied and lied to him, and then thrown money at him in an effort to protect herself. No wonder he'd had nothing but scorn for the people at the benefit. No wonder he'd wanted to hold Allison herself in contempt. Money could buy anything—an easy conscience, a fancy house. And it could even make a child disappear.

"The rest is one more version of the same old story," J.T. said with a shrug. "I hit the street running and I never looked back. I was sixteen when I started breaking into Buck's shop. It felt like home, you know? Reminded me of my father. Sometimes I think he was the one who...steered me there. Like a guardian angel, or something. But a man like my dad would never get to be an angel, would he?"

"Angels come in all different shapes and sizes, Jesse." Allison squeezed the words past the knot in her throat. "I'm sure that he...he never left you."

J.T. turned, and it was as if she was seeing him for the first time. She had reached up and torn off the mask he wore to fool the world, to protect the abandoned little boy who still lived somewhere inside him. He came to her and knelt on the blanket. "Did my father send you to me, Allison?" J.T. whispered, framing her face with the callused roughness of his hands. "I wonder. God, you look like an angel in the middle of all this hell."

"Let me be your angel, Jesse. Even if it's just for today. Make love to me. Here. Now. I love you so much."

J.T.'s face twisted with something almost like pain, a need so primal it rocked Allison to the core of her soul. "No. This sob story about when I was a kid doesn't change anything."

"It changes everything. Damn you, Jesse, I forced you to tear out your heart. Don't you see, I want to fill the empty place I left there with something. Something beautiful."

"Allison, you don't owe me—"

"Something beautiful, Jesse! Can't you just reach out your hand and take it?" Her fingers were on the hem of his shirt, tugging it upward, her mouth on the tanned skin she bared.

He groaned as she pulled the garment over his head, her hands and lips devouring him as if she were trying to kiss all the secret, scarred places he'd kept hidden for so long. She lingered over the gauze patch that now covered his wound. She dipped her fingertip into the indentation of his navel.

"Ali, this is crazy." J.T.'s breath hissed through his teeth. "We're leaving tomorrow. It's over."

She looked up at him, her splayed fingers seeking the most sensitive places on his chest, his belly. "And if you leave then, if we never take this time together, Jesse, I'll regret it forever. Don't we both have enough regrets in our lives? Do you want to spend forever thinking of this moment, knowing that we missed our only chance at touching heaven?"

Heaven . . .

J.T. had a fleeting image of his father, how he'd tried to love someone from a different world. A world as different as Allison's was from J.T.'s own.

It had ended in tragedy.

Had Tyler James ever regretted it? Or had he known, as Jesse did, that men like them could never expect to stay in heaven. They could only steal tiny pieces of it, to hold for a little while.

Eyes burning, J.T. reached out for Allison.

He stripped away her blouse an inch at a time, tasting his way to the lacy cups of her bra with the hot point of his tongue. He unfastened the delicate undergarment and lowered his head to her breasts, drawing life, drawing sustenance from this woman as if he were reborn. He worshiped her breasts, her throat, her face. He kissed her forever—on and on and on, a sweet seduction of lips and tongue and sweet desperation.

J.T.'s large hand tunneled under the baggy hem of her shorts, and she gasped as his fingertips skimmed the lacy band of her panties. They were damp and silky and soft, but not half as alluring as the treasure that they hid. With his other hand J.T. unfastened the fly of her shorts, un-zipped them.

His groan shook his chest as he spread the placket wide to see ice blue satin with creamy dollops of lace and tiny cherry red ribbons. Like some kind of sensual confection, they were fashioned to drive a man crazy.

He got her to lift her hips, and eased off the shorts. Then his eyes held hers for a moment, and he could see his head reflected in her wide, eager eyes.

"Did you wear those for me, Ali? Just for me? Did you think about me finding them underneath your clothes? Stripping them away." He hooked one scarred finger in the top edge of the panties and ran his knuckle along that tender, pale flesh.

"I've thought about—about this ever since . . . since you kissed me at HomePlace. And on the beach. I . . ." She whimpered as his middle finger slid down to find the tiny crease buried in dark blond curls. "Yes, Jesse," she breathed. "I wanted you to see these, I wanted you to—to . . . think they were . . ."

"Hot as hell? Beautiful? Do you have any idea what it does to a man to wonder what his woman is wearing under those damn proper clothes? To imagine satin and lace and deep Vs that cut down to here?"

He dipped his head and planted a burning kiss just above the rim of gold curls.

"Ah, Ali. God, I want you."

He ripped away all of her clothes except the dainty pant-ies, and mounded the garments behind her, to shield her skin from the wooden surface. She was golden and glori-ous, sexy and innocent dressed in nothing but that wisp of lace. And she was more than J.T. would ever have dared to dream.

A tight knot of worship formed in his throat, and he didn't want to frighten her with the wild, pulsing passion that he was barely able to hold in check. It took every ounce of strength he possessed to tame the raging need inside him, but he lifted her foot in his hand, and kissed the dainty arch of her instep. He trailed his tongue to her knee, he pressed kisses on her quivering thigh and the soft indentation of her navel. She was gasping, shuddering with pleasure as he reached the slick satin. He pressed his tongue against the point that made her writhe, then guided the panties down her legs until he could kiss softer, silkier places, dark gold and glistening in the sun.

She'd offered him a chance to steal heaven. And he wanted to give it to her, too. He wanted to imagine for just this moment in time that they had forever.

She gasped, protested when he opened her to receive his most intimate kiss. "No! Jesse . . . I—"

"Shh. Let me, angel. Let me show you . . ."

She writhed and clutched his hair, fought—oh, God, how she fought against her own release.

"J-Jesse, I want you inside me. I want you!" she almost sobbed. "If you stop again, I'll . . . k-kill you."

He looked up at her, smiled, a smile that could have charmed St. Peter out of the holy gates. "Is that any way for an angel to talk?"

"I mean it, Jesse," Allison gasped as his fingers—those clever, skilled fingers—took up the torment his mouth had been causing moments before. "Your wallet is in the—the bag."

J.T. couldn't believe it, but he was laughing. And it felt good, so damn good.

"Don't you laugh at me!" Allison said, glaring just enough to make his heart twist.

"I'm not laughing at you, sugar," he soothed. "I'm just so damned glad that you—you're mine. For today. Today."

He got out the protection, but she snatched it away.

"P-probably drop it as an excuse," she said, ripping at the foil package with fingers that shook. Then J.T.'s amusement died.

Delicately, so delicately, she took him in her hand. Her eyes were huge and green and astonished as she smoothed those soft, elegant fingers along the part of him that felt ready to burst into flame. She learned him by touch, leading him toward nirvana with the most sensual caress he'd ever known. He gritted his teeth against the waves of excruciating pleasure, almost fearing he'd lose it altogether as Allison made the ritual of protecting her into something worthy of some sultan's harem.

And as he watched her hands on him, all he could think about was how much he wished he could rip away the thin sheath of latex, just bury himself inside her with nothing between them. He imagined making love to her again and again, giving her his child.

With a savage groan he finished sheathing himself in the condom, then grabbed Allison by the arms, forcing her back on the blanket. He positioned himself between those sleek, silky legs, kissed her breasts, her eyelids, her lips. He could feel her against his shaft, wet and hot as she arched against him. J.T. drove himself deep, a cry tearing from his chest that was half triumph, half despair.

God, she was so tiny.... "Easy, angel," he breathed against her, holding himself back. "I don't want to hurt—"

"Jesse, please." She rocked her hips upward, seeking him, gloving him more deeply. "Please, Jesse . . ."

Gritting his teeth, he stroked slowly once, twice, a little deeper, easing deeper. He tried to discipline himself, hold back, but Allison wouldn't let him.

With a frustrated cry she twined those long legs around him and pulled him with all her strength, until with a groan of surrender J.T. drove himself full length into her tight warmth.

She took all of him. All of him. The pleasure almost undid him. He forced back his own clamoring climax, his breath rasping in his lungs as he let her get used to the feel of him inside her.

Then his mouth closed on her, and he kissed her fiercely as he took her higher, deeper, stronger, sensations rushing through him as mercilessly as if he had leaped from the top of the fire tower and suddenly soared.

She was liquid flame in his arms, driving out the darkness, leaving light in her wake. Blinding light, painful light, so beautiful J.T. had to bury his face in the soft cloud of her hair. Her fingers dug into the muscles of his shoulders, her legs clutched at him.

He felt her quicken around his shaft, heard her keening cry of release. Bracing himself on straight arms, J.T. flung his head back, seeking his own climax. He heard Allison whimper as that soft little mouth skimmed his chest, and those lips, still bruised and wet from his kisses, closed on his nipple, flicked it with such torturous pleasure that J.T. gave a guttural cry. The peak burst through his body with a force that stunned him, unnerved him as nothing in his life had before.

With a moan J.T. collapsed against her, holding her, just holding her, his cheeks wet with the tears he was trying to hide.

"Are you...all right?" he whispered. "I didn't mean to be so— Damn, I wanted to be gentle with—"

"You were everything I ever dreamed of," Allison whispered, stroking his hair. "I love you, Jesse. Don't you see? Couldn't we find a way..."

The words were like a knife thrust to his heart. Oh, God, if there was only some way they could stay here forever. Lock themselves away at Arawak and spend the rest of their lives skimming across the water in the sailboat. Nothing but the two of them, no one but the two of them.

He closed his eyes, wanting to hold on to the vision, but all he saw was the front porch of HomePlace, the kids shooting hoops. All he could feel was the cold penetrating his jacket as he walked the streets, finding kids behind dumpsters and in doorways, scared, alone.

"No, angel. There's no place for you in my world."

"Why? Because your mother didn't belong in your father's world?"

"Damn it, Allison—"

"I'm not like your mother, J.T. Melissa was too stupid and selfish to know what she threw away. I'm not. I'm going to hold on to you with everything I am. I'm not going to lose you. Not without even giving us a chance."

"Oh, I can see it now. We're going to set up housekeeping in my apartment over HomePlace? Three little rooms with leaky plumbing and about as much privacy as a street corner during the Macy's parade? You'd be miserable there."

"You're sure of that? Maybe I'd surprise you. God knows, in the past week I've surprised myself. Maybe I could find some way to help, be a part of all the good that you do. But how will we ever know, Jesse, if you don't even let me try?"

But what if it doesn't work out? J.T. wanted to shout at her. What if you leave when things get ugly and hard? This time there wouldn't be any place for me to run.

He looked at her face—ivory and roses, green forests reflected in her eyes. "And if it doesn't work? Then what?"

A shadow passed over her face, but she met his gaze squarely with her own. "Then I'll go. Without blaming anything or anyone. Without a word."

His hands were shaking, the fear in his gut so deep and dark and terrifying that it threatened to consume him.

Allison...in HomePlace...in the infirmary, in the kitchen. Out in the porch swing with the sunlight in her hair. The image was too compelling to resist.

He could protect her, couldn't he? Keep her safe. He'd die before he'd let anything hurt her.

But if it didn't work out? Would he ever be able to pick himself up and go on?

No! Just this once, couldn't he let himself hope without stopping to tally up the consequences? Couldn't he believe?

It was hard, so hard to trust himself to take that single step.

But she was his angel, wasn't she?

She wouldn't let him fall.

Chapter 13

The first glow from a street lamp slanted in through the narrow window and inched across the cramped office's floor. J.T. sat at his desk, buried in enough paperwork to keep any of the longtime residents of HomePlace firmly planted at the other end of the facility to avoid him.

It was common knowledge that anything that kept him behind a desk more than five minutes at a time made him as surly as a rhino with an alligator attached to its leg. So he had learned early on to lock himself in his office during his monthly battles with the staggering amount of red tape involved in running even a private shelter. And everyone, from the youngest runaway to Buck, mentally saluted him when he gave the order that he was not to be disturbed during these sieges, unless the building was on fire.

The days he'd been barred in his office had always been miserable, but he had learned to focus his energies at laser-beam intensity to get through it as quickly as possible. But today he hadn't been able to concentrate for ten minutes at a time. Because even though his door was locked, someone was with him. Haunting his thoughts, crowding his emotions.

Allison.

From the moment they had delivered Raine—otherwise known as Molly Lane—into the arms of her father, Allison had shown that she had a gift for cutting through people's anger and hurt, to draw out love. It had been a sight J.T. knew he'd never forget—Allison's sunshiny smile, her face wet with tears as Raine had clung to her and thanked her. Most beautiful of all, Ali had given the girl a gold locket as a reminder to the teenager how special Allison thought the girl was.

Though Allison couldn't replace the treasures Molly had lost that had been from the girl's own mother, Allison had told the girl that this was a gift she had gotten from the mother she could barely remember. The only gift Allison still had. The sight of her fastening the necklace around the girl's throat had made J.T.'s own eyes burn, his heart ache and soar at the same time.

Most wonderful of all, Molly's father had vowed not to let his daughter out of his sight again. He was going with the girl under police protection, until everything was worked out. As J.T. had watched the burly construction worker hold his daughter in his arms, tears running down his weathered face, J.T. had been certain that Molly was going to be fine.

It had been good to know, even better to share that knowledge with Ali. But the reunion of father and daughter had been only the first of Allison's many triumphs.

It seemed as if in the past ten days she had insinuated herself into every corner of the shelter. The classrooms, the game room, even here, in his office. Even though he should be working on state reports about the newly processed kids, his gaze kept straying to the documents that had arrived from the zoning committee three days ago, and he couldn't stop grinning.

Allison Crawford was a hurricane in high heels, and the commission hadn't even known what hit them. She'd pulled in favors, recruited old friends, even taken on the neighbors where J.T. had planned to start the mother-and-child facility. By the time she'd finished, even the most judgmental biddy on the block had been volunteering to crochet baby afghans out of leftover yarn.

In spite of all J.T.'s reservations—reservations that had only been underscored by the unspoken disapproval in Mike Flaherty's too-readable face—he'd begun to wonder how HomePlace had ever survived without her.

Without her teasing, without her laughter. Without her quick wit and her tenderness, her fierce protectiveness of the kids, and that hard-driving determination that would have done a bulldozer proud.

If anything, J.T. found her more beautiful, more sexy, more irresistible when she was ordering Buck around, or twisting city aldermen around her elegant fingers.

But she was most beautiful of all late at night, when she left the official bedroom assigned to her for appearances' sake, and crept up the back staircase that led to his apartment.

There, in his bed, they made love and talked. Planned and laughed. He stifled his amusement at her righteous indignation when she raged over the insensitivity of one of the commissioners. He laughed when she told him how she pulled rank on the stuffy jerk, and then let him know it in no uncertain terms. And he cradled her in his arms and let her cry, just a little, after she'd processed a child into the shelter with a story that broke her heart.

J.T. should have been happy. Hell, he was. Sometimes. Most of the time. Every second with Allison had been precious. Every laugh, every smile. She'd driven him crazy, flashing those sexy-as-hell garters at him from beneath the hem of her skirt when no one else could see, patting the back of his jeans in intimate caresses that had made promises about the night to come.

And the fight in her when she had run up against opposition had made J.T. so damn proud of her. Once the lady sank her teeth into something, she didn't let go.

Why was it, then, that sometimes when he watched her, J.T. would get that familiar tightening in his belly, that needle-sharp sensation of panic as if he were waiting out there for something to happen—something just waiting to take it all away?

His hand clenched on the pencil he held, and he forced back the unsettling thoughts. He wished to hell it was time for bed, so he could shove away the shadowy fears and bury himself in Allison's love. He could tell her about Sonny's score on a social studies test, and that the boys had painted a new mural on the back fence. She'd kiss him, and her eyes would shine so brightly they'd drive away the darkness.

He glared at the mound of paperwork. Hell, she was probably asleep herself, by now. For the past three days he'd come downstairs and found her in the dining room, her head on the table, a half-eaten dinner getting cold on her plate.

She'd been spending time at the new building, decking it out. He'd given her free rein, and she'd been so obsessed with getting the new shelter ready in record time that J.T. had almost felt jealous. She'd charmed four of the boys into helping her, and had had them painting and patching up everything in sight. He'd been anxious to see the progress himself, but there had been so much to catch up on, between HomePlace and the police reports, that he had barely had time to breathe.

He gripped the pencil more tightly, and started once again to attempt to add a column of figures. If he didn't get this finished, he'd never get out of this damned office. And for the first time since he could remember, he was eager to go up to the apartment above the HomePlace complex—because Allison would be waiting for him there.

The buzz of the phone made him jump, and he grabbed the receiver. "HomePlace," he said brusquely. "This is J. T. James."

"J.T.? Thank God you're there!" Mike Flaherty's voice was as tight as a bungee cord.

"What's wrong?"

"Everything. Everything. That bastard, IceMan? He slipped through the net, man. He claimed he was having chest pains, so we were transferring him to the hospital. He got away."

J.T. swore, a lethal fear building inside him. "What the hell? Did you warn Molly's dad?"

"Already took care of it. She's being taken to another safe house. Truth is, I don't think the bastard'll stick around here long enough to make trouble for any of you, no matter how ticked off he is. Logic says he'll get as far away as possible as fast as possible."

"Logic? Don't give me any crap about logic. What's your gut tell you, Mike?"

"The guy knows you were involved with the witness. There's always a chance he might be stupid enough to think he can get to the witness through you. And you fingered him in the lineup, then didn't take any pains to hide it. I don't know, buddy. It's always possible the thought of wasting you might just be enough to tempt him. We just have to hope he's got enough willpower to resist."

"Right." J.T. felt a cold knot of anxiety in his gut. He'd had a target on his back before and hadn't even missed a beat. Why was it that now every nerve in his body was jumping?

"J.T.?" Mike hesitated. "I'd tell Allison to keep her head down, too."

It was as if just by mentioning her name, Mike had yanked that nameless terror into focus. J.T.'s hand all but crushed the phone.

"Far as I know, IceMan doesn't have a clue she's involved, but you never know about these crazies. If he had any idea you two are an item he might not be overly picky about who he nails.''

J.T.'s jaw clenched. How many times had he seen it on the street? Blood vengeance. Brothers or sisters blown away to teach an unruly pusher a lesson. Girlfriends brutalized, then flung back to their lovers like broken dolls.

"The bastard won't get near her," J.T. snarled, feral protectiveness like a living thing inside him.

"I'm gonna get him back, J.T. I promise. I'm sorry as hell about this."

"You didn't unlock his cuffs, Mike," J.T. said tightly. "I'll keep my eyes open. Just nail him, damn it. Fast."

"Don't pull any hero stuff. You see anything suspicious, you call down here. I'll have the place swarming with cops in five seconds."

"You got it."

J.T. banged down the receiver, his face grim. He should've known better than to get feeling too damn relaxed. Son of a bitch! They had to get that animal back behind bars. Until they did, there were going to be a few changes around the shelter.

He'd keep a couple of extra staff members on duty. Keep the kids on the grounds. And Allison…hell, she'd just have to stay out of danger until this thing got straightened out.

He stalked to the door and went in search of her. But though he was able to warn a few of the staff members and the older kids, Allison was nowhere to be found.

It was dark now, well past time for her to be indulging in her favorite pastime, playing with little April while Annie studied toward her GED.

But when J.T. went into Annie's room the girl was balancing April in one arm, a textbook in another. She looked up, her eyes a little worried.

"Where's Allison?" J.T. snapped more stridently than he'd intended.

"I don't know. She was supposed to quiz me on the Constitution at about four, but she never came. I figured she was still at that zoning thing."

J.T.'s heart skipped a beat. "The zoning meetings are all over."

"Then she must be at the new shelter. I'm sure she just lost track of time, or something."

Allison? Miss Punctuality Crawford? J.T. couldn't see it. And the phones hadn't even been hooked up in the new place yet so he could call to check on her. Or, he thought with a sudden chill, so she could phone for help in an emergency.

"Sonny went with her to finish painting the bathroom over there today," Annie said. "But I saw him on the basketball court with the other guys hours ago."

Hating the anxiety bubbling in his chest, J.T. went to Sonny's room. The kid was sprawled on his bunk, playing a video game.

"Where's Allison?"

Sonny dropped the game, his eyes wide. "Isn't she back here? She was just going to finish putting some toy thing together, then she was coming right home."

"You left her there alone?" J.T. hated the edge in his voice.

"Yeah. I..." Sonny paled in the face of J.T.'s displeasure. "She was coming right home, and the guys were having a basketball game. She told me to go, J.T."

"When?"

"That was..." Sonny looked at the clock. "That was four hours ago. Hey, you don't think anything's wrong?"

J.T. didn't even answer. He dug his keys out of his jeans pocket and ran out into the night. Flinging a leg over his motorcycle, he kicked it into gear.

By the time he steered the bike in front of the old Victorian house, he felt as if he'd taken a beating.

A single light shone in one of the upstairs windows. The door was wide open to the evening breezes—the breezes and far more sinister things that might prowl the darkness.

He swore, taking the porch steps three at a time, yanking open the screen door. "Allison?" he bellowed, tearing through the house, searching. "Allison, where the hell are you?"

"Up here! Jesse! Help!" The cry was distant, strained. He bolted up the wide sweep of staircase, the dim house a blur.

When he flung open the last door he expected a scene from his worst nightmare—Allison helpless, hurt.

What he saw was a playroom, with Allison seemingly trapped in the web of a half-assembled Kid Gym.

Her hair straggled around her face, and dozens of screws littered the floor, along with various and sundry tools. She had a Garfield bandage on one finger and a smudge of dirt on her nose.

And if he hadn't been so damned worried he would have had a healthy respect for the outrage in her eyes.

"Are you hurt? Did somebody—"

"Nothing's wounded but my pride." She banged one of the blue-painted tubes. "I can't get this stupid thing together. Ten cribs, five baby swings, three sets of shelves went together without a hitch. Then I get this thing, and the screws aren't the right size."

"Damn it, Ali, you scared the hell out of me. You were supposed to be home hours ago. Annie said you were supposed to help her study."

Allison squirmed out from under the apparatus. "Annie! I didn't even think—"

"Yeah, I noticed. You left the door wide open. Anybody could've walked in."

She smiled, that honey-sweet smile he'd learned to be wary of in the past two weeks. "The biggest danger on this street is being run down by blue-haired old ladies who can't see over the steering wheel. Besides, after tangling with this stupid piece of equipment for five hours, anybody who dared to irritate me would be taking their lives into their hands. They'd have wrong-sized screws sticking out their ears."

"After everything that happened the past few weeks you should know this isn't a joke. Hanging around in an unlocked house alone after dark is asking for trouble."

"Thank you for the lecture, Mr. Safety Patrol," she sassed him. "Don't sweat it. I've got my can of Mace in my purse, a rape whistle on my key ring, and in two weeks I'll get my black belt in tae kwon do." She took up a mock fighting stance. "Chill out, James. The bad guys are behind bars, remember?"

She looked so self-confident, her eyes shining. But when he looked at her, all he could see was a little girl, lost in the park, not aware of the danger all around her.

He hesitated. "Not all the bad guys are behind bars, Allison. At least, not anymore. Mike called. IceMan's back on the street."

He saw the color drain from Allison's cheeks. "Raine— I mean, Molly. What about her? Does Michael think that this IceMan will try to hurt her?"

"Mike swears the kid's so far underground IceMan would have to dig to China to find her. No. The kid is safe."

"What about you? You're the one who identified him in the lineup. And fouled things up when he tried to murder her. Oh, Jesse—"

"Nothing's going to happen to me." He went to her, took her in his arms. J. T. James had never been afraid for himself. How could he explain the wild, irrational fear that was eating him up inside right now? Fear for this woman who was at once so strong and so damned fragile.

"I just think we're going to have to take a few precautions until Mike's men bring him in again. That means no more work here."

Her unease shifted to astonishment, then plain old stubbornness. "You've got to be kidding! I have electricians coming at nine o'clock tomorrow morning, and a plumber at twelve. I got the cribs put together, but I haven't gotten the beds for the mothers assembled. And I've got donations of baby clothes coming in from all over.''

"I said we're locking this place up until IceMan is back behind bars."

"Don't be ridiculous, Jesse. This IceMan has never even seen me. Why would I be in any danger?"

"I didn't ask for your opinion, Allison. You do what I say. If you're going to stay on at HomePlace, my word is law. That's the way it is."

She gaped at him. "Excuse me, Mr. Mussolini, I think you missed your exit to the Dictator's Ball." She planted her hands on her hips. "I've spent my whole life hiding behind my security locks waiting for the bogeyman to come get me. Between my own fears, and my father's fears for me, I was wrapped so tight in cotton batting it's a miracle I could even breathe. Then I came to HomePlace, and I found out what it was like to be free. It's pretty damn wonderful, mister. If you think you can just hand out a decree and put me back in some vault because you've come down with some caveman protect-my-woman virus that's out of control, you can forget it."

"Quit being a smart ass, Allison. I'm not trying to be unreasonable. But nothing, damn it, nothing is worth—" Losing you, seeing you hurt. J.T. suddenly realized he'd never been more frightened in his life.

It was crazy fear. Allison was right. IceMan had never seen her. Couldn't possibly know...

But if the guy was lying in wait for J.T., sizing up the situation, IceMan would be cunning enough to figure things out. Animals like him always knew how to go for the jugular of an enemy, and Allison was the most vulnerable weakness J.T. James had ever had.

She had barely been at HomePlace for ten days, and she was already in danger.

J.T.'s fists knotted and he stalked to the light switch, turning it off.

"Jesse, I'm not finished!" Allison snapped in outrage.

"Oh, yeah, you are, sweet thing," he said. He grabbed her by the wrist and dragged her out the door behind him.

Downstairs he barely gave her time to snatch up her purse. Using Allison's keys, he locked the big front door. But instead of returning them to her, he pocketed them himself.

Allison made a fierce grab for them. "Those are my keys, Jesse."

"They belong to HomePlace Foundation. Now get on the damn bike."

He stalked over to the motorcycle and flung one leg over it.

His eyes scanned the area by instinct. The night should have seemed peaceful in the warm old neighborhood, with the trees lining the street and the sounds of people laughing drifting from open windows. The yards were littered with dilapidated tricycles and abandoned watering cans instead of broken glass and garbage.

But all J.T. could see was IceMan's soulless eyes glittering in the streetlights, the sick pleasure that had been in the killer's face as he'd tried to jam the needle into a helpless girl's arm.

What kind of chance would Allison have against ugliness like that? What kind of chance did she have in J.T.'s world? Even here, on this quiet street, the security he'd hoped to find here for Allison was just an illusion. A dangerous illusion that he had allowed himself to believe in since the day they had made love in the fire tower.

He started the motorcycle and Allison slammed herself down on the seat behind him. She was mad as hell. He was glad.

He drove the way his father had—fast, too fast. The wind whipping his face, tearing at his clothes. The powerful motorcycle flew across the streets, weaving in and out. He wanted to believe that if he drove fast enough, far enough, he could outrun animals like IceMan, protect Allison from the stark realities of life that no angel should have to face.

No, he was going to see that she was protected if he had to lock her in a damn closet and slip food under the door.

When they pulled in to HomePlace Allison jumped off the bike before it was fully stopped, and ran into the house without a word.

Steeling himself for the confrontation to come, he marched up the steps, but before he could follow her to her room, Buck stopped him, the older man looking curious as heck.

"Yo, J.T. There's someone waiting in your office to talk to you."

"Tell him to make an appointment. I've got no time—"

"I think you better see him. If you don't, he's gonna come track you down. He's a suit, but he's got a hell of a mad on right now."

With an oath J.T. stormed down to his office, flinging open the door. The man Buck had told him about was pacing the office, his expensive suit crumpled, an obscenely huge diamond glinting on his clenched fist. He looked like a prizefighter, ready to take somebody down.

J.T. would have loved the release of taking a swing at him.

"Listen, mister, I'm real busy right now. What the hell do you want?" J.T. demanded, then froze as the man turned full face toward him, glaring at him with shrewd green eyes.

"I want my daughter back."

J.T. had seen plenty of pictures of multimillionaire Andrew Crawford—raiding companies, foreclosing on tycoons. He'd seen press clippings of the man with actresses and dignitaries. But as he looked into Crawford's face now, all he saw was a distraught father.

"Is she here?" Crawford demanded.

"Yeah. She's here." The anger went out of J.T. in a rush.

"My God, she's never done anything like this before!" Crawford paced the room like a caged tiger. "When her driver told me she'd moved into a runaway shelter, I caught the first flight home. If I'd had any idea the girl would get this carried away with her charity work, I would have put a stop to it!"

J.T. laughed without mirth. "I'd like to have seen you try. I'm J.T. James, the director of HomePlace."

"Andrew Crawford." The man extended his hand.

"I know." J.T. regarded it with a wry kind of humor, then gave the man a firm handshake. "Before you tell me it's good to meet me, or some other accepted social platitude, I'd better warn you that I'm the one who convinced Allison to come here and check the shelter out after the benefit. Things got a little out of hand."

J.T. could have sworn the temperature in the room dropped twenty degrees. "You consider getting tangled up with drug dealers and criminals 'a little out of hand,' Mr. James? I've devoted my whole life to keeping Allison safe. Do you expect me to congratulate you for throwing her in the middle of a war zone? Are you out of your mind?"

"There are plenty of people who'd testify to that under oath." J.T. crossed to his desk chair and sank into it, wondering if the old man knew how close he'd hit to the mark. That was exactly why he'd brought Allison here. He'd been out of his mind in love with her. Temporary insanity.

Crawford stalked to the desk and flattened his hands on the surface, glaring across at J.T. "I'm sure the work you do here is admirable. Financially, name what you need. I'll write you a check. But that's exactly where my daughter's involvement stops. I don't give a damn what she says. If you care about her well-being at all—"

"I love her." J.T. snagged the old man's gaze.

Crawford fell back a step, his face gray. "What did you say?"

"I love her. She loves me. That's the reason Allison is here."

Crawford groped for the other chair and sat down, looking sick. "My God."

"Mr. Crawford, I know this isn't exactly great news to you. Truth is, I have a lot of doubts about all this myself."

"Doubts that Allison's stock portfolio have put to rest, I suppose."

J.T. rounded on the older man. "I don't give a damn about her money. I didn't want this in my life. And I sure as hell didn't want to mess up hers. It just happened."

"You fell in love with my daughter, so you brought her here, made her a part of this." Crawford waved expansively. "Do you really believe that she can ever belong here? What happens when her zeal to save the world wanes? When she wants a husband, children? Are you prepared to give that to her, Mr. James?"

The words tore like shards of glass in his chest as he pictured Allison in a rocking chair, cuddling his baby against her dainty breast. He pictured the infant taking her rosy nipple to suckle. And he pictured Allison's soft smile, her eyes bright with love.

"Are you prepared to give my daughter a family, Mr. James?" Crawford repeated.

J.T. looked away. "I don't know."

"You don't know. My God, man, can't you see how impossible this is? Allison can't survive in this kind of an atmosphere. She's not strong enough. Not tough enough. Just working with these kids would break her heart. And as if that's not bad enough, she would be a target for every lunatic who wanted to get their hands on my money. She was kidnapped once, in spite of all I did to assure her safety. Surely you can't be fool enough to think that you can protect her?"

"No." The single word took the wind out of Crawford's sails.

"Wh-what did you say?"

"I can't protect her. At least, not now. That's why I'm planning to send her home."

"But I don't understand. You led me to believe—you seemed so determined to pursue this insanity."

"I didn't say I intended to leave Allison forever. Just—I want her safe *for now*. One of the men involved in shooting me escaped today and I don't want Allison anywhere nearby if he decides to pay me a visit."

Crawford tugged his tie, as if the news made it harder for him to breathe. "At least we're agreed on that much. The airport limo dropped me off. I'll call my driver and have him pick Allison and me up."

"You'll do what?"

Both men wheeled to the door where Allison stood, white-faced, dangerously still.

"Allison." Crawford crossed the floor, sweeping her into a hug that showed just how alarmed he had been on behalf of his daughter. "Thank God you're safe."

"Daddy, what on earth are you doing here? You're supposed to be in Paris."

"Business finished up more quickly than I had imagined, so I caught a flight—"

"You mean you called Ernie and got the most recent Allison report, so you cut the trip short." She was getting that uppity look about her that J.T. was starting to dread.

"It doesn't matter why I came home. I'm here. And you are going to pack your things and come back uptown with me."

"This is where I live now, Daddy. With Jesse."

"Mr. James and I have decided it's best for you to go home."

Allison wrenched out of her father's grasp and shot J.T. a fulminating glare. "I'm a grown woman. I'll decide what's best for me on my own."

"Don't be stubborn, Allison," J.T. cut in. "You'll only be away long enough for Mike to get IceMan back behind bars. As soon as it's safe—"

"Safe? And when is it ever really safe down here? Aren't you the one who told me this isn't Mr. Rogers's neighborhood? Once IceMan is behind bars, something else will come up. And then something else. And something else. What are you going to do, J.T.? Send me away *every* time there's any kind of danger?''

''Yes, if I think it's for your own good. Your father and I agree on this.''

''Well, that's just peachy for both of you. But it's not your decision to make. My father has treated me as if I were a helpless little girl ever since the kidnapping. But I'm not helpless, and I'm not frightened, and I'm not hiding anymore.''

J.T. remembered the images she'd painted in his mind, the horror of the kidnapping. He knew how hard she had fought to tap into the core of strength she'd lost for so long.

''Allison, be reasonable,'' Crawford pleaded, but it was as if he wasn't even in the room. Allison had no eyes for anyone but J.T.

''I love him, Daddy. And I'm not leaving.'' She glared at J.T. ''I'd go insane waiting in that apartment, wondering if you were hurt, if someone was—'' She stopped, swallowed hard. ''I thought I proved myself when we were at the cottage. That I was strong enough to handle things.''

She was searching for his affirmation of her strength. Needing him to tell her that he believed in her. But even the thought of betraying her was not as potent as the image of Allison hurt, dead.

He stalked to the window. ''The truth is, I'm the one who's not strong enough,'' he said. ''I'm not strong enough to ignore the fact that someone like IceMan might have a rifle sighted in on your back. I'd be so crazy worrying about you, I'd lose my edge and that could get you killed, or the kids hurt—God only knows what.''

''Oh, Jesse.'' Allison came to him, her arms encircling his waist. She felt so small, so vulnerable, but her chin was set at a determined angle. ''I know it'll be hard this first time. You're scared. Maybe I'm a little scared, too. But I'll stay here, and we'll get through it, then the next time it won't be so bad."

There was so much trust in her eyes, such blind faith. As if she believed that the guys in the white hats always won, and that somehow, J.T. would take care of her.

He'd die for her in a heartbeat. Gladly. But killers like IceMan only made bargains on TV cop shows. Even if it hurt her, he couldn't allow her to risk being caught in the cross fire.

He moved away from her, forcing the mocking sneer he'd used as a defense for so long. "You took care of a bullet wound. You kept watch at the cottage. That may seem like the cutting edge of danger to you, princess, but it isn't exactly grappling with some creep for a switchblade."

He waited for a flash of betrayal in those incredible eyes, anger, hurt, anything except the quiet strength he found there.

"I know what you're trying to do, Jesse, and it won't work." Her voice was sad, yet strangely determined. "I'm not going to hide from life anymore. I'm not going to let people protect me or make my decisions. You showed me how strong I can be. I can't go back to pretending I'm something different. Not even for you." There was a finality in her voice that made J.T.'s gut churn, his chest ache.

"Then I guess we've got a problem, Legs." J.T. forced the words past a knot in his throat. "You're leaving HomePlace. Now. That's just a simple fact."

"If I do," she said with quiet conviction, "I won't be coming back."

J.T. felt as if she'd slammed a sledgehammer into his chest, freeing the nameless dread that had been haunting him these past days. And he knew in that instant that he'd been expecting this moment from the beginning. Preparing himself to have Allison torn out of his life. He would have sacrificed anything to hold on to her, keep her with him.

Anything except Allison's safety.

"It doesn't have to be that way," he rasped. "Just go home for a little while. That's all I ask. As soon as this is over, I'll come for you."

"By then it will be too late." ·

He was standing on the edge of a precipice, looking down at the stark loneliness that had been his life. The only difference was that now he knew what it was like to have someone loving him, just him. Someone to trust, to share. To open all the dark places in his soul to the light.

Despair ground down on him with merciless savagery, and he wanted to grab Allison and kiss her until she couldn't breathe. He wanted to beg her to come back to him when this was through.

Instead, he jammed his hands in his jean pockets. "Then I guess there's only one thing left to say, Ali," he said softly.

He heard her cross the room, felt her fingertips tremble against his jaw. The kiss she pressed to his lips was an agony so precious he knew he'd hold it deep inside him forever.

"Goodbye, Jesse," she whispered, then she turned and walked away.

His eyes blurred, his fists knotted with the effort it took to let her go. After a heartbeat he caught a glimpse of Crawford, hovering in the door.

"I won't pretend I was thrilled at the thought of my daughter with you. But... thank you. For... for convincing her to..." Crawford's words trailed off.

Thank you for cutting your heart out, a voice inside J.T. finished. *Thank you for throwing away the only dream you ever held in your hands.*

He didn't trust himself enough to speak. He just nodded, then listened as Crawford walked away.

J.T. crossed to his desk, feeling old, tired. So damn tired. She was leaving, and he wouldn't lift a finger to stop her. Maybe it was better this way—quick, clean. Facing the inevitable.

He gave a bitter laugh. At least he'd be out of his misery, no longer waiting for the day when she would miss her privileged life and walk away from him forever. Like his mother had. Like his grandparents had.

It was a necessary pain. A merciful ending.

One he'd been unconsciously bracing himself for since the first day he saw her.

Then why did he feel as if he'd been blindsided by a semi? Why did he hurt so much he couldn't breathe?

Leaning back in his chair, he thought back to the magical day he and Allison had spent at Arawak, the laughter, the loving.

He had called their time together heaven. And it had been the only time in J.T.'s life he'd believed in angels and forever. Even so, he'd known from the beginning that paradise didn't belong to someone like him. But he had taken it, anyway, in some kind of blatant defiance, not giving a damn what came after.

He should have known what punishment would wait for any man bold enough to steal heaven.

In the end, the poor bastard had to crash back down to earth.

Chapter 14

Allison sat on the splintery park bench a hundred yards away from her car. She had driven around the city late into the night, not sure where she was going, knowing only that she needed to go there alone. By bare instinct she found herself in the neighborhood she had known as a child. The gates to Willowshade Park had been closed, but Allison had parked her car and climbed over the fence. She had wandered along paths illuminated by wan streetlights, and had been chilled by how things had stayed eerily the same.

She had come here a hundred times in her nightmares, trapped inside the stone fence by monsters disguised as swing sets and sliding boards, men in ski masks lurking behind every tree.

Allison sat in the predawn silence, remembering how small she had been, how frightened when she had been lost in this park so long ago. In the years since, she had clutched that same fear in her fist, like a butterfly. Until J.T. had unfolded her fingers, and she had finally been able to set it free.

Would he ever know what a gift he had given her? The sense of soaring that single act had made her feel?

At the sprawling new shelter she hadn't looked over her shoulder once. She hadn't run downstairs to check locked doors, or hesitated, her heart skipping beats, at the sound of a car backfiring, or a baseball hitting the side of the house.

For the first time in her life, Allison had felt safe.

Safe—with a wounded man and a runaway girl.

Safe, despite the fact that IceMan was on the street.

She'd taken a deep breath, and trusted herself. Plunged down into Jesse's world without any net to catch her except for his love.

And she had begun to hope that Jesse loved her, too. Enough to plunge past his own terrible fear. Enough to trust her.

But at the first sign of trouble he'd done exactly what her father had done so many years ago. He'd tried to lock her in some castle tower, so that he could fight all her dragons. He hadn't been willing to let her share, not only his love but the fight he was having to make.

And as she'd stared across the cramped office, Allison had known she could never allow anyone to lock her away again, safe, protected. Because there wasn't any safety in that huge, empty tower. There was only loneliness and fear.

The kind that Allison had seen in Jesse's eyes when he'd told her about his mother. The kind that crippled and maimed and left you bleeding more certainly than any bullet wound could.

She grimaced. She'd been so damn determined to prove to Jesse and her father that she could stand on her own now. But in the end, she hadn't realized that Jesse had used her determination against her when everything else had failed. She had played right into his hands, and left. Not just for the night. Not until the danger was past. But forever.

Forever.

And he had let her go.

Was it possible that, from the moment he'd carried her suitcases into her room at HomePlace, he'd been waiting for her to walk away? That he had escalated this whole incident on purpose, until he backed them both into a corner with no way out?

Allison tensed, remembering how many times he had told her there was no room for her in his life. That she would be miserable. That she would be in danger. She could remember the stark yearning in his eyes when he reached for her, the barely concealed despair.

What are we going to do, Jesse? she had asked him by the side of the lake.

We're gonna do what we have to do, he had whispered against her skin. But as she had held him, it was as if she'd felt pieces of J.T. shatter inside, slowly breaking away to reveal the loneliness that lay hidden in the angry crusader, J. T. James.

He'd been alone from the day his father died. He'd been alone when he'd lived on the streets, thrown away by his selfish mother. He'd been alone, even in the houseful of kids who idolized him, because even kids like Sonny and Annie didn't really know the whole man—couldn't see into the corners that J.T. kept hidden inside himself. Tough. Strong. Indomitable. He was all those things.

But he was also tender, gentle, temperamental and scarred, deep where he never let anyone see. He was an uncertain angel to the children he protected. A man who fought like hell for them, but wouldn't fight for himself.

Because as generously as he gave love, he didn't think he was worthy of receiving it. That was the legacy his mother had left him. Rejection of the most brutal kind.

And now he was shoving Allison away, as well, masking it behind their clash of wills.

And she had let him do it, feeling as if it was her only way to assert the new strength she had found.

"No, Jesse. I'm not going to make it that easy for you," she muttered to herself. "*I'm* the one in control of my life now. You can yell, stomp, throw things. Heck, you can bodily throw me off the shelter grounds. But I'm going to come back. I'm going to keep coming back until you quit running. Until you believe . . ."

In miracles. In heaven. In the fate that had brought them together, and given them a chance to catch their dreams.

Allison slung her purse over her shoulder and marched to where her car was waiting.

An unnatural hush blanketed the shelter, as if some magic had put it to sleep. J.T. vaguely remembered some kid's story about kind fairies who had cast a spell like that on a castle, to keep the residents from mourning a princess who was waiting in a tower for Prince Charming to kiss her awake.

But this time the princess was gone. And there wasn't a chance in hell that there would be a happy ending.

Worst of all, everyone in this particular castle, from Buck to Annie to little April, seemed to miss her, terribly.

J.T. winced at the memory of their faces as they'd questioned why Allison had left—without a word to anyone. He hadn't had it in him to offer explanations or comfort or any of the million and one platitudes they needed to hear. He'd just tunneled himself away in his apartment, trying to escape. What he'd done was fall smack into the eye of the storm.

He shifted against the mound of pillows at the head of his bed, his fingers curled around the T-shirt Allison had worn in place of a nightgown the evening before. She had come to his room, still dressed in her jeans, meaning to stop only long enough to tell him about an idea she'd had for the new shelter. She'd planned to go back to her room and change into something sheer and delicate and sexy as hell before bed, but Jesse hadn't given her a chance.

He'd been crazy to get his hands on that creamy pale skin of hers. He'd been desperate when he'd pressed her down on the bed, driving them both to shattering climax again and again and again.

He'd dismissed the desperation as raw desire. God knew, every time he touched the woman it was spontaneous combustion. But now, as he sat staring into the night, he wondered if he had known, somewhere in his soul, that it would be their last night together.

He stared out across the empty apartment, remembering how he'd anticipated the sound of her footsteps on the stairs the past week. He'd kept that damn back door locked for as long as he could remember until Allison.

Now it was like some kind of symbol for what she'd done to his whole life. She'd opened so many doors he'd kept closed for so long, and now, even though she was gone, he couldn't shut the damn things again.

J.T. got out of the bed that still held the subtle scent of her shampoo. He walked to the window.

In those months after his father had died and his mother had deserted him, J.T. had shut down, piece by piece. He'd put all his pain and hurt and grief in a box and nailed it shut, wrapping himself in nothing but anger.

Just thinking of his father had caused him so much pain that the only legacy he'd allowed himself from Tyler James had been the motorcycle parked outside, the way he rode it—more than a little reckless, as if he were invincible.

In reality, it had been because J.T. didn't give much of a damn whether he lived or died.

But now he kept wondering if his father had been scared as hell. He wondered what Tyler James had thought the first time he'd held his son at the hospital where J.T. had been born. A kid, without so much as a high school diploma, suddenly responsible for an infant. An infant whose mother had never really wanted him.

After his father had died, Melissa had made a point of telling J.T. they had named him Jesse James as a joke. That they had laughed about it together. The knowledge that they had had some inkling of the relentless teasing that would come from such a name had hurt J.T. more than he could have expressed.

But now, as he looked out the window, he suspected his father hadn't been laughing inside. He'd been a kid, trying to do his best. Naming his son something he thought was strong, cool, tough. Cloaking his own fears about being a decent father behind that laughter.

And as for Melissa... All these years he'd believed it was his fault that she'd abandoned him. Because he was unlovable. But Allison had delved into every corner of his soul, and she had embraced everything about him. Loved him, with a complete openness that had almost made him believe...

No. Damn it, he had to stop raking through this in his mind. He had to get on with his life. Stop imagining her body beneath his hands, the delicious give of her breasts beneath eager fingertips, the shuddery sighs when he found her most secret places.

Something hot and tight balled in his chest, his eyes burning as he tried to force it back.

He had to stop listening for her laughter, for the light tread of her footsteps on the stairs.

He had to stop hoping against hope that she would come back. If she did, she'd just be putting herself back in danger.

A groan slipped through his lips. Oh, God, this hurt too damn badly. He couldn't take it. He couldn't—

The creak of a stair made J.T. freeze, his heart thundering against his ribs. Another soft sound came through the crack in the door. Another.

"Allison?" Hardly daring to hope, he crossed the room, knowing if it was her, he'd never have the strength to send her away again. He flung open the door, praying and dreading that he would see golden hair, forest green eyes.

Instead, he met the cold glimmer of the barrel of a Beretta 92.

IceMan.

J.T. knew if he lived forever he would never forget the pure malevolence in the killer's eyes, but he figured "forever" wasn't what IceMan had in mind.

"Get in there, and don't make a sound," IceMan snarled.

J.T. backed into the room.

"I've been itching to get my hands on you ever since you screwed things up in that alley," IceMan said, shutting the door behind him.

"If you had any brains, you'd be three states away by now. The cops don't like it when scum like you catches them sleeping. They're going to be hot on your trail."

"They won't catch me. I'll be out of here just as soon as I finish up my business with you."

"You must want me dead bad."

"You *and* that stinking kid. I'll get her, too."

"The hell you will. She's under police protection."

"She'll have to come out of hiding when Earl goes to trial, won't she? With the two of you dead, the only time I'm looking at is for breaking jail. And even if I can't get to the kid, she's hardly a star witness. Runaway, druggie boyfriend. It shouldn't be too hard to prove reasonable doubt. You're the real problem. A goddamn Boy Scout. The jury'd believe you if you said I was frigging Santa Claus."

J.T.'s eyes flicked to a pair of scissors on the desk across the room.

"Do anything stupid and I'll blow your head off," IceMan snapped.

J.T. raised his hands. All he could think about was that if he'd allowed Allison to stay, she would have been in this room, in his bed. She'd be watching this scene unfold, terror in her luminous eyes. Thank God he'd sent her away.

"You pull that trigger, there are fifty people who'll hear the shot. And they all know that you might be paying us a visit. One of them'll have the sense to call the cops."

"Or I could take out a bunch of those brats of yours before the cops arrived, and you could watch. Wouldn't that be entertaining?"

"You're sick."

"Smart, too." IceMan withdrew a silencer from his pocket, affixing it to the barrel of the gun. "You screwed my life up, but good. Knocking off that kid was going to make me a rich man. I was going to live out my days on a beach somewhere with a dozen whores to keep me hot and bothered. Now my boss wouldn't give me the butt of his cigarette if I was dying for a smoke."

"You're breaking my heart," J.T. grated, his mind on the kids sleeping downstairs, the volunteers and staff that would be arriving soon to start up the day's work. The thought that even one of them could be in danger was enough to make J.T.'s skin crawl. He had to get the bastard out of HomePlace, no matter what the cost.

"You think you're such a genius?" J.T. challenged. "Prove it. I'm the one you want. You off me here, you attract a lot of unwanted attention. But if we leave through the back door now, you can take me someplace where you can put as many bullets in me as you want. Promise not to hurt the kids, and I'll walk out. I give you my word."

IceMan's lips pulled back over his teeth in a feral smile. "A dead man's word ain't worth much. No, James. I've got something lots more creative than a bullet planned for you."

There was something in the killer's eyes that chilled J.T.'s blood.

"You're gonna be headline material, James. The kind of shock TV loves to get their hands on. You're gonna die of a drug overdose."

"Nobody would believe it. I've never done drugs."

"I've got a kid ready to tell every talk-show host in the country that he sold you everything from cocaine to heroin. The name Eli Ramsey sound familiar?"

J.T. went still, remembering the last time he'd seen the boy, Allison's hundred-dollar bills clutched in his hand.

IceMan sneered. "That kid's got a real itch to see you crash and burn, James. See, the two of you used to shoot up together. Then, one night when you were stoned, you made some—shall we say, not too pleasant advances toward this kid. He refused, and you threw him out of your shelter."

J.T.'s hands knotted, white, bloodless.

"When the cops come, they're gonna find some real ugly stuff in your apartment. Between that evidence, and the kid's testimony, well, you know how it is with stories like this. Even if they're a load of bullshit, once they're in print people believe them. Everything you've worked for will be shot to hell."

IceMan took a small plastic bag filled with drug paraphernalia out of his pocket and tossed it onto the scarred table. "And if you don't do exactly what I say, I'm gonna go one step farther than just wrecking up your life. I'm going to hunt down that woman you've been screwing. The blonde with legs up to her neck."

J.T. trembled. "You touch her and I swear I'll come back from the grave and tear your damn heart out."

"I'm shakin' in my shoes. Truth is, I'm a reasonable man, James." A perverted pleasure lit the killer's eyes. "You do what I say, the lady's got no problem. Cross me, and—well, that high-society bitch and I are gonna get real cozy. Now that bag on the table's like a frigging candy store. And I'm gonna be a nice guy and let you choose your own poison. How do you wanna check out? Acid? Crack?"

J.T. stared at the plastic bag. He had to buy time. Look for an opening.

"Grab the tourniquet," IceMan ordered.

J.T. moved as slowly as he dared, opening the sack with numb fingers. A syringe and a spoon lay among an assortment of drugs that would have given DEA reason to celebrate if they had taken them from some user. Eight rocks of crack, papers of LSD and God only knew what else.

He shoved up his sleeve, then he took the tourniquet and wrapped the thing around his bicep. The strip of elastic was a burning path around his arm, making the veins stand out in a tracery of ropes beneath the skin. Slowly, J.T. withdrew the syringe, then glared at IceMan.

"You have to give me your lighter, genius. This rock doesn't suction into a syringe too well."

IceMan pulled a red plastic lighter from his pocket and tossed it at J.T. He caught it in midair.

"You know how to work that thing, don't ya?" IceMan taunted. "You can't have hung out with losers on the street for so long and not know how to shoot up. I'd love to see the faces on those stupid kids when they find you here."

J.T. hadn't even considered that—Sonny or Annie or any one of a dozen other kids, bounding up the front stairs to find him dead.

"For God's sake, take me somewhere else. Decorate the apartment like a damn Christmas tree if you want, but don't—"

"Shut up and grab the needle. I want to see you jam it in a vein, James. I want to watch you push the poison in. Now."

J.T. took the syringe, grimly preparing the drug. Damn, he was out of time, out of ideas. IceMan was getting twitchy as hell. One little shove, and the guy might go off the deep end. And God only knew how many others he'd drag over the edge with him.

J.T. filled the syringe, and flicked it with his fingernail to drive out any air in the cylinder. He was going to die. The certainty rocked through him. But there had to be some way to take IceMan down with him. It was a gamble J.T. was going to have to take, because once he was dead, there were

no guarantees what this lunatic would do—to HomePlace,
to Allison.

J.T. touched the point of the needle to his vein, his muscles bunching. It was now or never. Take the son of a bitch
out or die trying.

"No!"

The sound of the voice, mingled with the creak of the
door swinging open, made him drop the syringe, even as
IceMan cursed, the killer sweeping the gun to where a figure was silhouetted in the doorway.

J.T.'s heart leaped into his throat. Allison. Oh, God,
what was she doing here?

"Run!" J.T. bellowed, diving for IceMan. But the killer
fell back, the gun aimed squarely at Allison's chest.

"Take one more step, James, and I'll blow a hole in her
the size of your fist."

J.T. held up his hands in surrender. "Don't hurt her.
Damn it, don't—"

"Get in here, bitch, and shut the door!"

Allison did as he said, her eyes never straying from the
gun in his hand.

Hot terror pulsed through every fiber of J.T.'s being.
Why hadn't she run? Why was she just standing there?
Looking almost calm, serene? He could only imagine what
was going through her mind.

"Jesse, are you all right?" she asked.

"Oh, yeah, this is a goddamn party." He was so scared
for her.

"Don't look so worried, Jesse." She looked at him with
heart-wrenching love in her eyes. "Mr., er, IceMan is not
going to hurt me." She shook back her glossy hair. Her
voice was as cool as iced champagne. "You're a businessman, aren't you, Mr. IceMan? Far too intelligent to waste
a chance at turning an unexpected profit."

"Damn it, Ali, you can't bargain with a murderer!"

"Let her talk." IceMan cut him off. "I'm a real good
listener when money's involved."

Allison almost smiled. She slipped her hands into the pockets of the white jacket that hung open from her shoulders. "I can give you the chance to have so much money you couldn't spend it all in a lifetime. More than any petty drug lord or bad cop could possibly hope to pay you. My father's a very rich man. He'd pay any amount to secure my freedom. If I decided to cooperate, you could have a cool million in your hands and be on a chartered plane bound for wherever you wanted in the space of an hour."

The man positively stank of greed.

"There's only one condition. You let Jesse go now. Take me in his place."

"No!" J.T. took a step toward her, then thought better of it. "Goddamn it, Allison, I won't let you do this."

IceMan chortled. "This ain't your call, James. You're just one of the walking dead right now. As for you, little lady, well, after I off James, your daddy'll still dance to my tune."

"You're too smart not to realize that I could make things easy for you, or I could be a whole lot of trouble."

Was she crazy? Christ, what was she doing? Talking to the bastard as if she could reason this away....

Or stall him long enough to give J.T. an opening. Counting on J.T. to find a way out. That she should love him so much, trust him so much broke J.T.'s heart. He forced himself to calm down, his eyes narrowing on IceMan, hoping that the son of a bitch would be distracted. But the killer kept his gun aimed squarely at Allison.

"It's not easy keeping a hostage alive that doesn't want to stay alive," she continued. "And if anything really did happen to me—well, there isn't a rock on this earth you could hide under where my father wouldn't find you. Money can buy anything, Mr. IceMan. Especially the corpse of a two-bit crook like you."

IceMan flushed. "Stuck-up bitch! Been spit on by women like you all my life. I'll teach you some manners once I get you alone."

"Of course," Allison continued as if she hadn't heard him, "if I decided to cooperate, it could be much...nicer for you."

She was so damn close to the man—and he saw Ice-Man's eyes flick to her breasts, saw him lick his lips.

"If she's willing to do this for you, James, you must'a been hot in bed." IceMan's eyes were glazed with lust as he flung a glance J.T.'s way. "A night with her just might be worth letting you—"

Allison's hand flashed out of her jacket pocket. She flung herself at the killer's gun arm, and at the same moment something in her hand hissed.

The faint sound of the gun firing was lost in IceMan's screams as he fell back, clawing at his eyes.

Mace. Allison had zapped the bastard with Mace!

J.T. was already moving—launching himself across the table, barreling headlong into IceMan's midsection as the weapon flew across the room. IceMan cursed wildly as he hit the floor.

Again and again J.T. drove his fist home, as if he could beat the horror out of his own body with the fury of his attack.

He was crazy—crazy with a lifetime of anger. Crazy with fear. He barely heard Allison's voice pleading, barely felt her hands on his shoulders.

"Jesse! Jesse, stop! He can't hurt us now!"

Footsteps thundered up the stairway, people shouting in alarm. But J.T. didn't stop pummeling IceMan until Buck was beside him, grappling with the killer's limp form, dragging J.T. off him.

The room was spinning, sick panic leaving J.T. drained, dizzy.

"It's over J.T., over." Buck's voice seemed to be coming from the next county. "The kids are calling Mike. Help's coming."

J.T. turned to where Allison leaned against the wall, her arms wrapped around her, her shoulders trembling beneath her open jacket. He wanted to shake her until her teeth rattled. He wanted to crush her in an embrace. He wanted to say so much. Instead, he heard his voice rasp out, harsh, angry.

"I told you to stay the hell away from here!"

"You're too used to getting your way, Jesse. Must be that outlaw mystique."

"This isn't funny, woman. Do you have any idea what he would have done to you if . . ." He couldn't even form the words.

"I had my Mace. I was prepared."

"Against a murderer?"

"Yeah, well, my tae kwon do classes don't start till next week."

He grabbed her by the shoulders. She winced, but he gave her no quarter. "I could shoot you myself for being so damn stubborn."

She looked up at him, her lips crooking in a wan smile. For the first time, J.T. noticed that her skin was ice white, her eyes huge in her face.

"Jesse, what was it you said that first night at Arawak?" she asked, her hand coming away from her body, her fingers red with blood. "S-shooting me would be redundant."

Chapter 15

Allison stood at the bedroom window, staring out into the night. Twinkling lights spangled the darkness, the heartbeat of the city almost palpable as she pressed her hand against the glass.

The spacious grounds of HomePlace were cupped in the city's palm—something tender and protected, brightened by banks of lights that were beacons drawing troubled kids home.

She heard the shelter van start up in the driveway below, then head out onto the street. Whoever was driving it tonight had the stereo tuned in to vintage rock at a decibel that would have made an audiologist blanch.

In the house, below, Allison could hear the sounds of the kids—muffled, a little subdued. Still shaken, no doubt, by the events of early that morning.

It seemed as if it had all happened an eternity ago—the mass confusion of police arriving to take IceMan back to jail, Buck trying to calm the kids while Jesse, Jesse had cared for her wound so tenderly, so patiently.

It had been only a gash where the bullet had grazed her arm. But just looking at the wound seemed to have hit Jesse like a shot through the heart.

He'd met her assertion that hospitals were for wimps with stony silence, and hadn't cracked so much as a smile when she insisted she wanted to go to the lake, as he had. The only thing that had saved her from a trip to the emergency room was the arrival of Dr. Reed—coming to the shelter infirmary for weekly rounds. The doctor's assurance that her injury wasn't serious had seemed to calm J.T. a little. But then J.T. had perversely refused to let the physician touch her.

J.T. had bandaged her himself, with an expertise gained through tending countless injuries on the kids who came through HomePlace's doors. And she knew instinctively that each wound he'd ever touched with those strong, healing hands had left a scar in this sensitive man's heart. But the most vicious scar of all had been left by the small gash on Allison's arm. It was a scar she knew he would never be free of, unless she could find some way to reach him.

Bandaged, with one of J.T.'s shirts serving as a nightgown, she'd been tucked into the bed he had shared with her on such magical nights.

Then Jesse had gone away.

It was only logical that he had the shelter to run. The business of HomePlace couldn't grind to a halt just because of what had happened. Teenage boys had bottomless stomachs to fill, there were volunteers waiting to be assigned work and there were heaven only knew how many panicky kids to calm down.

Annie had been hysterical, Sonny ashen, the fear in their faces something Allison would never forget.

But worst of all had been J.T.'s face when he had slipped in to check on Allison from time to time during the day. Stoic, resolute, he had reminded her of an Indian warrior walking through his enemy's flames. It was his relative silence that alarmed her far more than the notorious Jesse James temper ever could have.

It wasn't J.T.'s way to bottle his anger up inside him, to hold back the words she knew must be choking him. He was blunt and ruthlessly honest and all too happy to vent his temper when riled. That he did not could mean only one thing.

He was going to send her away. For good this time, with no middle ground or compromises, no promises about loving her in some secret haven where he could keep her safe.

Allison's throat constricted. She had returned to HomePlace that morning to force J.T. to see reason, convince him that she could survive in his world.

But the altercation with IceMan had ripped away the curtain hiding J.T.'s most hideous fear, showing him just how deep his terror for her could cut him, just how helpless forces like IceMan could make him. Just how much danger a woman would face if J.T. dared to make a life with her.

The sound of footsteps on the stairs made Allison turn. He hesitated in the door, one hand against the jamb. Jeans faded almost white encased his long legs. The sweater he'd worn to the lake the night he'd been shot covered shoulders that were just a little bent with the weight of the scene to come. Allison's eyes burned at the memory of how she'd mended that sweater for him—awkward stitches, set by uncertain hands. His eyes had shone like every dream she'd ever known when she had surprised him with the treasured garment.

His eyes weren't shining now.

He looked as if he'd been dragged through hell. Maybe he had.

"You should be in bed," he said.

"I'm not tired. I like to watch the night, you know? The cars passing by. That old couple across the street, sitting on their porch. They're playing cards. I think the old man cheats."

J.T. paced into the room. He went to a light switch and turned it on. "Ali, we need to talk."

She was certain he'd been framing speeches in his mind for hours, noble garbage about keeping her safe.

Her heart ached. It was that soul-deep caring for others buried beneath his renegade facade that had made her fall in love with him. Was it possible that it would now cost her the only thing she'd ever really wanted?

"I told you to stay away," J.T. said quietly. "Why didn't you listen?"

"If I had listened, you'd be dead." Allison wasn't going to be shaken or morose. She wasn't going to let him focus on what might have been. Instead, she had to make him see what *was*. She tried to force a teasing note into her voice. "This is the second time we've beaten the odds, Jesse. Take me up to Arawak and say thank-you again."

"Thank you? You could have been killed! God, do you know how scared I was? I could have lost you."

Tenderness clouded Allison's eyes. "I know exactly how scared you were. When I opened that door and saw you with that—that needle, heard what he was going to do to you— Oh, Jesse. . . ."

She hadn't cried when the bullet struck. She hadn't cried when she'd walked out the day before. But she felt hot tears well against her lashes.

"You should've run, Ali. Why didn't you run?"

"You know the answer to that, Jesse Tyler James. Because I love you." Her words were hurting him. She could see it. As if she was tearing him apart with the love in her eyes.

His jaw knotted, and she could feel the stark determination in him to make her see the reality that was more glaringly clear than ever after what had happened that morning.

"You have to see now, angel. Understand why you can't stay here."

"What do I have to do to prove myself to you, Jesse? Prove that I can cut it in your world, that I belong here as much as you do? I took care of your bullet wound, got things cleared up for the new shelter. I maced a bad guy who had a gun."

"You got shot! Ten inches to the right, and we *would* be in a hospital right now, with you on a respirator, or maybe on a slab in the morgue. What do you think that would do to me, Ali?"

"The same thing it would do to me if you had been killed. But we didn't die, Jesse."

"*This time.* Next time, who the hell knows—"

"It's a risk I'm willing to take. I'm not totally naive. I know there are adjustments to be made. That's why I got the Mace and signed up for tae kwon do lessons. I'm not a victim. I'm not hiding anymore. And I'm damn good at what I do here." She gestured to their surroundings, then flushed, realizing her hand was pointed to the bed. She smiled, a little sheepish. "I'm even good at working at the shelter."

"Lady, this is crazy."

"It is. I'm crazy in love with you, Jesse. And this shelter is like walking straight into your heart. You don't have to save the whole world, Jesse. Don't you see? Just the pieces of it that fall into your hands. You owe it to these kids to show them that life is good and rich and full. And the only way that can happen is for you to open yourself to a life of your own. With someone to love you. With me to love you. We deserve a life together."

"Do you think I don't want that? You as my wife? Children?" His voice tore, ragged. "I've been dreaming of it a hundred times a day. But I can't believe. Don't you see, it hurts too damn bad? I'll be waiting for—I don't know—for something bad to happen. I'll be waiting for..."

"Me to leave you?" Allison asked softly.

"Yes, damn it. How can I expect you to keep loving me? You have the whole world at your feet. I have this little corner, three steps away from hell. How can I expect you to love me, stay with me, when my own mother wouldn't?"

He covered his face with one hand. "Oh, God, Ali, there's so much ugliness inside me. I don't want to poison you with it. I don't want you to see—see whatever made my mother walk away."

"Let me show you what I see, Jesse." Her eyes blurred with tears as she went to him, gently pulling his hand away from his face. That fallen-angel face that could warm a runaway's heart, and could seduce a woman into madness.

She turned his palm upward, cradling his hand in hers. Her fingertip ran down the faint tracery of a scar. "I see strong hands, callused hands, hands with a gift for healing everyone but yourself." She skimmed the knuckles he'd bruised on IceMan's face. "These hands are never too tired or too busy to reach out to anyone who needs them. And I need them, Jesse. On my skin, in my hair. I need them when they're hot and hungry and they make me forget everything except how much I love you."

"Allison, don't," he groaned.

But she slid her caress into the hair at his temple. "I see a mind where there's no room for the word *impossible.* Where the dreams you dream for all children become like—like a holy quest you'll never let go."

He was trembling. She reached up on tiptoe, brushing her lips against the hard line of his mouth. She drew back and traced the sensual curve with a fingertip, feeling the ragged catch of his breath.

She smiled. "This mouth is pure trouble, Jesse. Lethal when you're angry, but when you smile...it's like a—" She paused, then reached up to sip at one corner. "Like fudge still warm from the pan—sinful, delicious. So tempting I feel like I'll die if I don't get a taste."

His hands sought out her waist, like a penitent touching a shrine. "When you do taste me, I want to kiss you forever."

She could see his resolve starting to crumble as her hands smoothed down the wall of his chest. "Jesse, it's your heart that makes me sad sometimes. So sad."

He touched her cheek. "Angels should never be sad."

"It's a good kind of sad." She cupped her palm over the steady beat of his heart. "As if the whole world's pain is right here, and I can touch it. But I can also feel hope. So much hope, more than you even know exists. You're a real live hero, Jesse. The kind they put in fairy tales and legends like King Arthur. But you're also a man, with needs and weaknesses and pain. And I love every piece of you—dark and bright, bitterness and humor, anger and tenderness. If any one of those facets were missing, you wouldn't be the man you are."

Her fingers went to the buttons on his shirt. She opened them slowly, reverently, pressing tender kisses upon the skin that she bared.

"Look through my eyes, Jesse," she whispered, pressing a kiss to his heart. "See how beautiful you are."

J.T. reached up, his fingers hot and unsteady as they curled around her wrists to stop her. "God, Ali, I want you. So damn much, but we can't. You're hurt."

"I do hurt. Deep. I thought that I'd lost you forever." She tugged free of his grasp. "Find me, Jesse."

He scooped her into his arms, carried her to the bed. Before she had tasted his fire, his passion, his anger, his pain. But as he stripped away her shirt and sculpted her body with his hands, there was so much tenderness in his touch that it broke Allison's heart.

"I love you, angel," he breathed, raw need tempered with reverence.

He nudged her to the edge of madness in tiny stages, and when he took her hand and plunged over the edge, Allison soared with him, devouring every sensation, reaching deep inside his soul to where the scars were, promising without words to heal them.

And when the climax came, Allison felt the last of his walls shatter, leaving J.T. gasping and new.

Afterward they lay curled in each other's arms as reality settled around them once again—a gentle coverlet of familiar surroundings, familiar sounds.

Allison smiled as she heard a commotion somewhere downstairs—somebody dropping something, the sound of laughter. A basketball thudded with hollow, rhythmic sounds as it was bounced on the sidewalk under the window.

She looked at the half-open door. "I'd better put my skill at cutting red tape to use, Mr. James. Get a marriage license fast. You know, there are a lot of impressionable kids around here. It wouldn't be good for your image to be living in sin. Not that you'd be living at all after my father got hold of you. Of course, I'm sure he'll eventually see reason."

Jesse was quiet, so quiet and still that a tiny bubble of fear pushed against Allison's joy. "We don't have to get married if you're not ready. I didn't mean to press."

"Do you have any idea how long I've been waiting to find you?" J.T. braced himself on one elbow, his fingers tracing her cheek. "All those years I was on the streets...I looked up at the sky. I couldn't see past the pain. But you were out there, even then. Waiting for me."

He buried his face in her hair, and she could feel him shake, feel something hot and wet against her skin. Tears.

"I know it's been hard, Jesse. What you've been through with your mother and...and everything. I know it makes you angry and hurt and—"

"How can I hurt anymore, angel? I have a piece of heaven to hold in my hands forever. The rest doesn't matter anymore. It was in the past, Ali. You're my future."

Allison stroked the shaggy ends of his hair fiercely, wanting to reach behind the recklessness, the danger, to touch the Jesse that used to be.

A little boy with dark hair and his daddy's leather jacket, waiting at the window for a mother who would never come.

"I love you so much." Her fingertips skimmed his cheeks as if she were smoothing away every scar life had left on her own renegade. "You'll never be alone again."

Epilogue

It was widely known in Chicago's finest circles that even after four years of marriage noted social crusader J.T. James would have walked through flames for his wife. But the sacrifice he was making on this particular evening was of a magnitude so great that J.T. figured he might never recover.

He scanned the glittering assemblage of guests until he caught Allison's eyes. With enough theatrical finesse to fill a New York stage, J.T. hooked a finger under the black tie around his neck and pretended to stagger from lack of air.

Allison stood on the far side of the room, surrounded by two congressmen, a matinee idol, a beaming Leah Madsen and Buck—complete with a black silk bandanna around his head. J.T.'s heart melted as Allison flashed him a smile so brilliant it made the diamonds around other women's necks look dull by comparison.

It was her night. A national gala, honoring Allison and three other women for their contribution to society. And, God knew, Allison James deserved it. BabyPlace—the home for teenage mothers—had grown beyond even J.T.'s wildest imaginings. Her love and generosity, tolerance and understanding had helped to fashion frightened girls who were almost children themselves into responsible parents with a vision for their own and their babies' futures.

Looking at Allison now, in her old-fashioned velvet gown, her blond hair set off with a rope of pearls, J.T. thought she looked as elegant and untouchable as the first night J.T. had seen her.

But this time J.T. knew exactly how touchable the woman was. HomePlace, BabyPlace and the James residence next door had been chaos for the past week, the uproar almost beyond bearing. Every girl in both shelters had voiced their opinion of how Allison should do her hair, wear her makeup, accessorize with jewelry. J.T. had shaken his head in amusement at these female rituals. Rituals that had been cut short when one of the girls had gone into labor right in the middle of trying Allison's hair in an intricate French braid.

Allison had been at the hospital all day, coaching the girl through labor, until her twin baby daughters were safe in their bassinets.

She'd been late, bolting upstairs, her face soft with that familiar satisfaction that always came after a safe delivery, but when she'd burst into their bedroom, planning to change for the gala, she'd taken one look at Jesse and slammed to a halt, as stunned as if she'd found Mel Gibson jumping on their bed.

J.T. had been wrestling with the black tie of a tux—and cursing himself for thinking up this little surprise for his wife. But when he saw her face, any regrets vanished. There had been nothing cool about the lady in that instant. Only a slow heat that simmered in her eyes. The kind of heat that still made his hands shake as if it was their first time.

They'd already been late, but it hadn't mattered. In no time Allison had locked the bedroom door and tugged free the ebony studs it had taken him half an hour to fasten.

It had been good, so damn good that even here, in the middle of this crowded room, J.T. felt himself harden at the thought of it. He grimaced with wry humor, and tried to cool his blood with a swig of champagne.

He figured it was a miracle he could think of anything pleasant at all, while imprisoned in this kind of social affair that he loathed. But it was hard to play Joe Wet Blanket when Allison was so incredibly happy, and he could distract himself whenever he needed to by watching the antics of his tiny son.

J.T. scanned the room until he found the dark-haired moppet, who was currently trying to squirm down from Andrew Crawford's lap. Tyler Andrew James was one hundred percent outlaw, a miniature Billy the Kid whose smile could charm candy out of store clerks at twenty paces.

The three-year-old was a mirror image of Jesse, from his silver eyes to his identical tux. Proof positive that Tyler would share any fate with his beloved daddy—even the cruel and inhuman punishment of spending an evening in formal clothes.

"Down!" Tyler demanded, wriggling from his doting grandfather's lap, while mischievously snitching a piece of gum from his pocket. "Alli-gators unner the tay-bull! Got to stick their teef together with gum or they'll eat Tyler's toes!"

Jesse watched as his son played his current favorite game, skittering under the tablecloth as if it were a tent. J.T. wished to hell he could climb under there with him.

He gave the child a few minutes to hang out with the alligators, but when the white tablecloth beside his father-in-law stopped moving, J.T. went to peek under the hem. Tyler had scuttled down the fifty-foot length of the table as if it were a prairie dog tunnel. He was currently sitting Indian style, fascinated by what looked like some silver beading on a pair of women's shoes.

J.T. figured he'd better get down there before Tyler decided to pry the beads off to add to his "sparkly collection."

Trying to gauge how far down he'd have to go, J.T. started after his son. But he'd taken only a few steps when he saw the tablecloth erupting, Tyler popping out like a jack-in-the-box. The dark-haired toddler clambered to his feet and looked up at the woman before him, his hands on his hips.

J.T. stilled for a heartbeat, watching as Senator Alexander's wife stared down at the child, her perfectly groomed face more than a little disgruntled.

J.T. worked his way toward them, a strange tightness around his heart.

"You shouldn't hab jools on your shoes," Tyler was saying. "The ally-gators like to gobble them up like gumdrops. Hey, you got any gumdrops, lady?" he asked, flashing her his baby outlaw smile.

"Don't you know that it's very naughty to run away, little boy?" the woman lectured. "Your mother will be very worried."

"I didn't runned away, silly!" Tyler said, exasperated. "There were ally-gators. I was tryin' to stick their teef together. 'Course, my daddy doesn't stick teef. He tickles the ally-gators until they laugh so hard they can't eat me. He's the bestest daddy in the whole world."

"He certainly can't be a very good father if he isn't watching you—"

Tyler stomped his foot. "My daddy's the best daddy in the whole world! He chases monsters out of the closet an' takes me for rides roun' the parking lot on his motorcycle with a helmet and a jacket and—"

Tyler caught a glimpse of J.T. as he neared them, and the child flung himself headlong against his father's legs. Mrs. Alexander's eyes collided with Jesse's as he scooped his son into his arms.

"Don't like that lady," Tyler complained, jabbing an accusatory finger in Mrs. Alexander's direction. "*She* said you were bad."

Silence fell for a beat, as J.T. felt the warmth of that wriggly little body seep into his heart. "It doesn't matter, Tyler," J.T. said softly.

"Tyler?" the senator's wife echoed.

"His name is Tyler. Tyler James."

For an instant those perfectly made-up eyes seemed to water. As if she couldn't stop herself, she reached out one finger to touch the chubby hand that was crumpling the front of Jesse's shirt.

"Would you like to hold him?" J.T. asked softly.

"No! Don't want to!" Tyler started to squawk. But J.T. soothed him.

"It's all right, buddy. This lady and I are...old friends."

Grudgingly the little boy allowed Mrs. Alexander to take him. "I knew a Tyler once," the woman said to the child. "A long time ago. You look a little bit...like him."

"I look like my daddy, silly! Now, you holded me enough. Put me down! I gots to see my grampa."

She held him a moment longer, then set the toddler on his feet. Tyler bolted away. J.T. followed his progress until he saw the child climb onto Andrew Crawford's lap. Tyler was tugging at his grandfather's Rolex. J.T. was dead certain Crawford would feed it to the alligators himself, if it would make his grandson smile.

"Your little boy is...beautiful." Mrs. Alexander's voice was just a little thick, her gaze fixed on Tyler. He saw a lightning flash of emotion in her face. "You look just like him, you know. You always looked like him."

J.T. knew she wasn't thinking of his son, but rather a seventeen-year-old renegade who had seduced her away from her family, her life.

"Thank you," she faltered, "for—for letting me..." Her voice trailed off uneasily, as she waved her hand toward the oblivious Tyler.

"It's okay."

"I have to go now. My son—" She tripped over the word. "Peter is back in town for the weekend, and—"

"Wait. Just a minute," J.T. asked. She looked a little alarmed as he peered into her pale face for a long moment. "You look good, Melissa. Content."

"I am."

"I'm glad." He was startled to realize just how much he was.

"I'm glad, too. That you are... You've done some amazing things."

"Things work out the way they're supposed to." It was the closest J.T. could come to making peace with what had gone before. He wished the woman with the brittle smile and flashing diamonds could do the same.

He watched his mother turn in a whirl of elegance and walk to where her husband was waiting.

A heartbeat later J.T. felt a hand on his shoulder, and turned to find Allison there, her eyes soft and dark, filled with dawning realization and gentle amazement.

"She's the one. Oh, Jesse. You never said anything, not even to me. You never let anyone know. If you had—"

"You can't make someone love you, Ali. I learned that the hard way."

"You learned a lot of things the hard way, Jesse." Heartbreaking tenderness filled Allison's eyes. "I wish that I could take the pain from all those lessons away."

"Don't you know you have, lady?" He touched her face with a gentle reverence. "You taught me the most important lesson of all. When someone *does* love you, you can never make them stop. Even when you're a renegade hard case with an attitude."

"A beautiful renegade with an attitude," Allison said. "My renegade."

As if they were the only two people in the world, J.T. caught her lips in a melting kiss, showing her without words the healing power her love had had over his heart. "I love you, angel. More than you'll ever know."

J.T. James put his arms around his own piece of heaven. He would never let her go.

* * * * *

HE'S AN

AMERICAN HERO

January 1994 rings in the New Year—and a new lineup of sensational American Heroes. You can't seem to get enough of these men, and we're proud to feature one each month, created by some of your favorite authors.

January: CUTS BOTH WAYS by Dee Holmes: Erin Kenyon hired old acquaintance Ashe Seager to investigate the crash that claimed her husband's life, only to learn old memories never die.

February: A WANTED MAN by Kathleen Creighton: Mike Lanagan's exposé on corruption earned him accolades...and the threat of death. Running for his life, he found sanctuary in the arms of Lucy Brown—but for how long?

March: COOPER by Linda Turner: Cooper Rawlings wanted nothing to do with the daughter of the man who'd shot his brother. But when someone threatened Susannah Patterson's life, he found himself riding to the rescue....

AMERICAN HEROES: Men who give all they've got for their country, their work—the women they love.

Only from

IMHERO7

Take 4 bestselling love stories FREE

Plus get a FREE surprise gift!

**And now for
something completely different
from Silhouette....**

SPELLBOUND
R O M A N C E

Unique and innovative stories that take you into the world of paranormal happenings. Look for our special "Spellbound" flash—and get ready for a truly exciting reading experience!

**In February, look for
One Unbelievable Man (SR #993)
by Pat Montana.**

Was he man or myth? Cass Kohlmann's mysterious traveling companion, Michael O'Shea, had her all confused. He'd suddenly appeared, claiming she was his destiny—determined to win her heart. But could levelheaded Cass learn to believe in fairy tales...before her fantasy man disappeared forever?

Don't miss the charming, sexy and utterly mysterious
Michael O'Shea in
ONE UNBELIEVABLE MAN.
Watch for him in February—only from

Silhouette
R O M A N C E™

It's our 1000th
Silhouette Romance
and we're celebrating!

Join us for a special collection of love stories by the authors you've
loved for years, and new favorites you've just discovered.

**It's a celebration just for you,
with wonderful books by
Diana Palmer, Suzanne Carey,
Tracy Sinclair, Marie Ferrarella,
Debbie Macomber, Laurie Paige,
Annette Broadrick, Elizabeth August
and MORE!**

Silhouette Romance...vibrant, fun and emotionally rich! Take another
look at us!

As part of the celebration, readers can receive a FREE gift AND enter
our exciting sweepstakes to win a grand prize of $1000! Look for
more details in all March Silhouette series titles.

**You'll fall in love all over again
with Silhouette Romance!**

CEL1000T

As seen on TV!
Free Gift Offer

With a Free Gift proof-of-purchase from any Silhouette® book, you can receive a beautiful cubic zirconia pendant.

This gorgeous marquise-shaped stone is a genuine cubic zirconia—accented by an 18" gold tone necklace.

(Approximate retail value $19.95)

Send for yours today...
compliments of  Silhouette®

To receive your free gift, a cubic zirconia pendant, send us one original proof-of-purchase, photocopies not accepted, from the back of any Silhouette Romance™, Silhouette Desire®, Silhouette Special Edition®, Silhouette Intimate Moments® or Silhouette Shadows™ title for January, February or March 1994 at your favorite retail outlet, together with the Free Gift Certificate, plus a check or money order for $2.50 (do not send cash) to cover postage and handling, payable to Silhouette Free Gift Offer. We will send you the specified gift. Allow 6 to 8 weeks for delivery. Offer good until March 31st, 1994 or while quantities last. Offer valid in the U.S. and Canada only.

Free Gift Certificate

Name: _____

Address: _____

City: _____ State/Province: _____ Zip/Postal Code:_____

Mail this certificate, one proof-of-purchase and a check or money order for postage and handling to: SILHOUETTE FREE GIFT OFFER 1994. In the U.S.: 3010 Walden Avenue, P.O. Box 9057, Buffalo NY 14269-9057. In Canada: P.O. Box 622, Fort Erie, Ontario L2Z 5X3

FREE GIFT OFFER   079-KBZ

ONE PROOF-OF-PURCHASE

To collect your fabulous FREE GIFT, a cubic zirconia pendant, you must include this original proof-of-purchase for each gift with the properly completed Free Gift Certificate.

079-KBZ